Jessie rolled onto her side and drifted off to sleep. A swirling mist drew her to the edge of the woods. She couldn't see anything through the dense fog, only a narrow pathway twisting around the trees. Enticing, the foggy haze seduced her to move one step closer. Jessie paused. She didn't want to go in alone. Panicking, she started to turn back before it was too late.

"Jess," Matt's faint voice called out to her. He sounded wheezy and breathless, and she could hear the pain in his voice. Where was he? She glanced around, hoping to see his familiar face.

"Jess…" The call came again. She shivered. Matt was in the darkness, and death had come to play. The faces of those tortured young men danced in the mist before her. Her feet refused to move. She was paralyzed with fear. The silence around her was deafening.

"Jess," he screamed out her name once more, trusting her to aid him. Tears filled her eyes, spilling down her cheeks. This time there was no way she could help…

Praise for Iona Morrison

"Morrison's Blue Cove mystery novels are quite simply a joy to read. The town is filled with great characters and Jesse and Matt have that 'X' factor. The stories are well put together highlighting important issues for all of us. The books are a great read with plenty of 'edge of your seat' moments. I have no hesitation in recommending the books to all my friends."

~*Brian Mulholland (Ireland)*

"I am a devoted fan of her stories…I find her characters to be like family to me now and the setting, Blue Cove, is where I would like to live, which I do in her stories. I hope she keeps writing because I can't get enough!"

~*Vickie Atencio*

The Final Flashpoint

by

Iona Morrison

A Blue Cove Mystery, Book 6

The Final Flashpoint

Contact Information: info@thewildrosepress.com

Cover Art by *Debbie Taylor*

The Wild Rose Press, Inc.
PO Box 708
Adams Basin, NY 14410-0708
Visit us at www.thewildrosepress.com

Publishing History
First Fantasy Rose Edition, 2018
Print ISBN 978-1-5092-2196-7
Digital ISBN 978-1-5092-2197-4

A Blue Cove Mystery, Book 6
Published in the United States of America

Dedication

Dedicated to the memory of Dorothy Gates, my aunt.
Married for 72 years she left a legacy of love to all who
knew her.

Chapter 1

"Why? God, why? My life can't end like this." His anguished cries flooded her mind. Jessie lifted her head, tossing aside the book she was reading. *Where was he?*

"Please help me find him," she uttered, glancing at the noisy surf. The normally calm cove looked like a cauldron of churning water. Dark clouds were gathering out at sea. The wind was blowing stronger than when she had first arrived; an afternoon storm was in the early stages. The angry ocean thrust wave after wave onto the beach, spilling its contents on the sand.

His tormented cries intensified. The scene that played in her thoughts propelled her out of the chair and onto her feet. She scanned the coastline. The beach was empty except for a few joggers. Yet, the sobbing persisted. Pushing her glasses on top of her head, she walked closer to the water's edge. Warm, humid air swirled around her in the wind. Shivers danced down one arm and then the other. The water seemed fixed on thrusting something caught in its grasp closer to the shoreline. *Driftwood perhaps.* It was getting closer, whatever it was. And then she saw someone sitting alone on the rock jutting out into the water as the incoming tide inched closer to him. "Are you all right?" she asked, taking an unguarded step toward him. He lifted his head, stared out to sea, and then his eyes locked on her face. It was happening again! In one intense moment, she knew it was this man's body inching closer to land.

Frozen in place, she shielded her eyes from the sun's glare and together they watched the waves move his body, pushing him, tumbling ever closer until the moment the ocean spit him ashore near her feet. Shock rippled through her, and a vivid scene flashed in her mind.

"Move, don't just stand there," she hissed. Reaching for the phone in her purse, she snapped a picture and made the call, trying to steady her shaking hand. "Matt," her words tumbled out, "his body landed at my feet. He's dead. Hurry!" Tears spilled down her cheeks.

"Slow down, Jess. Who's dead?"

She took a deep breath. "Some man," she stammered, "the waves pushed his body ashore. I'll send you a picture." She walked away from the prone form, but not from his piercing eyes. "He's a young male. And just between us," she gasped, "his ghost is watching me at this very moment."

"Damn, Jess. Where are you?" Matt asked. She could imagine the look on his face. He was every bit the cop planning his next moves.

"I'm at my favorite spot down from the Inn." She shuddered when she looked at the motionless body. "Please hurry, the guests from the Inn will make their way here soon. I'm not feeling comfortable being alone with him, either."

"I'm on my way, sweetheart. Hang in there. I know you'll have more to tell me when I get there. I can hear it in your voice. Stand guard over the body and don't let anyone near the area. It's a crime scene now."

"I'll do my best," she told him.

"Phone Katie for me, will you? Let her know we're closing the beach for a while, my orders. Tell her to send her guests to the marina."

"I'll call her." Jessie could see the ghost standing over his body. What must he be thinking, or did they think? "See you soon…the sooner, the better." She pressed her hand to her throat.

"I'll hurry."

She sat on the edge of the chair and made her next call. "Katie, you have to keep your guests away from the beach area today. A body has washed ashore, and the police are on their way. The beach is closed as of now, Matt's orders."

"Are you kidding me? Of course, you're not. Why do I even bother to ask?" Katie grumbled. "What should I tell my guests?"

"Tell them what I told you. The police have closed the beach. Encourage your guests to go to town or the marina for the day. I'll let you know when the beach reopens again for them to use."

"All right, but I'm not happy about a body on the beach. You'll need to keep this quiet. No one will come back to the Inn if they find out. Geez, a dead body on my beach. Just a minute." She heard Katie tell a guest the beach was closed. "I'm back. Tell the guys they can eat dinner here tonight when they're finished. It's the least I can do for the police working in the area. I'll want details as soon as you have some you can tell me." Jessie heard her take a deep breath. "Dylan, how I love the man, is tight-lipped when it comes to cases. Kind of like you in that regard."

"I tell you what I can and so does he, I'm sure. I'll

let the guys know about dinner."

"Perfect, then they can answer any questions my guests might have about why the beach was closed, instead of me. Hopefully, without talking about a body."

"A good plan; talk to you later." Jessie jumped to her feet.

"Okay, you can always come early to help." Katie disconnected the call.

"I wish you could tell me your story." Jessie glanced at the spirit following her. "We'll figure this out in time, but it would be nice if you could talk," she whispered. "Or maybe not. I'm sorry. It must be hard to be displaced from your body in such a horrific way." She turned her head away from his constant presence.

A sudden chill wrapped around her as a swirling cold mist. He was near. Jessie straightened; her shoulders tensed. Yet—there was something else—a new presence, as warm as his was cold.

She didn't want to look, but couldn't seem to stop herself. Her feet had a mind of their own. The closer she got to him, the faster her heart raced. "What are these strange burns all over you?" She scowled, bending closer to get a better glimpse of the strange round marks. "You suffered," she said under her breath. "The question is who would do this to you and why?" Squatting there beside him, a warmth enveloped her. Taking a deep breath, she closed her eyes aware of another presence she couldn't see.

"Are you all right, sweetheart?" Matt called down to her.

"Yes." Jessie shot to her feet. She was happy to see him appear at the top of the stairs with Dylan and a few others.

"Let's take a look at what you found." Matt grabbed her hand when he reached the bottom stair. "Are you sure you're okay? You seemed lost for a few moments."

"I'm fine now that you're here. It was strange being alone with his body." She added under her breath, "Well, not quite alone." Did the young man know she could see him? She had no idea.

****

Matt slipped on his gloves and squatted down. "Is this where he came ashore?" he asked her, pointing at the victim.

She nodded."He hasn't been moved or touched."

"I'll take over. You can relax now." The victim was stripped to his boxers. No place for an ID. He hadn't thought there would be. It would have made notifying the family easier, but then again, it was never easy. A quick look at the victim's face might reveal more. "Marcy, you can snap your pictures now." Matt motioned to her. The man's hands were tied behind his back with some kind of electrical wire. The wire had rubbed open wounds on his wrists. A few snaps of the camera later, Matt rolled the body over enough to see the young man's face. He took note of the tape across his mouth. Depending on how long this body was in the water, some of the evidence was already gone. He couldn't tell from the victim's swollen face how old he was or how long he had been dead. From the wrinkled condition of his skin, he must have been in the water at least thirty minutes.

The strange marks all over the body stumped him. Each one was small and circular like the tip of cigarette, only larger. Someone had tortured him. *Why?* Dave would be needed to figure out an estimated time of death and the weapon which made all the marks on his body. Otherwise, there weren't any gunshot wounds or other visible signs of trauma. He stood beside Jessie. "Tell me what happened."

"At first, I couldn't see anyone, and then I caught sight of the waves pushing what I thought was a large piece of driftwood. The young man, or ghost, I should say, on the rock over there"—she pointed to where he sat—"let me know it was him. The body washed up, and I saw for a brief moment what had happened to him. If what I saw is real, he was tortured before he was killed."

"What did you see?" Matt took out his notepad.

"The details are sketchy, but he suffered. They used some sort of an instrument to shock him. It looked like some kind of electric rod. It must have made those unusual marks." She pointed at the small circles. "There were a few people involved, or at least it appeared that way."

"I guess we'll have to wait until Dave gives us a better idea of the cause of death to know for sure. What you saw is probably spot on. He couldn't have been dumped too long ago; the body is still in fair condition." Matt's brow creased. "How old do you think our victim is? You keep calling him young."

"I would say late teens or early twenties at the most." Jessie glanced to see if the ghost was still there. His tormented cries saddened her. She closed her eyes. "Much too young to die."

"Damn, I was afraid you'd tell me that. Dave will let us know for sure once he can ID this guy. For now, we'll wait to hear."

Marcy snapped several more photos. Dave and his assistant did what they could on site. They prepared the body to transport back to the lab. The others combed over the beach searching for any clues which might have washed ashore with him.

Matt leaned toward Jessie when her face paled. "What is it, Jess?" His hands clenched at his side, waiting for her answer.

"Unless I miss my guess, another body may soon wash ashore if it hasn't already somewhere else. My friend has been joined by another ghost. A second young man."

"Damn." His brows rose. "Are you sure?" He pressed his lips together.

"All I know is there are two of them watching us now as we stand here." Jessie rubbed her arms and folded them close to her body.

"Dylan, we'll need to check the shoreline along the cove. There's another body somewhere." Dylan gave him a questioning look. "Trust me, we need to check." Matt's phone rang. He walked away from the group to talk. He rejoined them after a few minutes. "Listen up, everyone, we have the location of a second body. A local man found another victim on his morning walk." Matt shook his head and glanced at Jessie. "It beats me how you get this stuff, but I'm glad you do." He squeezed her hand. "Dave, you may as well follow us to the next site if you have room to carry another body."

"We do. I'll follow you." Dylan and Kip prepared to help Dave and his assistant carry the stretcher up the stairs.

"If you finish before dinner, Katie told me to tell

you she'd be happy to feed you all at the Inn."

"I'll be there," Kip said. "I never turn down a dinner invitation."

Gary chimed in, "Me, too."

"Tell her to expect me," Dylan smiled when he said it.

"Of course, you'll be there. You always are." Kip elbowed him in the ribs.

"I'm sure most of us will be there. It may be late, and we'll be hungry." Matt ran his hand through his hair. *Two bodies and no idea why.*

A few miles down the road at a private beachfront home, the owner had discovered the second body. Jessie had called it right, a young male with dark hair was sprawled on the beach. He too had been stripped down to only his briefs, with his hands tied behind his back. The same circular burns could be seen on various parts of his body and tape covered his mouth.

Murdered somewhere else, they had been dumped unceremoniously at sea by their killers. The difference in weight and the precise moment when they were heaved overboard could make up the difference in distance of where they came ashore. Matt's mind was already beginning to process what he was seeing. He didn't like the conclusions his mind was drawing. It was only a theory at the moment, but something to consider about their deaths. Hopefully, he would know more soon.

****

Jessie had placed the last serving bowl with mashed potatoes on the table as Matt and Dylan walked in. "Your timing is impeccable. She smiled at them. Her smile broadened when Dylan went right to Katie and kissed her. Her friend glowed.

"You were right, the second victim was also a young male," Matt said quietly as he slipped into the chair beside her. I have a bad feeling about this one, Jess. Let me know if you see or hear anything, will you?"

"Of course." She glanced at him. "What are you thinking?"

"The victims are both young, and torture was involved. I can't help but think it's some kind of hate crime or drug related. I'll know if I'm in the ballpark when Dave gives me his piece of the puzzle." Matt placed a spoonful of potatoes on his plate.

"How strange it must have been for the young man to watch his own body come ashore. His sadness was palpable. It hung heavy in the air between us. I can never look at violent acts with indifference again. I've seen the toll it takes on the families, but I've also seen it with the victims, as well. For me, it changes everything." She sighed. "Do you think he was shocked to see himself lying there?"

"I have no idea." Matt shook his head. "I understand lives are impacted by crimes of violence; families, friends, and acquaintances, but I can't say I ever thought about the victim being on the scene when I was. My mind never went there until I started working with you."

"You're better off not to go there. I leave this side of my life alone the best I can. It shows up when it wants to and leaves when it's ready to." Jessie took a sip of her water.You know that my Gramma Sadie and my great-grandmother had these premonitions. I guess you could say it runs in my family."

"I guess it had to come from somewhere. All I know, Jess, you were right on about the two victims."

"The fact that they are males has me feeling more skittish. I've only seen female ghosts up to this point." She pursed her lips.

Matt glanced sideways at her. "Why?"

"I don't know. Maybe they might be more aggressive." Her hands fiddled with the napkin in her lap "It may not make sense to you, but being a woman, I was taught to be wary of men in some circumstances."

"I get it. I know the statistics." Matt buttered his bread.

"And yet," she paused, her voice quiet.

"What?" He leaned closer to her.

"I also felt a different presence this time. I can't explain it, but I will when I understand it." She closed her eyes savoring the moment again.

"I trust you to tell me when you figure it out." He smiled and abruptly changed the subject. "What were you doing at the beach anyway?"

"I was reading. One of my favorite things to do on my day off." She frowned. "That stretch of the beach is a nice, quiet place to chill. If it's going to get stormy, it's usually later in the afternoon and today was no exception. Although, I'm not sure it will ever be quite the same for me."

"Sure it will, in time." Matt's hand brushed hers.

"I'll adopt a wait and see policy." Jessie's brow arched, and she gave him a half smile.

Matt ate a few bites. "I'll bet you'll be down there on your next day off. You love the beach."

"You're probably right." She ate the last bit of salad on her plate. Jessie watched the guys devour their food. They didn't talk much when food was around. Her eyes crinkled, turning her lips up at the corners. When they were finished, they were done with little or no fanfare.

"Katie, thanks for another great meal." Kip pushed away from the table. "I'll see you all on Monday. I'm off tomorrow."

"Wait up, Kip. I'll ride back to the station with you to get my car." Gary stood. "Thanks, Katie."

"See you guys later." Katie followed them to the door.

Jessie helped Katie clear the table and clean the kitchen. "I've never seen you happier. It makes me happy to see you with Dylan." Jessie placed the last cup in the dishwasher. "We need to plan a trip to New York and begin the search for the perfect dress."

"Sounds fun. We're still thinking about the date and what kind of wedding we want. I want an outdoor wedding, so it has to be warm. Dylan thinks the fall would be nice. This summer is too soon, and he's not sure if we should wait until next spring. We'll figure it out soon enough. My mom is going crazy with the whole idea. She wants to move Dad here. So far he's holding out."

"Maybe your mom would like to go dress shopping with us. It would be a good way to get them both here for a visit, and your mom could work on convincing him. I bet she'll win eventually. I mean both of her kids live here now, and there's always the possibility for grandchildren too." Jessie teased.

"Whoa with the grandkids. I'm not ready to be anyone's mom, yet." Katie laughed. "I'm warming up to the idea of being a fiancée and all the perks that come with it. For now, I want to savor it." Katie fanned her face playfully. "One thing I know for sure, I'm glad you're here to share this time with me." Katie hugged Jessie.

"Me too." Jessie placed the dishrag in the sink. "Are you waiting for me?" she asked Matt.

He nodded. Matt pushed away from the doorframe where he had been leaning. He took hold of her hand as soon as they stepped outside. "Katie told me you have a birthday in a few weeks."

"I do."

"You could have told me." He turned her to face him. "A guy needs to know this stuff."

"I should have, but I didn't want you to think I was fishing for a gift." She grinned at him and started walking again. "I don't know yours either," she said when he caught up to her. "A sure sign that we need to spend more time in small talk and getting to know each other as well as talking about cases."

"Fair enough. I have made plans for your birthday, so don't make any."

"Are you asking me or telling me?" She turned her face to hide her smile.

"Both." He stopped her. "I want it to be a special day for you. We'll do all the small talk you want to do and a whole lot more. I think you'll approve what I have in mind." He gazed into her eyes.

"I'm sure I will." She took a deep breath. "In a couple of months, I will celebrate the anniversary of my move to Blue Cove and of course, meeting you. I love my life here and all my new friends. It's been an enlightening time for me." They started walking.

Matt chuckled. "Enlightening for all of us." He

touched the sapphire ring on her right hand. "I see you're wearing my reminder."

"Every day." She smiled as she twisted the ring on her finger.

He took the key from her hand and unlocked the door. He gave her a quick kiss. "Sleep well, sweetheart." He turned to leave and then stopped. "I'm coming in, any objections?"

"Not from me." She chuckled as he walked past her on his way to the sofa, grabbing the remote along the way.

He patted the space beside him. "Come on, sweetheart, let's watch TV and do some serious kissing." He grinned, placing his feet on the table.

Chapter 2

It was Monday, and Matt wanted answers. He hoped Lewis had some for him. He picked up his phone to call the coroner. "Dave, I was hoping you might have something for me."

"I have one tentative ID. I'm waiting on the confirmation. No ID on the second victim yet, but I have an idea about the marks all over their bodies."

"Lay it on me."

"The wounds came from a picana."

"A what?" Matt repeated the word. "I've never heard of it before."

"It's an electric device developed from a cattle prod that's been modified for human torture. The shocks are high voltage and low current."

"Damn," Matt shook his head, "Jessie thought he had been tortured. What are we looking at?"

"It's a device that works at a very high voltage to maximize pain and minimize the marks it leaves. The power can be supplied by a car battery. The prod enables the user to cause painful shocks in a precise area, and the damn device is portable."

"Humans can be barbaric at times." Matt wrote notes in the open file.

"If the killers wanted to maximize the intensity of the pain and reduce electrical resistance they would have thrown water on the victims first. Considering the places of the marks on their bodies, these two young people suffered immensely before they were murdered."

"Why?" Matt tapped his pencil on his desk.

"That is always the question, isn't it. Even if we hear the answer, it's almost impossible to believe someone is capable of doing such a heinous act."

"You're right, Dave. Still, we have to ask it to make sense of an act that makes no sense at all. What was the final cause of death?"

"There is no obvious cause of death like bullet wounds or blunt force trauma. Until I can do an autopsy, I'm only guessing. I think they were smothered, which would have been easy to do in their weakened condition."

"Strange, with torture involved, you would think they would have executed them." Matt circled the notes he wrote.

"We're running some checks on identities. I hope to have some answers for you later today."

"Thanks, Dave, I'll wait to hear from you."

Tortured and smothered; it didn't make sense. Matt called the front desk."Kenny, get me Tom Maxwell on the phone. I need to run something by him."

"Sure thing, sir, I'll patch him through as soon as I have him."

Were the kids local or from somewhere else and dropped in the area? Matt frowned. He didn't like what he thought when he examined the bodies. There was something familiar about one of the faces, Matt pulled out the missing persons file. His eyes widened at the young man's face staring back him from the page, the same face that had been on the evening news a few days ago.

Matt picked up the buzzing phone. "I have Tom on line one for you," Kenny told him.

"Thanks." Matt pushed the line. "Tom, we have a big problem here." Matt told him about the two bodies washing up on shore. "I'm waiting on their identities, but I'm pretty sure that one is the missing college student we keep hearing about on the news."

"Damn, I wasn't expecting to hear you say that. What are we looking at?"

Matt repeated what Dave Lewis had told him. "This should bring the Feds into it, I'm convinced."

"No doubt. Tell Lewis no autopsy until we know what the family wants and the country's protocol is. Keep this quiet until I talk to my superiors to find out who's investigating his disappearance. Blue Cove is about to be overrun again with Feds and the media once the story breaks."

"You can count on it. I'll keep it quiet, but remember, a local man found the young man's body on his beachfront property. It won't take long for him to put it all together and for the news to leak out."

"I'll get right on this, Matt, and get back to you. If not me, the lead investigator will call you."

"Thanks, Tom. I'll sit tight. I'm sure Dave will have his ID soon." Matt called Lewis next. Dave had the same ID on one of the young men as Matt had, but was still working on the other male.

"Dave, keep this under wraps until I know how the Feds want us to proceed."

"I will. I'll keep working on the other ID and get back to you as soon as I know who he is."

Matt turned his chair and stared out the window.

Torture was never a good thing. It usually meant some bad people were involved. Add to the mix the identity of his victim, and it became a veritable and potentially explosive mess. He tapped his pencil on the arm of the chair. Lewis would have to do a tox screen. Damn, he hated to wait. Every hour took the killers farther away.

****

Jessie was placing some books on the counter when the bell above the door rang. She smiled when Evan and Adriana Foster walked in the door carrying a small bundle wrapped in pink. "You brought her to see me." Jessie's voice filled with excitement as she walked toward them.

"Of course, we had to introduce the two of you." Adriana handed the sleeping baby to Jessie.

"She's beautiful." Jessie sat in the chair and uncovered the little girl. "Perfect." Jessie held up her tiny fingers. "She's a miniature Adriana. So amazing. I wonder how you can get anything done with such a precious bundle to take care of."

"Thankfully I have time before I have to go back to work. I can't imagine leaving our little Jessie Lynn with anyone. I cry just thinking about it."

"To be fair, love, you cry about a lot of things right now." Evan patted his wife's shoulder.

"You're right. I do. I'm grateful to be here. It could have ended differently. I'm happy to have every moment I have with our baby. This is our first outing since she was born, and I wanted to see you and say thank you, Jessie. When I think of what might have happened if you hadn't come to Palm Springs, if you hadn't seen me in your dreams, and kept looking for me." She shook her head wiping at the tears forming in her eyes. "I guess you get my drift."

"I do and I'm thankful it all worked out. Radar was the real hero in finding you," Jessie handed Adriana a tissue. "I'm glad you came for a visit." Jessie snapped several pictures with her phone. "My friend owns the coffee shop next door. Would you like something to drink or eat?"

"No, we'll be eating soon at Evan's mom's house."

"Sounds perfect, an outing to Grandma's where she'll be spoiled even more." They spent the next hour in a conversation interrupted only by customers needing to check out. Jessie held her sweet little namesake, her eyes getting misty when Adriana and Evan left.

She would have blubbered outright, but another customer came in; a beautiful young woman stood near the door. "May, I help you?" Jessie asked her. The girl's eyes were dark brown like chocolate, her hair a shiny black, and with her olive complexion, she was simply stunning.

"I was wondering if you have a place where I can put these posters up?"

"I have a community board. Feel free to put them there." She pointed to the spot. Jessie noticed the face on the first poster the girl stuck on the board. "Do you know this young man?" Her pulse began to race.

"He's my boyfriend, and he's been missing for several days. This is his best friend, and he's missing too."

"I want you to talk to someone. Do you mind if I call a friend?" Jessie didn't know what she should tell the young woman.

"Why? Do you know something?" Her brown eyes glanced at Jessie with hope.

"I'm not sure, but I know someone who might be able to help."

Jessie called Matt and gave him a quick rundown of the situation. The one face she thought she recognized, the other one she wasn't sure of. Could it mean there was a third man out there somewhere? She hoped not.

"He'll be right here. Would you like some iced tea while you wait?" Jessie asked the girl.

"Please," she said softly.

"My name is Jessie, by the way. I'll be right back with the tea." Jessie was happy to see the young woman was still there when she came from the coffee shop with two glasses.

"I am Darsha Sarin. My parents immigrated here from Delhi in northern India."

"Your name is lovely. Does it have a special meaning?"

"It means to see or perceive. I only wish I could see what happened to my friends." Her expression became sad. "This is not like either of them to be gone and not call."

What were the odds of this happening? She rubbed her arms. The tiny shivers felt like spiders walking up and down her back. Jessie stood when Matt walked in. "Matt, this is Darsha." A customer ready to check out sent her dashing to the register, giving them a chance to talk. Darn, she wished she could hear what they were saying, but their conversation didn't last long enough.

"Jess, I'm going to take these posters and Darsha with me. I'll be in touch soon."

"Thank you." The girl looked at Jessie with tears in her eyes.

"You're welcome." She followed them to the door, watching until the car was out of sight. Coincidence? No way; they had met for a reason. There was something big going on, and she was in the middle of it again. Jessie held the door open for Reba. Her arrival was the only confirmation Jessie needed.

"Hello, my dear girl. Who was that lovely young woman leaving with your Mr. Parker?" Reba got right to the point.

"Her name is Darsha Sarin. She wanted to put up a poster of a missing person on the community board."

"The person wasn't missing though, was he? A body was found, if my dreams are right. A few days ago my rest was interrupted by nightmares of torture and death. There is something awful going on. Make no mistake about it, she was supposed to come into your store. Did you find the body?"

"Let's just say he found me." Jessie explained what happened.

"Darsha is in danger too. Be sure to tell Matt. She has seen and heard more than she should have but may not be aware of it. Things hidden in the shadows have a way of coming to light."

"I'll tell him." It sent a tingle of goosebumps up her arms.

"I will get my book and be on my way." Reba picked the book she wanted off the shelf. "Hatred has no limit. For those snared by its force, it's a bottomless pit. Hate will take them down and many around them."

Jessie was unsettled. Those were strong words, but she knew they were true. "What happened to those young men was pure evil. Why? Both of the men were so young."

"I'm sure we'll understand soon enough whatever the agenda was, but I doubt it will ever answer the question why. It would be nice to live in harmony on this planet we call home." Reba shook her head. "The sad thing is we're all too busy blaming someone else for our problems. You know, dear, the other."

"Who is the other?" Jessie rang up the book.

"Anyone who looks, thinks, or believes differently than we do." Reba handed Jessie her credit card.

"It's such a waste. I saw the emotion of the young man as he watched his own body come ashore. Hate extorts a steep price." Jessie placed the book in the bag and handed it to Reba.

"A sad truth, which leaves the families to pick up the pieces of their lives." Reba took the bag. "Jessie dear, all of this will get easier for you with time. It did for me. You feel each of these deaths so personally right now. Soon it will be more about the living and finding justice for them. It will replace the sadness."

"I know what you're saying is right. I've had moments when it was all about the justice, but this was different." Jessie handed Reba the receipt to sign. "You'll enjoy this book."

"Reading has been a comfort to me, I guess it's a good way to get away from my own thoughts from time to time."

"Not to change the subject, guess who was here earlier?" Jessie walked with Reba to the door.

"Who, dear?"

"Evan and Adriana Foster brought their baby girl by to meet me. She is so precious."

"A sweet reminder. We may not save every life, but we can help a few." Reba walked out the door

Jessie held open. She patted Jessie's arm as she passed. "Have a good day, dear."

"You too." She watched Reba leave. It seems those who they helped were too few in numbers.

Chapter 3

Everything happens for a reason. Mom and Sadie had told her that often enough growing up. And time would tell soon enough why Darsha picked her store to put her posters in. What was Matt learning about the young man? She couldn't wait to hear from him. Molly waved at her through the open doors, and she waved back. "I'll bring the glasses back later."

"I'll come get them. I want you to try one of my new salad creations before I put it on the menu for customers. I want your honest feedback. I have a few folks who have tried it."

"I'd love to. I've been Katie's guinea pig for years and believe me, when she started out she wasn't as good as you are."

"Wow, it looks like we're about to get busy." Molly pointed to the bus pulling up across the street.

"I hope they spend their money, my friend." Jessie was happy to see the bus.

Jessie got to work as several customers wandered into her store. She loved busy mornings; time seemed to fly by. Business was booming. Customers and a good mystery kept her mind and hands busy. Darsha was never far from her thoughts. Her investigative juices were flowing.

Her first break in the crazy morning came at lunchtime. She sat at the small table and took her first bite of Molly's lovely salad. It was pleasing to the eye as well as delicious. Besides the mixed greens, there were slices of grilled chicken, black beans, and corn, topped with crunchy tortilla strips. A southwest lime chipotle dressing completed the taste experience. The flavors were wonderful. It was a keeper. With the last bite she could possibly eat in her mouth, Jessie gave Molly a thumbs-up.

Molly walked in her store. "I take it you liked the salad." Molly gave a skeptical glance at the salad left on her plate. "You didn't eat much."

"Are you kidding me? I stuffed myself. This is a big salad. I would order it again." Jessie looked at the small dent she had made in the huge salad. "You could offer to box the leftovers up so I can munch on it later." Jessie handed her the plate. "I think it will become a favorite on your menu. Only one suggestion, make sure you offer a half-size salad on the menu too."

"What a great idea. I think I'll put your suggestion into practice with all of my salads. They're rather large servings, more conducive to a man's appetite."

"Hello, ladies," Matt stood in the open doors. "I'll be in to talk as soon as I get me a sandwich." He winked at Jessie.

"Sounds good." Her eyes lit up at the sound of his voice. His visits were a bright spot in any day.

"How was your morning?" Matt came back with his lunch and sat beside her.

"It's been a busy one, I'm pleased to say. Besides all my customers, Reba was here with some of her wise words. The best surprise of the morning was a visit from Evan and Adriana Foster, and their new little girl." Jessie's face softened. "Matt, she was perfect. I loved holding her." She showed him the pictures she had taken on her phone.

"How are they doing?"

"They seem to be fine. Although, I'm sure the new baby has changed their lives in a major way."

"I can imagine. I think that's why my parents travel so much now. No rowdy boys to worry about, they're finally free."

Jessie nudged Matt's hand. "Before I forget, Reba said to watch over Darsha. She's seen more than she should have and someone is aware of her knowledge."

"I'm waiting to hear from the FBI agent in charge of the investigation. One of them was reported missing a few days ago. I can't say much, but the life of anyone with knowledge of this case is in jeopardy. Darsha, her family, and people who know them are in danger." Matt rubbed his temple. "Let's just say this case is a big one and will have the Feds descending on Blue Cove along with the press when the story leaks out."

"I know you'll tell me what you can when you're able to. I'm sure of one thing; I was supposed to meet Darsha. She is important to this case."

"It's strange or maybe not so strange she came into your store." Matt grinned at her. "I'm starting to catch on to how this works. It's fate or some kind of destiny thing." He took a bite of his sandwich.

"I was hooked the moment I saw him sitting on the rock watching the body coming ashore. The big guys may come to town, but you and I will have our part in solving this case because the victims have come to us." Jessie frowned. "Where is Darsha anyway?"

"She's still at the station. We're waiting for her parents to come for her. We need to talk with them. I wanted to see you, eat lunch, and now it's back to work for me. I have more questions than answers right now." Matt stood. He wrapped the rest of his sandwich to take with him. "How's dinner sound?"

"Perfect, if you're there." Jessie walked him to the door. "See you later." She kissed his cheek and got back to work.

If she hurried, there was enough time to put a few books on the shelf and replenish the display table before her next customer. The cemetery at the church was in her line of sight as she straightened the sale sign in the window. Where was his ghost today? Were they both still in town, or had they moved on? Shrugging her shoulders, she moved to the counter which needed sprucing up.

The bell above the door rang, breaking into her thoughts. An odd little man shuffled into her store. He grabbed a magazine and sat down in a chair to read. More than once she caught him looking over the top of the magazine at her. He was making her nervous. The man was thin, with angry blue eyes, and he walked with a slight limp.

"Can I help you?" She smiled tentatively at him.

"No, I'll read here and pay for the magazine before I leave." His foot shook back and forth in front of the chair.

Two women in the coffee shop made their way into the store, chatting and laughing. They bantered back and forth, hardly taking the time to catch a breath. Jessie smiled. With their cups of steaming coffee and books, they sat at the table in the center of the room. "Do you mind if our book club meets here?" one of the women asked. "A few more will be joining us soon."

"This is a perfect place for your club to meet, and I'm happy to have you." The strange man wasn't pleased though, if his scowl was any indication. Jumping to his feet when the next group of women walked in the door, he limped to the counter to pay for the magazine, his frown making the wrinkles on his face more pronounced,

"Nice place you have here. I'll be back. I can guarantee it." The man's voice sounded gruff.

Jessie handed him his change, not liking the way he had said he'd be back. It sounded more like a veiled threat to her than a normal comment. "Would you like a bag?"

"Nope." He rolled the magazine hastily in his hands and walked into the coffee shop.

Pulling out a chair with force, he sat at a table where he could see in her store. The book club stayed all afternoon, and he was still in the same spot when she shut and locked the doors going into the coffee shop.

"Feel free to meet here anytime." She walked over to the table to meet the members in the group. "You might want to put your club time on the calendar and make this your regular place to meet," she added. "I'd love to have you."

"Good idea. We could meet every month. I'll talk to everyone and get back to you."

"Here's my card and number." Jessie walked the last couple of women to the door. The man was standing outside leaning against the lamppost. Locking the door, she turned the sign around to "Closed." Relief filled her when Matt pulled up in his cruiser, and the man moved on.

Chapter 4

When Jessie opened the door for Matt, she stepped outside and glanced down the sidewalk.

"Are you looking for something?" Matt grabbed her arm to pull her back. He held her around the waist.

"I am, but he got away." She tried to pull away.

"He who?" Matt frowned. He held on to her until she answered his question.

"I don't know who he is." Jessie told him about the odd little man who had watched her store all day. "He must have scurried between the buildings after he saw your car."

"I don't like the idea of someone casing your store, especially after Darsha was here earlier." He followed her back inside and took the keys from her hand. "Let's drive your car and go somewhere quiet to talk."

Jessie checked the door to make sure it was locked. "Quiet sounds perfect to me." She turned off the lights as she headed to the back room. "I know you've had to learn something today, and I'm impatient to hear the details. You know how I get. Once I heard our victim's cries, I was hooked."

"I've learned plenty. More than I wanted to know," Matt muttered as he closed her car door. He slipped into the driver's seat.

"Is it all right if I ask you something?" She turned in her seat so she could see him.

"Ask away. I'll answer if I can."

"Is it possible there's another body somewhere?" His expression told her what she needed to know.

"It's not only possible but highly probable." He started the car. "What made you think of another body? You didn't see another ghost, did you?"

"No, but I got a good look at Darsha's posters. I recognized the one young man, but the man in the second photo was not one of our victims."

"Good observation, sweetheart. You're right." Matt turned onto Main Street and headed out of town to the highway. "From what I learned today, I have a hunch a few more bodies might show up. With any luck, we won't find them in my jurisdiction. Lewis has his hands full with two." Matt adjusted his mirror. "Did I mention I talked to Agent Kaufman?"

"No. Is he the agent in charge of the case?"

"He was the lead agent in charge of the abduction and will work with us on the murder for now. Kaufman is on his way to Blue Cove and will be at the station in the morning. No one understands the reason for the torture or the murder. From everything the agency's investigation has uncovered to date, the victim was a good student, played by the rules, and was popular on campus. The boy's father was stunned when he received the ransom note."

"Have you seen the ransom note?"

"Not yet, I should see a copy soon. The families are in shock. Neither young man seemed to have any enemies." Matt continued to drive. "Both victims were only twenty. It makes no damn sense. "Too young to die, that's for sure."

Jessie brushed her hand against his. "It's sad and

kind of depressing. It makes me wonder what the world is coming to."

"I know. I can't imagine what the families are going through."

"Where are we headed? I forgot to ask you earlier."

"Dylan and I found a nice place a few miles out of town a few weeks ago on our way back from the city. We can enjoy a quiet meal together." Matt paused, becoming silent for a few minutes. He glanced at her. "It's liable to get hectic around here the next several days." He signaled his turn into the parking lot. "There's a tight lid on this case."

"I get it. I can't speak a word of it to anyone." Jessie fiddled with the purse sitting on her lap. His tension was making her uneasy. "What do we know so far? You know—details that we can discuss at this time."

"I've learned enough to know I wished those two had come ashore in the next town. We have a potential for a big mess on our hands. Dave has two bodies in the morgue, and I know the identity of one of them, which must remain a secret for the moment. When it gets out, it will be big news." He walked around to open her door. He took her hand when she stepped out of the car.

"I wish I could do more" She rubbed her thumb across the palm of his hand. "This will be a stressful time for you and our town."

"Having you around helps me more than you know." He smiled at her. "Let's eat. I'm hungry." Matt stopped walking. "I can breathe when I'm with you."

Jessie smiled at him. "I'd say breathing is a good thing."

"You know what I mean. I can rest when I'm with

you."

"Rest is good too. Personally, I think we're good together."

"The best. How are you doing?" he asked before they walked into the restaurant.

"I'm fine, but I can't stop thinking about that man's face when he watched his body coming ashore. It was surreal."

"I can imagine. I think we both need this time together." Their conversation ceased when the hostess escorted them to their table. "Have you seen his ghost since yesterday?"

"No." Jessie looked at the menu. "I'm not sure I want to either. I don't know if a ghost can be in shock or not, but he seemed to be. I don't want to be around when the shock wears off." She rolled her eyes. "I know, it sounds weird to me too."

After they had given the waiter their order, Matt filled her in on the details he could tell her. "Your idea of torture from an electrical prod was correct. The weapon of choice was a picana." He told her the details Dave had told him. "Those two suffered; the question is why? What did they do?"

"Do you have any theories?" She placed her napkin on her lap.

"I was thinking drugs, but after talking to Darsha, I'm not sure now." Matt waited for the waiter to place their salads on the table. "Darsha said he wasn't a user. Of course, he could have hidden that part of his life from her, or he could have sold drugs on campus and stole the money."

"I'm sure Darsha would know. Addiction to drugs is not easy to hide. Besides, he didn't look like the kind of kid who would do drugs to me, but I could be wrong."

"I wish it was easy enough to pick them out by their looks. We could save a lot of lives that way. The case is in the early stages; it could go so many directions from here."

"What about a hate crime?" Jessie took a bite of her salad. "Darsha is from India, one of the young men was white, and I don't know the other's ethnic background. Reba made it sound like hate could have played a part in it."

"I'm sure it did. There is an element of hate and passion in most murders." He twirled his wine in his glass.

Jessie watched him closely. He was pensive. She knew what it meant. He was walking a tightrope, guarding information, and still trying to bring her into the case. She loved how he included her. "I'm sure we'll know soon enough, and you'll tell me when you can." Jessie changed the subject to her day at work. He laughed in all the right places, but she knew he was far away.

****

Matt leaned his head back against his recliner. He had been downright boring tonight, not because of the company, she was mighty fine. Picking up the remote, he flipped through the stations hoping something would grab his attention. Jessie understood his crazy moods when he was at the beginning of a case. Hell, it was more like anytime during a case, if he was honest. She understood this quirk about him; not many women would. He loved that about her. Matt wanted to talk about the case, but he couldn't risk something slipping out until the right people were in place. Jess was in the middle of it all too; the body had found her and so had the kid's ghost. She must have needed to talk about it. Some listening ear he had.

Damn, who was casing her store? It concerned him more than he had let on. Why was he there? Darsha must have a tail. At least the Sarins were in a safe house for the night. He put his feet up and reached for his phone.

Jeremy answered on the third ring. "Hey, man, what's up?"

"I've got some research for you to do." Matt gave Jeremy the details that he had now without giving away the identity. "I want you to check out the group."

"I'll take care of it."

"Call me when you get anything, and maybe I'll be able to fill in more details for you soon."

"I will, and, Matt, people who use torture devices are not nice and don't act alone. Keep your eyes open and make sure someone has your back."

"I'll keep your advice in mind."

Chapter 5

Matt's day started out hectic and showed no sign of getting any better. Agent Kaufman met with his officers early in the morning and updated them on the investigation. Amir Baz was one of the victims. His father, a diplomat at the Kuwait Embassy in D.C., was the one who had reported his son missing. Matt had a copy of the ransom note Mr. Baz had received. After reading over it several times, he was still having a hard time understanding the hate-filled rant. Crudely written, the page had religious underpinnings and racial bigotry, which made little or no sense. There was a demand for a million dollars for Amir's safe return. The FBI had monitored all incoming calls into the embassy, but the kidnappers only called once, letting the parents hear Amir's voice before hanging up. They never contacted the family again with any instructions. Matt shook his head. They obviously weren't in it for the money. What was their motive?

Ryan Lucas was the identity of their second victim. The FBI was on the lookout for two more missing persons, Carlos Huerta and Shara Nachman. All of them were good students, leaders on campus, and well liked. Their common link, besides being good friends, was their leadership roles in a club fostering good relations between students of various ethnic backgrounds. Many students on campus participated in the club. Darsha, also one of the leaders, was late to the meeting that day. Matt penciled a note into the open file. It was strange how a matter of minutes could forever change a person's life.

He picked up the phone and dialed the coroner's office. "Hey, Dave, this is Matt. I was informed a short time ago that you can proceed with the Baz autopsy as soon as the family's mullah and representative get there."

"Okay, chief. I know how important it is to the family that we follow their country's protocol, the law, and their religious practices. I'll make sure the body is ready when we release him for burial. Time is of the essence in these cases. I've done a few before."

"I'm sure you have. I'm afraid this case comes with added pressure from our government. They want answers."

"Who doesn't? We'll have a few shortly, but the toxicology results will take longer. I'll call you as soon as we're done here."

"Thanks Dave." He disconnected the call.

What else did the kids have in common besides this group? Matt was sure there had to be more. The way they were tortured made him think they knew or had something their abductors wanted. Why pick on the kids? The next few days would consist of putting together their story in the days leading up to the kidnapping. Somewhere in the ordinary movements of their normal day were clues waiting for discovery. Jessie could help him with the details. His pencil tapped on the file.

Agent Kaufman knocked on Matt's door. "I thought you might like to see this." He opened up the box and pulled out the rod. "This is like the weapon used on those boys."

Matt held the device in his hand. Lightweight and easy to transport, with maximum torture capabilities—the authorities' worst nightmare. It had inflicted maximum damage to those kids. "I've never seen anything like this before. Usually, we deal with guns or knives." Matt turned it over in his hands. "How do you stop something like this?"

"I doubt it's a weapon of choice in our country, which makes me wonder if we have a foreign group operating in the area." Kaufman sat in the chair in front of Matt's desk. "We have a couple of agents at the school asking questions. We have the boys' computers, and we're going through them as we speak. I've scheduled a news conference for later today. I want to control the information getting out. Maybe someone saw something. Right now, the only thing we have connecting them is the group on campus."

"What about the other two missing students? Has anything turned up on them yet?" Matt placed the picana on the corner of his desk.

"Nothing, not a word. At this point, another ransom note would be nice. Not that the last one got us anywhere. I don't relish the thought of finding any more bodies of college students. I have a daughter about their age in her first year on campus. I'd like to bring her home where I can keep her safe. She'd never let me, but I'd still like to. How about you, any kids?"

Matt shook his head. "No, I'm not married yet, but getting close."

"I thought you seemed a little young for the position you're in. How'd you come by this sweet job?"

Matt explained how he came to have Anderson's job. He told him about Jessie and her help to the department. "She's the one that made the call when the body found her."

"Now I know I'll have to meet her. Tom told me about her. I didn't realize she was the one who found the victims."

"She has had some unique experiences since moving here."

"Is she some kind of psychic?" Kaufman asked.

"She'd tell you absolutely not. It is a mystery to all of us, especially her. I don't know what to call it, but I've come to trust her intuitive nature. Jessie has helped to solve more than one case along with her friend's tracking bloodhound, Radar."

"We should work on what we're going to say at the news conference. It's scheduled for two."

"Sounds good." Matt and Kaufman talked strategy for a while.

****

Jessie had finished her work at the church and stepped out into the bright sunlight. It was a beautiful day. Spring was pushing the last remnants of winter away. Good riddance! Warmer weather meant more time at the beach. She was daydreaming when she found herself face to face with yet another ghost. This one was a female, which meant there was a body somewhere nearby. Maybe if she ignored it and made her way back to the store, it would go somewhere else. Jessie didn't turn to look, but she could tell by the charged atmosphere the ghost was following her.

She opened the door to her store and smiled at Audrey. "How was your morning?"

"It was quiet and slow except for a strange little man who came in. He kept asking me questions. I kept saying I didn't know the answers and he finally left. It was the truth. I had no idea how to answer him." Audrey grabbed her purse from under the counter. "He was way too intense for me."

"What did he ask?"

"He wanted to know where you were which I told him I didn't know. I know that was a lie, but I didn't think it was any of his business. He asked if any foreigners had been in the store in the past few days. I told him only bus tours, and they are usually from the big cities."

"I hope he didn't bother you for too long." Jessie glanced through the mail.

"He left as soon as several women came in and sat at the table to talk."

"At least he didn't bother you for long. I'll keep my eye out for him. Hopefully, he won't be back anytime soon. Enjoy your afternoon." She waved as Audrey walked out the door. Jessie's stomach gurgled, reminding her she was hungry. A chicken salad sandwich sounded good right now. She waved Molly over to the open doors and gave her order. "I'll be over to pay in a minute."

Jessie called Matt and left him a message when he didn't answer. She explained there was another body somewhere nearby. *"You need to look for a female this time. I came face to face with her ghost."*

After lunch, her afternoon got busy. Evan delivered a new order of books, and she had several new customers stop by. She loved to spend time talking to people about books. The plans for her summer reading program were starting to take shape. Reading was a big part of her childhood, and she would like to do the same for the kids of Blue Cove.

The bell over the door rang when Matt walked in. She went to him and asked. "Did you get my message?"

"I haven't had time to listen to my messages. We had a news conference at two to release the names of the two students whose bodies were found." He grabbed hold of her hand and led her over to the chair. He shared with her what he knew about their victims. "Now we see if Blue Cove is inundated with the press." He leaned his head back against the chair. "What was your message?"

"I saw another ghost. I think the girl's body has to be somewhere close by."

"Damn!" He frowned.

"Was there a female abducted when the guys went missing?" She held her breath.

"Yes, but we were hoping she was still alive and a ransom note would be coming. I guess that was a stretch considering how they tortured the other two victims." He rubbed his temple. "I have no idea where to begin looking."

"You forget Radar. He can find her if she's in the area."

"You're right, I'll call Frank. Kaufman can get a scent item from her family. I hope it's not her, but my gut tells me that none of these kids will make it home alive to their families unless they leave one to tell the story for effect. I still don't get why they ended up here. We're miles away from the campus."

"Who knows why? Unless of course, we were the ones meant to find them and get them back to their families for closure. Frank told me once that getting them home, even when they are dead, is important for the families. I believe it. I can't imagine what it would be like to always wonder if they were alive out there somewhere."

"I have new information to fill you in on, but I have to get back to the station. We'll talk at dinner. I'll order the pizza and have it delivered to your house. Does six sound good to you?" He reached for her hand, pulling her up beside him.

"I'll be there." She walked with him to the door. "Before I forget, Audrey said there was a man in here asking questions earlier. He was the same man who was here the day Darsha came in. He's determined to find her, I think."

"We'll have to make sure he doesn't get near her." Matt kissed her. "See you."

He had a sexy walk. Why hadn't she noticed it before? The familiar heat moved up her neck and face. She hoped, for his sake, there wouldn't be another body found in the area. Matt didn't need it right now. It had to be frustrating for him to have the press descending on the town, along with the FBI, and the families to contend with while trying to do his job. He liked working behind the scene and not in the limelight—one of the qualities she loved and learned about him when the marina was bombed.

In her heart, she knew they would find the girl's body in the area. "It's meant to be," as Reba would say. Jessie was starting to understand what Reba was talking about each time she said those words. Jessie felt connected to all the cases she had been a part of, and she cared about the families involved. Matt did his job, never giving up until he solved the case. Together they made a way for the people to move through the grief and pain of losing their loved ones. "Keep him safe," she whispered as he drove away.

Chapter 6

Jessie made a salad and set the table. She reached for the glasses in the cupboard. What she wanted to do was to talk to Darsha while the details were fresh in her mind. Amir was her boyfriend, and she had spent a lot of time with him over the past several months. Darsha would know more than anyone what, if any changes, had occurred in him. Jessie made a mental note of questions to ask her when she got the chance as she placed the glasses on the table.

Distracted, she tossed the salad with dressing, sprinkling cheese and slices of pepperoni on the top. A quick glance at the clock told her Matt would be there soon. She placed the salad in the fridge and went to her computer to check her e-mails. A few names down the list, she found the one she was hoping for from Jeremy. He was working on something for Matt, but he had promised to keep her in the loop. The more details he learned from Matt, the more he had expressed his concern over the case. They were only a few days in, and Jeremy was already full of warnings. His message to her was short and sweet. *Call me when you get this!*

Jessie picked up her phone and called her friend.

"Hi, sweetheart, is Matt with you?" he asked when she answered the phone.

"No, but I'm expecting him any minute. He's coming for dinner. Why?" The hair on Jessie's neck got prickly.

"I need to talk to you both." Jeremy sounded troubled to her. "Call me back as soon as he gets there. Promise."

"I will. You've got me worried. Is something wrong?" she asked.

"It's fair to say you both have walked into a deadly mess, and we need to talk about the information I've found so far."

"Like what?" She stared at the computer screen.

"I'd rather wait and talk to you both, if you don't mind." His voice calmed when he changed the subject. "Did I hear right that Katie and Dylan are engaged?"

"Yes, I'm sorry it didn't work out between you two."

"It makes sense to me. I always felt that something didn't feel quite right between us. Katie tried, and so did I. I think she has always loved Dylan."

"You're probably right. You can still come to visit me anytime. I love seeing you." She waved at Matt when he walked in. "Matt's here,"

"Who are you talking to?" Matt asked her.

"Jeremy wants to talk to us both. I have it on speaker." She sat next to Matt on the sofa. "Jeremy, we're ready. You can start anytime."

"Hey, Matt. I wanted to let you both know what I've found out so far. The kids who participated in the group are devastated. These young leaders were well liked on campus. None of the students I talked to could make sense of it."

"Agents have found out the same info from their interviews." Matt grabbed her hand and held it tightly.

"One thing I found interesting was that a couple of

students told me there has been more hate rhetoric on campus in recent weeks. There were several scuffles between members of their Foreign Students' Club and a Neo-Nazi group new to the campus," Jeremy explained.

"Great, a hate group bent on stirring up trouble." Matt frowned. "They seem to be coming out of the woodwork across the country. Different names but the same old story."

"We have a climate ripe for it now, I guess," Jeremy added.

"Don't I know it. Dylan had to bust up a fight at the Blue Cove High School the other day over the same issues."

"I wish it were only a few scuffles that you have to deal with, Matt, I've been doing some research, and this form of torture has been used recently. It's turned up a couple of times now. What I've learned is a little frightening."

"What are we looking at?" Matt asked.

"It's only a beginning idea, but it's often used as a method to gain information from an unwilling victim. In our country, guns are the weapons of choice for hate groups, gangs, and almost anybody committing a crime. These foreign groups seem to play by different rules. Several groups routinely use the picana rod along with drug cocktails. We're talking about some tough characters who use these methods." Jeremy went on to tell them about a couple of cases he had found so far.

"Now that's scary." Jessie jumped up when she heard the door. She went to get the pizza and pay the teenager who delivered it.

"I hope you both understand your suspects mean business. Anyone who would abduct college students and torture them is serious about what they stand for. Whatever it is. It can be for some strange worldview ideology or as simple as a core belief that the races shouldn't mix. They may be from one of the countries of the students, or it might be a homegrown group which has adopted techniques from a foreign group."

"You've given us plenty to think about." Matt followed Jessie into the kitchen. "Keep digging into it, would you, and get back to me with anything new you find out. I'll keep you informed, too.'

"You're too quiet, Jessie. Why? It's not like you." Jeremy said.

"I'm thinking, Jeremy. I mean I've heard racist comments in my lifetime, and I knew these groups operated in the country, but to see it so blatantly exposed makes me wonder if I know people at all."

"We all understand this ugliness exists in secret, but you don't expect it to take center stage in the news. I'll get back to you if I find out anything new. Be careful, especially you, sweetheart, you find the good in everybody—sometimes to the point of being naïve."

"You've got that right." She frowned. "I'll have to stop it. When are you coming for a visit again?" Jessie changed the subject.

"I'll have to see when I can get away. Talk to you both later." Jeremy disconnected.

"Jess," Matt lifted her chin and looked into her eyes. "You're intuitive and smart. You care about people, but you're not dumb."

"I need to know this because…" Her voice trailed off.

"Because you're not naïve, you're caring, and there's a big difference." He smiled at her. "You can take care of business when you need to. I'm sure Roger and Adam would agree."

She blushed. "Let's eat while the pizza is still hot." She took the salad out of the fridge and placed it on the table. Handing him a beer, she filled her glass with iced tea. "Ummm, this smells good. I'm hungry."

"Me too. You can change the subject, sweetheart, but you can't change the fact you're the strongest woman I've ever met." He took his napkin and wiped off the tomato sauce that had landed on her chin.

"Messy, too, obviously." She smiled at him.

"Easy on the eyes and fun to be with." He opened his beer. "Shall we get down to business? I need your perspective on this case."

****

Matt had stayed later than he had intended. Jessie was falling asleep on the sofa when he told her to go to bed; he was leaving. A few incredible kisses later he was out the door wishing he could stay. Once his lips had tasted hers, he was lost.

After listening to her explain her ideas of the case, Matt knew it was important for her to talk to Darsha. She had a great list of questions to ask her—things he would have never thought to ask. She was his perfect counterpart. He would arrange a meeting between them. Darsha could be aware of something significant without realizing it. Some new detail would emerge; that's how it always seemed to work. He shook his head and smiled.

He was glad she was on his side. She was with him a hundred percent, and made him feel like he could do anything he set out to do. The only problem was leaving her at night when, in truth, he wanted to stay.

"Soon enough," he whispered, his fingers tapping on the steering wheel. With the twist of the key, the engine turned over.

Playing his earlier conversation with Jessie over in his mind, he didn't notice the car that tailed him. The car stopped when he pulled onto his property and into his garage.

Why had this case come to them? They had made plans tonight on how to proceed in between the glances and kisses. He tried to rehearse them in his mind, but he kept drifting back to Jessie all warm and gorgeous, leaning against his side. He had no discipline when it came to her. What could he say? He loved her.

Chapter 7

Jessie rolled onto her side and drifted off to sleep. *A swirling mist drew her to the edge of the woods. She couldn't see anything through the dense fog, only a narrow pathway twisting around the trees. Enticing, the foggy haze seduced her to move one step closer. Jessie paused. She didn't want to go in alone. Panicking, she started to turn back before it was too late. "Jess," Matt's faint voice called out to her. He sounded wheezy and breathless, and she could hear the pain in his voice. Where was he? She glanced around, hoping to see his familiar face. "Jess..." The call came again. She shivered. Matt was in the darkness, and death had come to play. The faces of those tortured young men danced in the mist before her. Her feet refused to move. She was paralyzed with fear. The silence around her was deafening. "Jess," he screamed out her name once more, trusting her to aid him. Tears filled her eyes, spilling down her cheeks. This time there was no way she could help...* Jessie awakened with a start. She looked at the clock. It was too late to call Matt. Jeremy was right; someone needed to watch Matt's back. Troubled by the thought that she might not be able to help him, her mind wouldn't shut down.

****

Matt had a restless night. The possibility of a third body in his town bothered him. Frank would arrive today with Radar. Matt wanted to get started looking for the possible third victim. Agent Kaufman had the scent items from both Shara's family and the Huertas in case Jessie saw another ghost. Matt was on edge and wanted answers.

He picked up his phone to call her. "Good morning, sweetheart." Matt poured coffee into his cup as he waited for her reply.

"Are you doing okay?" she asked.

Something was wrong; he could hear it in her voice. "I'm fine. What's up?" He put a bagel in the toaster.

"I had a strange dream last night. I almost called you. Jeremy is right. Someone needs to watch your back."

"I'll be fine." His bagel popped up, and Matt spread some jalapeno cream cheese on it. "Frank will be here this morning to search for Shara's body. Do you want to come along, or are you working?"

"I'm at the store this morning. I'm not sure if I can get anyone to sub for me on such short notice, but I'll try."

"I'll check back with you before we leave." He took a sip of his coffee.

"Maybe one of the ladies could answer the phone at the church so Audrey can watch the store. I'll let you know if it works out."

"Sounds good, and, Jess, don't worry about me. I'll be fine."

"Easier said than done." She sighed. "I love you, Matt, and I'm supposed to be concerned. I think it comes with the territory."

"I'm happy you love me. With you watching my

back, I'll be fine." He glanced at the clock. "I have a meeting. I need to get to work." He put the lid on his coffee mug. "I'll talk to you in a while. Dylan let me know earlier that the press is camping outside of the station. It's going to be a long day answering questions. I only wish I had some answers to give them."

"Let Kaufman do it," Jessie said.

"I will," Matt said his goodbyes and headed for his car.

He'd be happy if he could fill in a few more empty spaces in the victims' files today. They didn't need another body, but since Jessie had seen something, they'd be finding one before long.

He parked at the station and made his way to the door, dodging reporters and their questions. "Patience, fella," Matt said to one reporter who thrust a mic in his face. "We'll give you answers as soon as we have them. In the meantime, go eat some breakfast, get a cup of coffee, and try to chill. I'll get a schedule of upcoming news conferences to you sometime today." He stepped inside and closed the door.

"I see you made it in the door without punching anyone." Dylan chuckled and followed Matt. "It was a close call for the fella who shoved a mic in my face earlier, but I restrained myself. I didn't want to give the department a bad name."

"I'm happy for your restraint," Matt said with a chuckle. "Although, I'm sure your self-control will be tested over the next several days." Matt scowled. "Is Kaufman here yet?'

"He arrived a few minutes ago. I sent him to get a cup of coffee." Dylan pointed the way.

"As soon as we can, we should give the reporters a

schedule. They need to know when to be here, so they can come and go as they want. At least I hope they warm to the idea and won't constantly be underfoot."

"It's a nice thought anyway." Dylan got in step with Matt, and they walked into the lunchroom together.

"There you are, Parker." Kaufmann gave him an impatient glance. "I've put together a list to give the press. We have nothing to give them this morning, so I scheduled the first press conference at four p.m. Give it to one of your officers to hand out. We should get started going over our plans for the day."

"Dylan, make copies and have Kip hand them out to the reporters when I tell you to. We may need to keep the press busy at some point." Matt handed Dylan the list Kaufman had given him as the three headed down the hall.

"Will do, chief." Dylan went to make the copies.

Matt closed the door once they were in his office. "I have a bloodhound coming this morning, so we can do a search for Shara's body. If she is in the area, this dog should find her. Frank will be here with him by ten-thirty."

"Sounds good. Maxwell assured me this dog brings his A game and will do a bang-up job. I've never seen a search dog in action. It should be an interesting experience." Kaufman drank his coffee.

"You'll be amazed by his capabilities."

"I have to admit, I was a bit skeptical about Shara's body being in the area, but Tom said if Jessie saw it, we had better take it seriously. I'm willing to give it a gander. Hell, I don't know how you deal with this stuff." He shook his head. "I would have written her off as a kook the first time she came to me."

"I can't say I embraced it at first. In fact, I didn't want Jessie involved in my case at all. We fought about it." Matt grinned at the memory. "She got in my face, told me what she thought, walked out of my office in a huff, and did what she said she would do. Besides falling hard for her, I discovered she's invaluable when it comes to shaking up stuff." Matt told Kaufman about a few of the cases he had solved with Jessie's help.

"I would've probably arrested her for interfering in an investigation. I'll be the first to admit I'm intrigued and look forward to meeting her." Kaufman took a sip of his coffee.

"You will before long, I'm sure." Matt glanced at his notepad. "Before I forget, Jessie requested an interview with Darsha. Jessie has a way of putting people at ease and getting information from them that the police overlook. O'Malley, a precinct captain in New York, once told me she does it because she thinks like a girl. It'll make your head spin, but she gets what she's looking for. She's that good."

"I'll take your word for it. I'll arrange to have Darsha brought here and let her give it a shot. We haven't gotten much to go on from our interviews of her."

"Jessie will, believe me." Matt's phone buzzed. "This is Matt. Okay, Kenny, send him in. While you're at it, call Jessie and see if she can make it this morning. If it's a yes, tell her to watch for us and meet us at the church. Let me know as soon as you find out." Matt stood by his door and waved at Frank. "Thanks for making the trip here this morning."

Frank walked in with Radar on a short leash. "I

hope you don't mind. I didn't want to leave my dog in the car with all the action in your parking lot."

"It's crazy out there." Matt nodded. "He'll do better in here. Frank, this is Agent Kaufman. He's a friend of Tom Maxwell and has already heard about Radar." The two men shook hands. "Would you like some coffee?'

"No, I've had enough for the day." Frank sat down. "What's the plan?" He listened while Matt filled him in on the details.

"We'll start by the church and see if Radar can pick up any scent. Jessie was near the church when she saw the ghost of one of our possible victims. You know how she works, so I don't need to say any more on the subject."

"Affirmative." Frank eyed Kaufman's skeptical expression. "It sounds strange, but like the rest of us, I think you'll be amazed at how accurate she is. Our girl may be unconventional, but she's right on the money."

Kenny knocked on Matt's door. "Miss Reynolds said to tell you she'll meet you at the church."

"Great. Thanks, Kenny." Matt stood smiling to himself at Kenny's formality "Let's get started."

"How are we going to keep the press from following us?" Kaufman asked.

"Frank, you leave first. Drive around the block and meet us at the front of the building. If the press follows, we'll have to put up a police line and keep the reporters at a distance. I don't want Radar to be affected by all of the people."

"Good idea. Radar gets testy if people get in his space when he's working a track." Frank walked out the door into the hall with his dog. "I'll be at the front in about ten minutes."

Matt nodded. He buzzed Dylan. "In five minutes, you and Kip can begin handing those schedules out to the press. Keep them busy asking questions. We need to make our escape."

"We'll take care of it."

****

When Frank pulled into the church parking lot, Jessie was standing outside waiting for them.

"Jess, this is Agent Kaufman."

"Nice to meet you." She patted Radar's head as she talked to the agent.

"Let's get started." Matt handed Frank a plastic bag.

"Sounds good to me." Frank pulled one of Shara's sweaters out of the bag. He put Radar's line on, bent toward the dog, and held the scent item at his nose. "Hey, big fella," Frank said. "It's time to get to work. Find the girl. Let's bring her home."

Jessie walked beside Frank as Radar pulled him across the front of the church toward the cemetery. "She was at the front of the church when I saw her."

"It looks like he's on to something, and we're headed in the right direction." Frank held on as Radar tugged hard. He was in his zone and moved purposefully through the graveyard to the woods behind the church. After a few minutes, he veered off on a path to the right that led through dense underbrush and trees. He came into a clearing pulling Frank hard and stopped in front of a cluster of bushes. He pawed at the ground.

Jessie saw the foot before Frank did. "He's found something," she called back to Matt.

"Damn, we have another body." Matt called the

station for his crime unit. "Kip, see if you can find a pair of hedge clippers. Hank might have some in his shop. We need to clear some brush away without disturbing the body. If he doesn't have any, I have some in my garage at home."

Matt and Kaufman worked on lifting away any dead brush they could move without disturbing the body. Jessie placed it all in a pile. Once the team arrived, they made short work of it.

"I wonder why they dumped her here. How far is the highway, Matt?" Kaufman asked.

"Not far. It's an area dense with trees and undergrowth, but they could manage it. The victim doesn't appear to have been dragged, though." Matt studied the body carefully and took notes. Like the boys, she was stripped down to her undergarments with her hands tied behind her back. The same wire used on the male victims appeared to have been used to tie her hands. There was tape across her mouth, and her captors had used the torture prod on her. "I wonder what these kids got themselves into?" Matt shook his head.

The unit combed through the area, making their way through the trees and down to the highway. They searched for drag marks, shoe prints, or any other clues which could tell them more about who might have dumped her body and why in this location. Marcy took pictures.

"Were there marks like this on the other bodies you found?" Frank asked Jessie.

"Yes. All made by the same kind of electric torture device. Each of the victims had several marks on their bodies. It makes you wonder about people. I don't understand how we can be so cruel to one another." Jessie sat on the trunk of a fallen tree. "From what we have learned, these kids were great kids. It doesn't make sense to me."

"The longer you work with us, Miss Reynolds, the more you'll understand that murder rarely makes sense." Kaufman sat down beside her. "Explain to me how you knew there was another body in the area."

"I know you'll find it hard to believe, but this is the world I live in right now." Jessie explained how she had seen the ghost.

"Tom told me about you. I can't say I believed him when he told me about you leaping out of the tree to save them that night. The whole story of what happened was beyond the norm. Having watched this play out, I might have to rethink my position."

"I had to." Matt walked over to the group. "There are many things in life too hard to explain, and I've learned to place the way she solves cases in one of those categories." He smiled at her. "All I know is it works."

"Yes, it does." Jessie rubbed her forehead. The victim was young, with her whole life ahead of her. She wiped a tear as it made its way down her cheek. Murder was a nasty business and ruined so many lives in the process. The anger she felt rising up surprised her. Closing her eyes, she fought to tamp down her emotions. When she opened them again, Shara's ghost was watching her.

Chapter 8

Happy to be back at Idle Times before it was time to close, Jessie got to work. Pushing her hair behind her ear, she massaged her temple. *Long and disturbing* were the words that came to mind to describe her morning. It didn't help her emotional state that the girl's spirit had watched their every move. Were people always aware of what was happening to them after death? The expression of sorrow on the spirit's face seemed to indicate that she was aware. Jessie doubted any theologian alive would want to tackle this one.

She straightened the book table. Audrey had placed some of the new books on the counter earlier in the day. Carrying a stack of paperbacks over to the shelves, she slipped them into their places. She got the feather duster, flicking it back and forth over the books and shelves with gusto. After tackling the counter, she cleaned the glass on the front door. If a customer didn't come in soon, the whole place would be spotless.

"Idle Time Books, may I help you," Jessie answered the ringing phone.

"Hi, sweetheart, are you free later on?" Matt asked.

"No plans, I'm open to suggestions."

"How does dinner sound? I'm taking Frank and Kaufman out. It would be great if you came along. I think Dylan and Katie might come too. He's calling her now."

"Sounds like a good way to spend an evening." She loved the deep, husky timbre of his voice. "I'm always down with spending time with Frank, and you too, of course."

"The feeling is mutual, sweetheart." He paused. "Jess, what happened at the murder site? It's not like you to clam up. You left before I got a chance to ask you." He sounded worried.

"Has the girl been identified?" She turned toward the door when the bell rang.

"Yes, it was Shara Nachman." He paused. "You still haven't answered my question."

"Shara's ghost was watching us." She softened her voice and glanced at the woman who walked into the store. Her dark, short hair made her deep brown eyes seem huge on her attractive face.

"Ah, I thought so."

"It still troubles me when I see them looking at their own bodies. I heard Amir crying. Did I tell you that?" She turned her head and spoke quietly into the phone. "I'm sure I did." She ran the feather duster over the counter again "It's hard for me to forget the victims; they're real people whose deaths hurt many others. Honestly, I don't know how the police do their job every day."

"It can be brutal at times and murder is never pleasant, but most days are routine. Besides, I doubt there are many police officers who have the added burden of seeing the victims' ghosts staring at their bodies."

"True, I'll talk to you later." She smiled. "I have a customer."

"I'll pick you up at your house at six. I don't want

you to have to wait at the store after closing."

Jessie hung up the phone. "May I help you?" She walked to where the woman stood. Up close, she looked like an older version of Darsha. Her eyes were the same dark chocolate brown. A calm, peaceful aura surrounded her.

"I hope so." She glanced at Jessie, a serene look on her face. "I wanted to ask you if you would come talk to my niece, Darsha. She was quite taken with your kindness and needs to talk to someone. The sadness is bottled up inside of her so deep. She doesn't sleep or eat. Our family is worried about her." The woman extended her hand. "I'm Aisha Sarin, Darsha's aunt. The family is staying with us for their safety." She handed Jessie a slip of paper with a phone number on it. "Please think about it and give me a call if you will come."

Aisha was a beautiful woman. "I would love to talk to Darsha. I've wanted to talk with her ever since she walked into this store a few days ago. I'll give you call, and we'll arrange a time that will work for both of us."

"Thank you, Miss..." She gave Jessie a tentative smile.

"I'm sorry, where are my manners? I'm Jessie Reynolds." She clasped the woman's hand. Thrilled at the prospect of talking to Darsha, she walked Aisha to the door. Poised and unruffled, Aisha was like Reba— at peace with her world.

"Please call and come soon. My niece is not well. She is waning, and I feel helpless."

"I will." Jessie watched the woman get into the car in front of the store. She waited until it pulled away and couldn't be seen anymore.

****

A constant stream of customers came through her store throughout the afternoon. Being busy meant sales, which was always good. Another book club signed up for a time to meet at the store every week. Idle Time Bookstore was fast becoming a place to hang out for the community and her dream was becoming reality. Five o'clock rolled around before she knew it.

Jessie started and finished the routine of closing the store with a spring in her step. Darsha knew something. She was sure of it. Once the shock of their murders wore off, details would start to emerge in her mind. Flipping the light switch off, she locked the back door, and headed to the car. Only Darsha would be able to answer some of the questions they needed to have answered.

****

Matt pulled in beside Jessie's car. He got out to open the door for her as she walked up the path. "Hi, sunshine," he whispered in her ear before she slipped into the seat.

She smiled at him and turned her head toward the back seat. "Do either of you need more leg room? I'd be happy to change places with you."

"I'm fine," Frank said with a chuckle. "My legs are shorter than yours."

"You can stay put." Kaufman patted the headrest. "We're fine back here. After the day we've had, I don't want to move until I'm going into the restaurant."

"I hear you." Frank laughed. "One of these days I'll just have to lie down and let Radar drag me."

"I noticed he tugs hard. Your arm must be sore at the end of a track." Kaufman checked his phone.

"He's strong, and I'm not getting any younger. This darn knee of mine gives out from time to time." Frank rubbed his knee as he said the words.

"Where are we going?" Jessie latched her seat belt and placed her purse near her feet.

"A new place that Dylan suggested. He seems to know all the best places around." Matt glanced in his rearview mirror and then his side mirror.

"Are they going to come?" Jessie had her fingers crossed. "I haven't seen Katie for a few days, and it would be great to see her."

"Yeah, he was at the Inn when we drove by."

"You boys can talk shop, and us girls can talk weddings. It will make for a great night."

"To tell you the truth, Jessie, I'm interested in hearing more about you," Kaufman told her. "I'm fascinated by all this, and I've never heard anything like it in all my days at the Bureau. I have a list of questions I want answers to. The wedding plans might have to wait."

At the highway, Matt turned to the right. He smiled at Jessie. "Relax. We have about a twenty-minute drive ahead of us." He gave a brief glance in his side mirror.

Frank was talking to Kaufman, which gave Jessie time to talk to Matt. "Darsha's aunt came into my store to visit me today. She wants me to talk to Darsha. Her family is worried about her." She saw Matt check his rearview mirror.

"Huh? Isn't that what you wanted?" He glanced in the mirror again.

"Yes, I'm happy." Jessie turned to look in the side mirror. The car behind them turned when they did.

"Looks like you're going to get your wish." He

gave her a quick glance. "If we're ever going to find the people who tortured these kids, we might need to shake things up. You have a way of doing it, sweetheart."

"Thanks. I never thought of myself as someone who rocks the boat." She smiled at him and glanced at the side mirror again. Their tail was still with them.

"Take it as a compliment. We're going to have to turn up the heat and force our suspects to show their hand." He signaled and slowed for a turn, glancing in the rearview mirror as he did so. He frowned. "A trap or two, close the circle around them, and force them out into the open—those are all things you can do with your pen." Matt parked the car.

"I hope you're hungry." Dylan and Katie came over to Matt's car. "They have great food here. Kip told me about it, and we tried the place a few weeks ago." Dylan pulled Katie into his side.

"I could use a good meal." Kaufman started toward the door of the restaurant.

"Me too." Frank fell in step with the agent.

Matt held Jessie's hand. "We'll talk later. Enjoy some down time with your friend, sweetheart." He held the door open and followed the others in.

"Thank you."Jessie gave the car that had tailed them a quick glance as she walked through the door. The man bent out of sight.

****

Too close for comfort. Marshall popped sideways on the seat and then peeked over the steering wheel. "Phew." He wiped the sweat from his brow. They were inside. He'd have to be more careful in the future. "No slip-ups now, Marshall, you're too close to your goal." His fingers strummed the armrest. He'd been tailing the cop for a few days. Nothing of interest yet, but it was a side job, and they paid him well. Why they were interested in the cop, he had no idea. You didn't ask guys like them questions. You took the money and kept your mouth shut. Keeping quiet was something he knew how to do. It was a game of dead or alive, and he wanted to live. This was his last side job. Retirement was in sight after thirty-five years on the force, on a lousy beat. They should have promoted him, but the Chief never gave him a chance. He scowled. With the money he would make from this hire and his pension, he'd be sitting pretty—better than most retired cops. A nice warm place far away sounded about right to him. Marshall snapped a few pictures. He didn't want his new boss to think he was slothful.

Chapter 9

Matt looked for the car that had followed him when they walked out of the restaurant, but it wasn't there. He had noticed it twice in the last few days. He put his arm around Jessie. "Are you warm enough, sweetheart?"

Jessie leaned close. "I'm fine. Besides, your car is right there." She pointed at it. "Are you okay? You were quiet tonight."

"I'm fine. You know how I get when we're on a case." He unlocked the car.

"True, you do get edgy, but I was thinking it might because there was a car tailing us on our way here."

"You saw it, too? I should have known you would. You're becoming more observant." He smiled down at her.

"It could be, but it's more like the guy following you wasn't doing a good job of being discreet about it."

Matt chuckled. "You're something, you know it?" He opened the car door and chucked her chin as she slid in. As soon as they were all in the car, Matt turned to Kaufman. "We were being tailed tonight. The car was gone when we came out. Jessie noticed it too."

She shrugged. "He got a little sloppy at the end, which is the only reason I saw him."

"We'll have to be on guard. These guys mean business." Kaufman fastened his seat belt. "Jessie, after hearing your stories tonight, I definitely want you to interview some of the college students and Darsha. We can use all the help we can get."

She turned in her seat to answer him. "I'd be happy to if Matt comes along."

"Be prepared, Kaufman. Once she starts asking questions, the case will break open." He grinned at her. "It's happened every time."

Jessie laughed. "Don't let him fool you, sir, it's no big deal."

"You'll see, Kaufman; get ready for a hell of a ride." Matt signaled to pass a slow-moving car. "How long can you stay in town, Frank?" he asked.

"A few days, why?"

"I thought we might need Radar for one more track. Three of the four missing students were found in my jurisdiction. I find it strange. I may be wrong, but I can't imagine them dumping the fourth somewhere else, unless of course they're keeping him alive as a messenger or for ransom."

"I'll stay around. As long as I have a place to stay, which I do, and you feed me, you can count me in." Frank stretched his sore knee out and rubbed it. "Besides, I want to help make sure these guys are caught. I hate what happened to those kids."

"You and me both." Kaufman leaned his head back. "I'm tired. A meal after a long day makes me sleepy." It didn't take long, and he was out.

Matt turned off the highway at the Blue Cove exit. "Jess, see if you can take a day this week to go to the college with me. I want to talk to the kids while the details are still fresh in their minds. Kaufman has given you the go-ahead."

"I'll arrange for a day away from the church. Audrey can work the store maybe, or Reba might be able to come in for me. You're right; we need to go soon. Also, an article for the local paper and one for Neil would be the right touch to shake things up a bit." She let her excitement punctuate her words.

Matt parked beside her car. "Don't go. I'll walk you to your door." He strode over to open her car door. "I'll be right back," Matt told Frank and the snoring Kaufman.

"He's not going anywhere." Frank yawned. "I'm not either. I might join him before long."

****

"Thanks for dinner." She smiled at him when he grabbed her hand. "I enjoyed spending time with Katie. I love watching how happy she is with Dylan." Her breath caught when his thumb stroked the palm of her hand. "They're good together. Dylan has a calming effect on her."

"They seem happy." His thumb made a path across the palm of her hand again.

"I know she is." She exhaled. "Knock it off," she grinned at him. "You're distracting me on purpose. I won't be able to keep a straight thought in my head."

"Ah, it's working, then." He lifted his brows. "I would be happy to have more time with you. We haven't had much time alone the past few days. I hope that's not an omen for the duration of this case." Matt pointed at the second cottage. "How are your neighbors working out? Is Liam still checking on you every day?"

"I've hardly seen Liam or Connor. The pub has kept them busy." Her face lit up. "I think they're having a great time together. They work all the time, like anyone with a new business has to. It takes a while before you can hire help. At least for management. With the summer tourist season almost here they should be in great shape. They have a solid business plan." Jessie found herself rambling. Matt was making her nervous. Why?

"I know how you love plans." Matt held out his hand for her key. He leaned in close. "I love you, sweetheart." He kissed her until she relaxed in his arms. "I wish I could come in…" His voice trailed off, and he kissed her again.

Jessie walked in the door he held open for her. "Matt," she called as he turned to leave, "please be careful." Jessie saw him nod as she closed the door. The car tailing them tonight had reminded her of the dream still fresh in her memory. Maybe it was her feeling jumpy and not him. Jessie rubbed her hands over arms to ward off the sudden chill. Matt getting hurt wasn't something she wanted to think about.

The knock at the door startled her. Matt stepped in and pulled her into the circle of his arms, his chin resting on her head. "You forgot to lock it, didn't you?" He shuddered. "Don't worry, Jess, I'll be careful." He kissed her. "I'm not finished—we're not finished—it's only the beginning, sweetheart. I like that you worry about me," he whispered in her ear. "Lock the door behind me this time." He paused when he saw her notebook with bold letters written across it. He took a closer look. "Flashpoint? What's this?"

"The title of the article I'm working on." She folded her hands behind her back.

"Catchy." He placed the notebook back on the table.

67

"It's more than that. Some event or place was the flashpoint that set off this crisis. I'm in search of it. These kids deserve that much."

"Their families do for sure." He moved toward the door. "See you." He gave her a quick kiss and walked out.

Turning the lock, Jessie leaned against the door and sighed. The room always seemed empty after he left. Matt's love had blindsided her. Jessie had had her life mapped out, her short and long term goals in place. He was right; she liked to plan, but she wasn't sure her plans even mattered anymore. When had that happened? She pushed away from the door. Goals were good, of course, but relationships and people were more important. The last year had taught her the lesson well. He filled up the empty spaces in her life.

Jessie walked over to the computer and turned it on. A quick check of her e-mails showed nothing of importance. She wrote a brief note to her parents and to Sadie. While she sat there, she researched the weapon that had been used on the kids. What kind of people would choose to torture young people? The electric prod had become a weapon of choice in certain groups. It was designed only for the purpose of inflicting pain. If applied to the skin, the current would sear, burn, and scar the skin; inflicting high levels of pain on the victims. The picana took the current up to the next level to cause maximum damage. The more she read, the sicker it made her. How could parents live with the knowledge that their child had been tortured? Jessie couldn't read another word. Her conclusion was that sometimes people were cruel. Hate unchecked never ended with good results. She grabbed the remote and turned on the TV. When it came to ways of killing people, the bad guys kept inventing new methods. When would people learn to get along? She sighed and turned up the volume of her favorite show.

Chapter 10

Matt arrived at the station in time for the morning press conference. He was happy to let Kaufman deal with the questions from the reporters. The Bureau was sending a few more field agents to assist with the case. Between the press and the FBI agents, they'd be tripping over each other before long. Matt understood. This was a big case. It could be bad for international relations for years to come unless they solved it quickly.

"Sir." Kenny approached Matt when he walked in the door. "I have a call on line one for you from Tom Maxwell."

"Thanks, I'll take it in my office." He picked up the phone. "Hi, Tom, what can I do for you?"

"I'm one of the agents being assigned to help in this case. I'm coming for the sole purpose of watching your back. What's going on there anyway?"

"I don't need a babysitter," Matt snapped. "But we could use all the help we can get to solve this case."

"That's not how Kaufman sees it. You're being followed, according to him. It could be a part of this case or separate from it. I'll be there to watch you."

He let his breath out in mild exasperation. "You have to follow your orders, but I think you'll be coming for nothing."

"I wonder if Jessie sees it the same way," Tom

muttered.

"Probably not." He couldn't help but smile. "But she worries about me because she cares."

"Damn it, Parker, I care." Matt heard Tom chuckle. "I'll be there sometime today. I'll be staying at a motel and not the Inn when I'm not camping out at your house. My expense account won't allow the Inn this time."

"Dylan would stay in the room next to yours if you stayed at the Inn. He's not taking any chances when it comes to Katie."

"Hey, it worked the way it was supposed to. I know it, and so does Katie. I'm cool with it. I was only trying the relationship on for size. I could tell her heart was otherwise engaged. You could see it anytime Dylan was near, or when she heard his name. That last night at her brother's pub made it perfectly clear to me."

"You wouldn't like living in Blue Cove anyway. You'd miss the Bureau, and she would miss the Inn." He chuckled. "Like you said, it all worked out for the best."

"Kaufman was amazed by Radar. I'm sorry he had to find another body though. I wonder if the dog could help us in our search for the people who did this," Tom mused.

"Anything is possible. We've had one stroke of recent luck. The coroner found a fingerprint on Shara's body, and Dave is running it now. Hopefully, it will give us a name." Matt clicked his pen off and on.

"The thing about groups who use torture as their preferred method of killing is that they aren't what you'd call refined criminals," Tom said sourly. "He'll probably be in the system somewhere. They don't care about wiping off their fingerprints; they want you to know who they are. Fear and intimidation are their mental weapons of choice. He won't be in this alone. There's some kind of gang involved."

"I hope it gives us someone to put away for the sake of the families. The longer this goes unresolved, the harder it will be for all involved."

"One can hope. We're not looking for a single suspect—these folks roam in bands," Tom said. "Don't try to be a hero and go it alone. Wait until I get there."

"It'll be hard to be a hero sitting in my office with no clue where to begin." Matt turned his chair around to watch the people in the park.

"Good, you'll make my job a whole lot easier if you sit tight. See you soon."

"Sounds good."

What wasn't Tom telling him? There was more going on than the facts in front of him. The FBI must have a group in mind, maybe one they'd been watching. Hell, he didn't want someone to babysit him. Slamming his fist down on his desk, he went in search of Kaufman.

Matt found the agent in Dylan's office. He walked in closing the door behind him with a bang. "I think you have some information you haven't told me. I hate working with my hands tied behind my back. I would prefer you to put all your cards on the table so I know what we're dealing with."

"Do you want me to leave?" Dylan asked.

"No, stay. You need to be a part of this discussion." Matt glared at Kaufman. Maxwell told me he's coming for the sole purpose of watching my back. We have more field agents on their way here, and I want to know why."

"It's a big case." Kaufman sounded defensive.

"I'm well aware of the size of the case, but there's more to it than that, and you know it. Let's hear what you've got." Matt squeezed the arm of the chair. Hard.

"We're not sure if this is the group we've been keeping tabs on. They were operating around the edges south of the border when you captured the human trafficking group. They've never had any operations in this country, which would make this a first. Frankly, we have no idea why they would be involved with these kids. This is one nasty group, and they leave a lot of bodies wherever they operate."

"You didn't think this was an important fact for us to know?" Matt frowned. "If they are anywhere near our town, don't you think we should have been made us aware of it?" Matt stood. "If you have a theory, I want to know it. I would do the same for you."

"We're still trying to fit the pieces together. It may not be this group at all, but their use of torture is similar. We're bringing in a team of agents who have tracked these groups in our country and have learned from the CIA, who is tracking them on foreign soil. Our world is a whole lot smaller than it used to be, and you never know when one these gangs will show up."

"Tell me, have you learned anything about these students that would tell us why they might have become a target?"

Kaufman shook his head. "We're in the beginning stages of all this. You know as much as I do. What's this all about, Matt?'

"I don't want to be pushed aside while you take over my department and run roughshod over me. I learned a few minutes ago that I'm going to have a shadow, but no one told me there was even a need for one. I'm responsible for this town, and I want to know what you know so I can plan accordingly." Matt raked his hand through his hair.

"I wanted the protection for you in case we find a connection to one of your big cases. The closure of the organ trafficking group, for example, dried up the foreign group's resources for buying and selling. It could have made you a target, and that's only one of the groups impacted in the past year.

"Have you found a connection?" Matt asked.

"Not yet," Kaufman said. "You have to remember, you've dealt with some high-profile cases. Hell, most small-town cops never see this crap. Besides organ harvesting, you busted up a human trafficking group and a major weapons ring. Our concern is you've shut off the money source to some bad people, and you've created enemies. Are they connected? We have no idea if there's any connection to you. Or how the kids fit into it. We have a mystery to solve and want to prepare for any scenario." Kaufman paused. "You might start by telling me how long your stint at the Bureau was and why you quit." Kaufman held up a folder with Matt's name on it.

Matt's answer was brisk. "It wasn't for me."

"Why is that? You were on your way up and well-liked in the division."

"Two years was enough for me. It was too stressful. The threat level to our country is high and continuous. The Intel kept me awake at night." Matt leaned against the wall and folded his arms across his chest.

"I get it and so does anyone who works there. It's a damn pressure cooker. I had to ask because reading your file made me wonder."

"I guess that makes us even. From now on, I'll tell you what I learn, and I expect no less from you." Matt opened the door.

"Fair enough. Oliver Kaufman walked out the door with Matt. "I haven't kept anything from you on purpose, nor will I."

"That's all I ask." Matt walked into his office. *Could those days at the agency tie into this somehow? Not good.* He paced until he could finally sit down and then picked up his phone. He needed to hear her voice. "Hi, Jess, how's your day?"

"It's moving fast. I had a bus tour this morning, and the book club women are meeting here again. I'm happy to have them. It makes the store bubble with conversation, which I love." He could hear the smile in her voice. "I don't mind being busy." Matt heard the hum of people talking in the background.

"When can you go to the college to meet with Darsha?" Matt asked.

"Will Wednesday work for you? I talked to Darsha's aunt today, and she said Wednesday or Thursday would work for them. Kaufman thought an agent should bring her to the station. They don't want her aunt to be followed either."

"Damn Kaufman," Matt said under his breath. "What about the college student interviews?"

"Thursday morning would work for me. Reba said she could answer the phone at the church both days so Audrey could work for me."

"Perfect. How about dinner at Patterson's? Frank

will meet us there at five-thirty."

"I'll be there."

****

Jessie loved listening to the book club women arguing their points about the book they were reading. It was especially nice to have them there since the strange man was sitting in Joe's and watching her shop again. She wrote down what she noticed about him on a scrap of paper. Later she would check the police photos to see if she could find him in among the criminals. His eyes were blue. Stormy might be a good description. He was considerably shorter than she was, maybe five feet four inches or thereabouts. His mousy brown hair had a few streaks of gray running through it. It was fine and wispy. Did he have any scars or visible marks? Not any that she could see right off. He did have a piercing glare. Jessie held up her phone, pretending to scroll through the texts. She took a quick photo, hoping he wouldn't see what she was doing. She caught him at the perfect moment when he wasn't paying attention. Jessie glanced into the coffee shop again. Sitting at a table in the front was Amir—or rather his ghost.

Chapter 11

Amir's ghost followed the man who'd been watching her as she closed the doors into the coffee shop. Her eyes narrowed when she glanced toward them. Did Amir know this man? How were they connected? A cold, calculating man, he wasn't someone she wanted to turn her back on. What he lacked in size he made up for in anger. Not a nice man, if her feelings were correct. The cold clammy sensation took her by surprise. She pulled her sweater tight around her and blew on her hands. It was time to close up the store. Locking the front door, she shut off the lights. Movement by the cemetery caught her attention. Shara's ghost and Ryan's were flittering back and forth between headstones in the cemetery as if playing a game of tag. "And that makes three for the day," she whispered.

Grabbing her purse, she slipped her jacket on and locked the front door as she left. Patterson's was only three buildings down from her store; she could walk there. A brisk cool breeze swept past one side and then the other. She wasn't alone. The flurry of ghostly activity around her sent a cold chill through her body. Picking up her pace, she looked behind her. "I'll help you," she said softly. "We will find those who did this to you. I hope you're willing to help us too."

Jessie walked into Patterson's, and Joe, the owner,

greeted her. "I have the perfect table waiting for you and your friends. Matt called and reserved it." Patterson led the way. "I'm glad you decided to make Blue Cove your home, Jessie. You have brightened our town by being here." Joe smiled and handed her a menu.

"I'm glad I moved here, too." She sat as he pulled out her chair for her. "How's your wife?"

"She's doing well and still tolerates me. I'd say after all these years, that's a good thing. I'm a lucky man." Patterson grinned.

"You sure are, but so is she." She took the menu he handed her.

"You do my old heart good; enjoy your meal." Patterson placed his hand across his chest.

Jessie glanced over the menu. She should know it by heart; she had been here to eat many times. If Patterson only knew what she had brought to Blue Cove, he might help her pack her bag and escort her out of town. She fiddled with the napkin, finally placing in on her lap. Thank heavens for Reba. What would she have done without her? Speaking of Reba... Jessie frowned. She hadn't seen her for a few days. It was about time she showed up with some kind of new thoughts for her. A tap on the window startled her. Reba's smiling face was looking in at her. Jessie shook her head. She should have known. If she thought of Reba, Reba was thinking of her.

"Add another chair to Jessie's table, Joe; there will be five of us for dinner," Reba directed as she and her striking husband, Lawrence, made their way to the table where she was. The staff moved to add a chair.

Jessie adored Lawrence's loving glance at Reba as he pulled out her chair. She sighed inwardly. He must have been a heartthrob when he was younger. He still was a handsome man. His silver-gray hair made him look distinguished. "You could teach a few of the young men around town a thing or two about romance." She beamed at him.

"He sure could." Reba placed her hand on his as he sat. "He's a keeper."

Joe handed Reba and Lawrence their menus. "You folks enjoy your evening. Be sure to check out the dinner specials. The pork roast is especially good tonight, and so is the prime rib."

"What brings you here tonight?" Jessie glanced at the menu to see what came with the special.

"You know how this works by now, Jessie." Lawrence smiled as he picked up his menu. "Reba told me we had to eat at Patterson's tonight. So here we are." Lawrence's eyes twinkled when he looked at her. "I could no more say no to this dear wife of mine than to the man in the moon if he were to talk." Lawrence patted Reba's hand. "When it comes to my sweet wife, I'm never sure where her ideas will lead us. I've learned to go with it since she seems to be right every time. My guess is that she wanted to come to Patterson's for dinner tonight knowing she would run into you."

"Yes, I know she's always right. The funny thing is, I was sitting here thinking about her too." The fact Reba always showed up at the right moment didn't surprise her anymore.

"We are kindred spirits, Jessie girl. I hope your nice Mr. Parker will soon be here, too."

"I expect him any minute." Jessie watched for Matt out the window.

"The past few days, I've run into a few new friends. It has me wondering what is going on in our lovely little town."

"I have no idea." Jessie scrunched her face. "How about you, Lawrence? Do you have any theories?"

"None whatsoever. I'm only an observer in my wife's adventures. All I can say is that I know enough to take her seriously."

"Reba, let's talk about the menu or weather until Matt gets here. I want him to hear firsthand what you have to say. Speaking of Matt, he's here." She motioned him over when he walked in the door.

Matt brushed her shoulder as he slipped into the chair beside her. "Hi, sweetheart."

"Hi back at you." She smiled. "I thought you said Frank was coming. I guess we won't need the extra chair after all." Jessie moved the chair to the end of the table, so they had more room.

"He was, but he wanted to watch the game more. He picked up something to eat on his way to my place. Hi, Lawrence." Matt shook his hand. "Reba, to what do we owe the honor?"

"To be blunt, I wanted to see you, and that's why we're here."

"Why do you want to see me?" Matt's brows rose, a puzzled expression his face.

"I always talk to Jessie, but this time what I have to say concerns you more than her. I'll tell you as soon as we place our order." The waiter stood beside the table with his pen and pad.

Jessie leaned toward Matt after she gave her order. "How was your day?"

"I've had better." He grabbed her hand and laced

his fingers through hers.

"Are you making any headway on the murders yet? I heard about them on the news. Who would want to kill three young people?" Lawrence frowned as he asked the question.

"I've asked the same question myself." Matt took a sip of water. "We are getting tips to the FBI hotline, which is good. One of them should pan out. We also have a partial fingerprint on one of the bodies. The coroner is working on an ID."

Reba shuddered. "Murder is such a depressing topic. I can't figure out why anyone would want to hurt another person. Unless of course, they are pure evil, and as you know, there are some folks like that around." Reba placed her napkin on her lap.

Matt took a roll and put it on his bread plate. "In this case, I think we're dealing with bad folks."

"I know you are. I thought it was all about the kids at first, but now I'm sure that it is not." Reba reached for Lawrence's hand.

"What you do mean?" Matt's eyebrows rose as he frowned at her. "There are three dead and another one missing. I think it's all about the kids."

"Yes, of course, it is about them, but there is another dark shadow when I think about them, and it involves you, Mr. Parker." She paused, and Lawrence squeezed her hand.

"You may as well tell him, dear. We're here because of it, although I think the roast sounds good to me." He glanced at his wife.

"Your life is in jeopardy and so are the lives of others near you." Reba blurted the words out. "The hate, in this case, is two-pronged, and one of them is aimed at you. The other has marked our way of life as its enemy. It will take all your skill and strength for you to come out of this alive. I believe you will, and you must believe it, too, for there might be moments when you will doubt it." Reba took a tissue from her purse.

"I don't know what to say." He squeezed Jessie's hand tightly. She clung to it, her stomach sinking. She wanted to be shocked at Reba's words, to deny them, but...Reba was right. She knew it.

"I know you don't know me well." Reba's eyes were on her. "But I believe Jessie was warned, too. Weren't you, girl?" Jessie nodded at her, biting her lip.

"Chief, I've learned to take my wife's offbeat ideas seriously. She's not here to scare you but to warn you. You're no stranger to this stuff." He gave Matt a gentle smile. "Jessie has helped you solve some cases using unconventional means. These ladies," he pointed at Jessie and Reba, "are two peas in a pod. I never thought I'd meet another woman like my Reba in my lifetime, but here she is, living right in our town."

"I've always approached things logically. I admit that I don't have answers for everything, and Jessie has thrown me a curve with the stuff she's seen. I don't get it, but I trust her. I'll take what you say seriously." His expression was grave, and he didn't let go of Jessie's hand. "I'm not sure what I can do with the knowledge until I find myself in the situation." Matt glanced at Jessie, who was watching him.

"Your training will be enough. It will kick in at the precise moment you need it the most. I believe you will find out you're a much stronger man than you realize." Reba thanked the server when he placed her salad in front of her. "Blue Cove is lucky to have you as our chief of police."

Jessie had wondered what Reba was going to tell Matt. She was stunned and more than a little worried after the dream she'd had of him. The rest of the evening was pleasant enough. Reba always managed to deliver her words and move on as if she had said nothing out of the ordinary, but she knew Reba felt it deeply. More than once, she had seen how much the knowledge she was given had affected Reba's life. Would she ever be free from seeing ghosts and premonitions, or would this be a lifetime burden like Reba's? Only time would tell.

Chapter 12

When Reba and Lawrence left, Matt turned to Jessie. "How am I supposed to handle what she said to me?"

"I always ask myself the same question." She placed her hand on his. "Can you come over for a while?"

"Yes, I was planning on it. I'll take the time whenever I can get it." He stood and held her jacket for her. "Did you walk?"

"Yes." She preceded him out the door.

"I'll drop you off at your car and follow you home."

"Thanks." She scrolled through her photos on her phone and pulled up the one she wanted. "Before I forget, here's a picture of the man who's casing my place." She handed him the phone.

"Good job." He peered at it. "E-mail me a copy, would you? I'll have Tom run a face recognition scan on him. Maybe we'll get lucky and find him in the system."

"I also wrote down a few things I observed about him." She handed Matt a scrap of paper with the description she had written earlier. "I noticed Amir's ghost was watching him. When the man left so did Amir."

Once she was safely in her car, he followed her,

checking his review mirror. No one was behind him. Waiting for a break in the case set him on edge. Hell, Reba's words didn't help either. His fingers tightened on the steering wheel. What the hell had Reba meant? It didn't sound promising. He wasn't about to wait for something to happen. Damn, he hated all the suspense. "I won't be a sitting target," he muttered. He saw Jessie step out of the car and reach for something on the seat. He breathed deeply and pulled into the space beside her car. "Wait up," he called out as he got out of the car. "I want to walk with you."

"I was waiting." She fluttered her eyes him. "It seems I've been doing a lot of it lately." She tapped her foot playfully.

"Are you feeling neglected?" He watched her nod as she held back a smile. "I have the perfect remedy." He took her hand, and they strolled toward her cottage. He stopped to kiss her along the way.

"The weather has been perfect." She looked at the night sky filled with stars. "I can run outside again, which I love. The treadmill at the gym isn't the same as seeing the beauty of the ocean and woods when I run." She stopped on the path.

He took his time to stop and kiss her before they walked on. "I get it. Outdoors is better than being inside any day." Matt took the key from her hand. He unlocked the door and pushed it open. "We need to talk." He walked in after her and closed the door.

"About what?" She slipped off her shoes and sat on the sofa, curling legs her under her.

Matt drew a deep breath. She was as pretty as a picture sitting there. For the moment, he sat across from her in his favorite chair. "Tell me again about your dream."

She told him again what she had seen. "I'm not sure what it all means, but Reba seemed to have a similar warning, didn't she?" Jessie watched his facial expression change with her question. It passed from puzzled, to angry, to a stubborn resolve.

"Yes, and to add to the mystery, Maxwell arrived in town an hour ago. He's giving me a space of time to be with you tonight, but he's here to protect me. I have no idea why. I've had no threats, no strange calls, or anything."

"That small car has been following you, which isn't good." Jessie twisted the fringe on the throw pillow around her finger. "I saw all three of the ghosts in town today, so I guess they're still around, and Reba told me she has seen some of our old friends. I'm not sure what that means." She scrunched her face. "What's your take on the case, Matt? I trust how you work through it."

"We don't have a whole lot to go on yet. There's a fingerprint. We know the weapon that was used, but we have no motive. Tom seems to think they're a foreign group of some sort, a gang who enjoys torturing their victims. What are they doing here? It makes very little sense if you ask me. Why are they active on a college campus? I'm not connected to the students in any way." Matt rubbed his temple. "I need a toxicology report or at the least a confirmed cause of death."

Jessie patted the space beside her, moving her legs so he could sit. "Let's talk about something happy for a moment. The case will still be here tomorrow."

Matt moved over to sit beside her and laid his head on her shoulder. This was home. "You're right, I need to learn to shut if off for a while." He shuddered and then relaxed against her side.

She handed him the remote. "Check the score; you know you want to." She grinned.

"Oh, yeah." He chuckled. "You know me well." He turned on the game.

"Do you want a beer or something else to drink?" She walked to the kitchen.

"Water would be great. Hurry back," he called after her. "It's not the same without you next to me."

Matt drove home a while later. He hadn't been good company. Even the game couldn't hold his attention tonight. Once his mind zeroed in on the photo Jessie had given him, it was all over for him. She never failed to surprise him with how astute she was in getting the details right; quick thinking on her part. Tom should have his copy by now. He would send it on to the Bureau for a facial scan. With luck, within a few days, they should know who he was.

****

Jessie was ready early on Thursday. Plans had changed for the visit. Agent Kaufman was driving them to a secured place to meet with Darsha Sarin. The questions she wanted to ask were on the list tucked in her purse. Jessie was excited to jump into the investigation. She knew as they peeled away more layers, the *why* would begin to emerge.

Another agent showed them into a small room in a nondescript warehouse style building several miles from the college town. Matt held Jessie's chair out for her. "Are you nervous?"

"Not really. I'm eager to meet with her and have a chance to talk. She may have a memory or a small clue that will shed light on what happened to Amir and the others."

Matt took out his notepad. "Do you have your list?" He straightened in his chair, drumming his fingers on the table.

"Yes." She smiled. He was nervous. Reba's words alone were enough to make anyone nervous. Agent Kaufman came into the room with Darsha and her aunt. Aisha held tightly to her niece's arm. Darsha was pale and fragile looking. The difference from her appearance only a few days ago was striking. Jessie understood why Aisha was worried. "It's nice to see you again." Jessie stood to greet her.

"My aunt thought it would be good for me to talk to you." She eyed Matt warily. "I need to talk to someone. I can't sleep; my mind will not shut down." Tears filled her eyes.

"Sit, please." Jessie pointed at the chair across from her. "Can I get you anything? A glass of water perhaps?" She had brought two bottles of water with her.

Darsha shook her head. "I don't want anything."

"I'll leave this bottle right here. You might need to have a sip at some point." Jessie placed it within her reach.

"Thank you." Darsha looked at her aunt who smiled encouragingly at her.

"You remember Chief Parker," Jessie said as Matt sat down beside her. "He's my friend, and he's working hard to solve this case. He'll find the ones who did this to your friends."

"Are you sure?" Darsha dabbed at her eyes with the tissue. "I can't stop thinking these evil men will hurt others if they aren't caught."

"Matt will do everything he can, along with Agent Kaufman, whom you've also met. I need you to help them."

"What can I do?" Her eyes brimmed with tears. "I'm overwhelmed and can't even help myself."

"Of course you're in shock, but it will be good for you to talk about your friends. They were important in your life and maybe one small detail you remember will help solve this case," Jessie said, encouraging her. "You will not only help your friends but also help yourself by talking about them. I know how hard it is to let yourself feel again. Grief is powerful, but one day you will wake up, and it won't hurt as much. It will still be there off and on, but you'll find you can also laugh and smile again. Amir would want you to."

"Yes, I know he would want me to be happy, but I don't want to forget about him. I can't do happy yet. I still can't believe he's gone." She looked down.

"You can work to keep his story alive. Tell me about Amir and how you met."

Darsha warmed to the subject and began to open up. Every now and then, she smiled at a memory she shared. "We were both pre-med students with a tough schedule. We still managed to find time to hang out together. The five of us were in a study group and socialized whenever we could fit it in. Shara was pre-med, too, but Carlos and Ryan were studying sports medicine."

"Is that why you all were a part of the Foreign Students' Club?"

"Yes, it was an important part of campus life. Amir, being from Kuwait, knew what it was to have people not trust him. Every time there was a terrorist attack, someone would blame him for it as if he had committed the act himself."

"People can be cruel sometimes." Jessie opened her water and took a sip.

"This was more than cruel." She met Jessie's eyes. "It was hate-filled. At least with the club, we were able to band together and help each other through the hard times. Don't get me wrong, there were a lot of nice, welcoming kids, too." Darsha paused. "My relationship with Amir caused problems for some. Also, the fact that he was friends with Shara, a Jewish girl, didn't sit well with others."

"It's hard to get past people's bigoted ideas."

"They didn't just come from other students, but people in our own countries as well. We hoped by talking about it, we could foster better relationships."

"Did it work?"

"Somewhat, but lately, after the last couple of attacks, rhetoric became more heated from inside the school and also from off campus. It got so we didn't want to leave the campus. We were never sure who would say something. Carlos was born in this country, but his parents emigrated from Mexico. He was also gay, which made it all the harder for him. He was teaching his parents to speak English. Carlos was a gentle soul and one of kindest people I know." Darsha gulped to hold back a sob.

"Who else is involved in the club?" Jessie asked.

"Foreign students and American kids as well. There are several students from Middle Eastern countries and a few from Africa. Some are here on student visas, and some immigrated and are now citizens."

"Were you ever targeted for your beliefs?"

"We all were. I'm Hindu, Shara was Jewish, and Amir was Muslim. It's strange I know, but we got along fine."

"I admire the fact that you worked so hard to understand your differences but didn't hold them against each other." Jessie wrote in her notebook.

"I think most people want to live in peace." Darsha opened the bottle and sipped the water. "A few in our group have escaped from war and poverty in their own countries and came here looking for a better life. My parents wanted a better life for my siblings and me. Amir's family is in the U.S. in service to their country. Shara was born in Israel. Her father moved back to the States after her mother died of cancer. Shara was funny and smart. She made it her life's goal to save others in her mother's memory. There are many stories like this among our group. Most of the club members who are foreigners want an education so they can return home and make a difference in their own countries."

"I'm sure that's true, but fear seems to make us all look at each other differently, doesn't it? We tend to point our finger at someone who is different from us as being bad." Jessie wondered how many times she had looked down on a person's difference.

Darsha smiled at her. "You Americans are hard to understand for those of us who are new to your land. You have so much and are free to choose, but many don't take advantage of what's before them."

"You're right." Jessie shook her head, seeing it through Darsha's eyes for the first time.

"It's the same everywhere. Because of the wealth

of your country, I think foreign students are often surprised when they find unhappy and poor people live here, too."

"I can understand why." Jessie wrote a few notes. She continued to ask questions. The last question was the most important on her list. "Can you remember if Amir seemed troubled by anything lately?"

"A few days before they disappeared, Amir told us we needed to get together. He had received an anonymous letter that he wanted us all to read. We were supposed to meet at the coffee shop where we often met." Darsha took a deep breath. "I was late to the meeting, and so I have no idea what happened, only what I've learned from the police." She gulped. "Now they're dead, and I'm the only one living. I should have been with them." Darsha eyes filled with tears.

"I wonder what was in the letter. Did Amir tell you anything?

"We talked right after he got it and read me a small section. It was a hate-filled rant against him, his father, and the rest of our group."

"Had any of you ever received a note before?"

"Yes, of course, but this one was different." Darsha dabbed at her eyes with a tissue.

"In what way?"

"It threatened each of us by name and our families. That's why Amir wanted us all to read it. He thought we should go to the police, but he wanted it to be all of our decisions." Darsha dried her tears. "It was as if the person writing the letter knew us all or was stalking us. I should have been with them."

"Don't let yourself feel guilty because you survived. You were late, but not on purpose. Your friends need you alive, if for no other reason than to bring their murderers to justice. I know your family is happy to have you here to enjoy." Jessie patted Darsha's hand.

"It must have concerned him if he considered going to the police." Matt said.

"He was worried, and Amir didn't scare easily."

"Did you ever see any strangers hanging around your group?" Matt clicked his pen.

"Not that I can remember, but I'll think about it." Darsha took a sip of water.

"Could someone be following you?" Jessie took a quick look at her list of questions.

"I don't know." Darsha's voice was barely audible. "It's possible."

"Think hard for a moment. Did you see or hear anything odd?" Matt leaned forward in his chair. "This is important. You may hold an important key to breaking the case."

"I'm afraid." She looked away from Matt. "One day I met Amir at the coffee shop. He was talking to someone on the phone. The conversation was a heated one."

"Did he tell you what it was?"

"He told me it was better if I didn't know." Tears filled her eyes. "He said they were playing with fire and someone could get killed. His exact words were, 'They are playing a dangerous game.'"

"I wonder who he was talking to." Jessie twisted a strand of hair with her fingers.

"Is there anything else you can think of?" Matt asked her.

She sighed. "I did see a man pushing Amir a few

days before he went missing. When I asked him about it, he said it was a friend of his father. He didn't act like a friend. Amir was quiet on our date later that night. He never told me what they had talked about, but it wasn't friendly. It's all so confusing."

"There is something else, isn't there?" Jessie touched her hand.

"Yes." Darsha wiped the tears running down her cheeks. "His parents were upset that he was dating me. I am Hindu, and he was Muslim. They didn't like me. You can't help where you're born or whom you fall in love with, Amir told them, but they were not happy with him. Or with me for that matter. They blamed me for trying to seduce their son. It wasn't like that, though." She began to sob. "We were good friends, and we wanted to marry someday after we had enough money. We both tried to live by our parents' strict standards because we loved our families." She shivered. "Maybe if I had stopped seeing Amir and refused to date him again, he would still be alive."

"I doubt it, Darsha. You can't let your mind go there." Jessie handed her the box of tissues. "Do you think his family would hurt him?" Jessie asked her.

"No, but all religions have an extreme element that might." Darsha leaned her head on her arms.

"You're right. That's another angle to consider." Matt scribbled a few notes on his pad.

Jessie patted her hand. "Darsha, go home, sweetie. Eat something and begin to live again. You can go to school with an escort. Keep the group alive in your friends' names. If you see anything or anyone that is out of place, tell the woman the FBI has assigned to protect you while you're at school. She will look more like a school friend, a new girl on campus, and you'll be showing her around."

"I know you're right, Jessie, but I miss him so much it hurts."

"I know it does. I wish I could make it go away, but it will get better with time. I know." Jessie leaned closer to her.

"Keep your eyes open, and you could be the one to solve the murder of your friends," Matt told her. "I think we're done here for now. If you think of anything else, call Jessie or me." He handed her his business card.

"I will. Jessie, can I call you? Sometimes I miss my friends so much I ache." Darsha stood.

"Anytime you want." Jessie hugged her. She watched her leave with her aunt.

Chapter 13

Matt gazed at Jessie. He could tell she was lost in thought. "What do you think?" Matt grabbed her hand.

"The pictures in Darsha's head are jumbled. When she can think with less emotion, she may be able to put it together. As I see it," Jessie said, "we have three possibilities. It could be a hate crime or a religious zealot. Maybe it has something to do with the heated conversation Darsha overheard. I guess we should throw families into the mix, too." Jessie pursed her lips. "Well, that didn't narrow the field much."

"She gave us a good starting point. We need to question Amir's family, interview the students, and check Amir's phone records. I'll get Jeremy to check on incoming calls to Amir's phone. We need to know who called Amir in the days before he went missing."

She snapped her fingers. "Good idea, why didn't I think of the whole phone records idea? If you can find who the number belonged to, that would be great."

"It'd be great, as long as they didn't use a throwaway." Matt frowned. "Still, we have to give it a shot. You never know when something will turn up."

Matt texted Jeremy and gave him Amir's phone number to check the records. He scrolled through his text. "Bingo."

"What?" Jessie asked.

"Dave Lewis sent me the cause of death. The drug

found in their blood acts to shut down the respiratory system and suffocates the person slowly. They were tortured and drugged."

"No wonder there were no visible signs on their bodies like gunshot or stab wounds. One of our suspects has to have some medical knowledge."

"One more piece of the puzzle to put in place." Matt finished scribbling on his notepad. "Let's go have lunch."

"Sounds good to me." Jessie smiled at him.

"You never know if you're dealing with smart criminals or really dumb ones until you put it all together. I have no theory on this case yet, but I see a beginning."

"You amaze me how you can put the little clues together and come up with an idea." She opened her purse and stuck her pen in it.

"You're pretty good yourself, sweetheart."

Kaufman came up behind them. "There's a problem on the campus. I just got a text. The students are demonstrating near the Admin building. One of our agents said you're to go to the back of the building and up to the second floor to the student library. They have you set up to interview students there."

"I wonder what they're demonstrating about?" Jessie got in the car.

"Who knows?" Kaufman shrugged. "When it comes to students, there's always some life-shattering cause." He started the car.

****

After lunch, they arrived on campus. This was more than a demonstration. Two opposing groups marched in protest outside the administration building.

If the yelling was an indicator, the protestors were reaching a flashpoint. The campus authorities had called in the city police for help. Police cars flew past them as they pulled over.

****

Matt and Jessie spent the afternoon talking to students who came into the library. Each time there was a break in the interviews, Jessie found herself headed over to the window to watch what was happening on the street below. The students' angry voices wafted through the air, filling the library with their heated retorts all afternoon.

"This is what democracy looks like," the large group of students shouted in unison as they thrust their protest signs in the air. Jessie could read a few from her vantage point. *"Hate speech isn't free speech." "Liberty and justice for all." We are a country of immigrants."*

On the other side was a small group dressed all in black with their faces partially covered by ski masks. They were shouting, "Foreigners go home," as they held up posters with swastikas and the white power symbol on them. The crowd screamed back and forth at each other until tempers began to flare.

It was hard to pay attention to their interviewees. She watched from her safe perch behind the window as the police moved in to break up the protestors. It was starting to get out of hand. A fist flew, catching the jaw of a young woman and sending her sprawling to the ground with a thud. From where Jessie sat, she could see the girl's head bounce off the pavement.

Jessie stuffed her notes into her purse as a petite girl with a bubbly personality and long blonde hair walked into the library. "Are you the one we're supposed to talk to?" she asked Jessie.

"Yes, have a seat." Jessie pointed at the empty chair across from her.

"My name is Misty Carlson," she said with a lot of enthusiasm.

"Misty, I'm Jessie. How can we help you?" Jessie was sure she had to be a cheerleader. She smiled. The girl's energy gave her away.

"I heard you were talking to students today, and I have something I need to tell you." She opened up her notebook and took out a slip of paper. Misty pushed it over to Jessie. "I've been carrying this around with me for days. I'm glad I can give it to you." She pushed a photo to Jessie.

"How did you come by it?" Jessie recognized the man and gasped. It was the man who had been watching the store! Matt sat down in the chair beside her.

"I came into the library several weeks ago, and I saw these men. I thought they looked out of place. I'd never seen any of them on campus before except for him." She pointed at a scruffy looking young man in the photo. "He's been among the demonstrators. I took a picture with my phone. When I heard about Amir's kidnapping, I thought this might be important, and I made a copy just in case. Amir was studying at the time. When he left the library, they followed him at a distance. I watched."

Jessie showed the photo to Matt. "He's the same man as in the picture I sent you," she whispered in his ear.

"Do you remember what day this was?" Matt

asked.

"It was a couple of weeks before they went missing. Look, I liked Amir, and they were all my friends. I can't imagine anyone wanting to hurt them. The Foreign and Local Students' Club is great. So many friendships and bonds have been formed. The leaders of the group were the best. I hope this helps in some way."

"You have helped more than you know. We should be able to tie a couple of pieces together now." Matt handed her his business card. "If you remember anything or see any of these men around here again, please call Agent Kaufman or us."

"I will. May I ask you a question?" Misty looked at Matt.

"Sure, go ahead." Matt stood beside her.

"I haven't seen Darsha Sarin for a few days. Is she going to be okay? I've called, but she isn't answering her phone."

"She's grieving. We have her under police protection, and they are monitoring calls. Until we know why the kids were targeted, we're keeping an eye on her," Matt told her.

"No matter who did the killing, it's all about hate. The anger is getting scary on campus. It doesn't take much to make people turn on each other. If they emigrated from another country, it's worse. Walk through this campus for a few days, and you'll see what I mean. That was what the demonstrations were about today. There are people willing to take advantage of the anger to promote their own causes." Misty shook her head.

"We might have to do as you suggest." Matt leaned

his hip against the table.

"You'll see how heated it gets from time to time. Tempers flare, and people choose sides. Two women wearing hijabs were attacked at the coffee shop near the campus. Please watch Darsha. Don't let anyone hurt her." Misty shifted from foot to foot.

"We are going to do our best to see that she lives a nice long life." Matt smiled. "Thank you, Miss Carlson; you have given us some valuable information."

Jessie watched the perky girl leave. "She has given us some good info to think about."

"This picture links this man to the students and to your store. Next time you see him, call us, and we'll bring him in for questioning. I wonder if Tom was able to get a name to go with the face."

"I hope so." Jessie gathered her stuff. "I thought Tom was supposed to shadow you. Where is he?"

"We're with Kaufman and the other agent today. Tom is catching up on the case. Until the Bureau thinks it's safe while we are in public, he'll be with us. When I have time alone with you, he can sit in the car and be happy about it." Matt grinned at her. "Let's get out of here." He took her hand. Kaufman followed a few strides behind them.

****

If he hadn't been late this morning, he wouldn't be sitting in this damn car hungry. Marshall listened to the tune on the radio, keeping time to the beat of the music on the steering wheel. A stiff belt of whiskey would help, but it never ended with one, and it usually left him in a stupor for hours in the morning. He'd missed the cop leaving this morning. He had better not do it again, or he wouldn't see his next payday. Marshall only knew to head to the campus from the chatter on the police radio he'd listened to earlier.

He turned in his seat in time to see them walk out of one of the buildings. Positioning the camera, he snapped a couple of photos. The boss would ask him who the cop had met with, and once again, Marshall would have to do some fancy improvising to remain alive. Lying was his new daily routine. Coming up with good ones left him feeling drained. He was too old for this junk. Marshall frowned, the wrinkles on his face furrowed into deep, unsightly lines. He looked at his image in the mirror. Bloodshot eyes stared back at him. Damn, he was a mess.

Chapter 14

Jessie was glad to be home. All the sitting in the car made her long for fresh air and activity. She changed her clothes, tied her running shoes, and jogged her way to the path leading down to the marina. The ocean was beautiful with the sunlight dancing off the water. It felt great, her feet pounding the ground, deep breaths bringing oxygen into her lungs and giving her more energy, and the sense of well-being that increased with each mile she covered. Running wasn't a chore for her. She loved it.

The man casing her store was one of the men in Misty's photo. How did he play into the case? Did they need to worry about the family friend? It was hard to believe that Amir's family would have him killed. Jessie couldn't imagine it. She placed the family friend at the bottom of the list for now. Amir's letter was placed at the top, along with the strange little man who had come into her shop. What about the heated phone call? She turned around at the marina and started for home. What would any of this have to do with Matt? Why was his life in jeopardy? She knew it was, but how it all fit together was still unclear. How she wished the ghosts could talk and make it easy for Matt. Maybe they communicated by actions. She would have to be more observant the next few days.

Jessie took her ringing phone out of her pocket.

"Jessie speaking," she said breathlessly.

"I take it you're running." Katie's cheerful voice sounded in her ear.

"I am. It's a perfect evening for it. You should try it with me. There are lots of folks on the trail with me."

"You're nuts. I would never run anywhere unless my life depended on it. How you enjoy the pounding on your joints and getting all sweaty is beyond me."

"Come on, you know you want to." Jessie loved teasing her.

"I love the fads and the pretty exercise clothes, not the actual work of it. Let me Zumba in mixed company, mainly with Dylan, or do yoga poses in my new yoga pants. That's my idea of a good time." Katie chuckled. "Where are you?"

"I'm heading up the hill back to my place right now. I only have a few minutes left, and I feel great." Jessie smiled at another runner who passed her.

"I think you're making it up. No one feels good when they're working hard."

Jessie laughed. "You know me well enough by now to know that I don't do what I don't like to do."

"Yeah, I guess, but I still don't get it."

"Why did you call, anyway?" Jessie slowed down her pace.

"All this talk of enjoying running took me off track. I want you to come to the Inn when you're finished beating yourself into the ground. We have some wedding planning to do. I'll even feed you supper."

"Sounds good to me. I'll be there as soon as I shower and change." Jessie placed the phone back in her pocket and ran to her front door. She did a few jogs in place, walked around for a moment, and did some stretches.

After she had changed, she walked out her back door, locking it as she went. The days were getting longer, and the trees were budding. She was happy to see the changes. Jessie could almost feel the garden coming to life around her. Did the buds make sounds if you listened carefully? Fanciful is what she was being. Although, Sadie had told her when she was little that if she would listen with care, she could hear the flowers grow. Maybe if she started to listen, she could hear what was happening around her. Amir's cries had reached her ears because she could hear them. It was something to consider.

Katie was standing at the stove as Jessie peeked through the window on the door before she opened it. "What wonderful casserole are you making now, my friend?"

"Wait until you taste this one. It's brilliant if I do say so myself." She gave Jessie a taste from the spoon.

"Oh my, this is so good." She sighed with pleasure. "What is it called?"

"I'm calling it Katie's surprise. It has a little of this, a little of that, and it gives your taste buds a wonderful surprise."

"Well, I'm down for it."

After dinner, Jessie listened to Katie gush on about Dylan. They looked through endless wedding magazines and wrote down the ideas that Katie liked. From flowers to the colors of the bridesmaid dresses, Katie had a sense of exactly what she wanted. A simple, small, and intimate wedding at the Inn and a lavish dance reception at the marina began to take shape.

Later, Jessie strolled toward home feeling quite content. The stars filled the night sky. Wishing on the first star that appeared had been pure magic when she was a kid. Jessie never knew if any of the wishes had come true. It was more about hoping they would. Life needed doses of hope. Reality could often be a bummer. The first real test for her perpetual state of optimism was when her friend, Tessa, had died in middle school, followed a few years later by her Grandpa Max. Those were her angry years. How could life be so mean and yet so wonderful? It was perplexing at times. Jessie felt bad for the parents of Amir, Shara, Ryan, and Carlos. How were they dealing with the pain and loss?

Her phone vibrated in her pocket. She checked the caller's name. "Hi, Matt."

"I would like you to go with me to Ryan's memorial service on Saturday. Sometimes a suspect will show up at a service to gloat. I'd like you to write about Ryan and each of the kids, and you can always learn something great about a person at their service."

"It works for me. Saturday is my day off, and the store is already taken care of for the day."

"As soon as they release Amir's and Shara's bodies, we will be attending their services too."

"Sounds good. I'll go if I can." Jessie caught a strange sight out of the corner of her eye. "Oh my gosh," she squealed. All three ghosts were darting among the trees. She rubbed her eyes, not quite believing what she saw. A magnificent creature of light was following them. Its wing span alone was incredible. The angel lit up the night sky.

"Where are you? What's happening?" Matt yelled into the phone.

"Sorry, I'm walking home from the Inn, and I saw something strange. Something tells me you're going to find another body or something in the woods by my house."

"What did you see?" he shouted into the phone.

"Amir and the others are zipping through the woods. It's eerie; the night is extremely quiet except for the sound of their wailing. The strange thing is, I don't see a fourth ghost, yet. Still, it's active over here. Something is going on." Her breathing was rapid. She wasn't ready to share what else she had seen.

"Damn, Jess, I know what this means—Radar will be doing another track. I was hoping there wouldn't be anyone else." She heard him tell Frank "We'll be there in the morning."

"I'll be at work, but let me know what you find." She ran the rest of the way to her cottage, locked the door, and leaned against it. Gasping for air, she bent over. All these sightings were making her uncomfortable. Carlos had to be out there. She could still hear the cries of his friends.

****

Matt disconnected the call. He would have never thought to look in the woods by Jessie's place. The pattern of body disposals made no sense to him. He took out his file on the case. He needed to read it over again. What was he missing?

"Did Frank tell me right, you think there's another body?" Tom sat on the sofa.

"Yes. Jessie saw something, and you know what that means." He threw the remote to Maxwell. "If you're going to stay here to babysit me you may as well make yourself at home. I can't have you spreading the word that I'm a lousy host."

"I know you're not happy about this, Matt, but let's make the best of it." He turned on the TV. "Besides, your house is a lot more comfortable than the motel I was staying at."

"I hope it doesn't mean you'll be making a nuisance of yourself every time you come to town." Matt slipped his glasses on and began reading the file. "I like your company, but not underfoot."

"I don't mind hanging with you either, but do you mind if we don't throw in murder, ghosts, and general mayhem? I could come for a barbecue or some social event." Tom chuckled. "Or you could invite me here when another good looking unattached female like Jessie moves to town. Heck, if you're ready to break up with her, let me know. I'll help you out."

"You can forget it." Matt snorted. "I'm more serious about her than ever. I'll take her any day—right along with the ghosts she sees. Her strange dreams and the voices she hears are a part of what makes her endearing to me."

"Okay, I get it. Don't get all mushy. You're in love." Tom changed the channel. "I hope I don't have to come here often, either. Every time I do, it means something major is coming down. When it comes to Jessie and you, it's never simple."

"It's true lately. I'd like some downtime without any murders involved. I wouldn't mind a few traffic tickets, a couple of disorderly conduct arrests, or simple vandalism cases for a change."

"Hell, why would you want any of those cases? You're a regular damn hero on the fast track with all these major solves you have. Of course, you have an unfair advantage over the rest of us poor saps. You have someone giving you clues that the rest of us can't see." Tom grumbled.

"I'd say strange is the word you're looking for. I'm a logical person, and I don't know what to think of this unconventional way of dealing with a case. But I do love the messenger and the package she comes in." Matt took his glasses off and cleaned a smudge of the lens.

"Speaking of hero, why did you quit the agency? I got a look at your file; you were a damn hero then too."

"Not really. Besides, I needed to come back to Blue Cove." Matt shrugged his shoulders.

"Why?" Tom asked.

"Let's just say I needed to deal with some things and leave it at that. My days at the agency gave me a healthy dose of fear. I couldn't imagine having a family and working in that unit."

"How's it working for you here?"

"Fine."

"Are you sure about that? You've had your share of trouble in your safe little town." Tom pointed out.

"I'm fine." Matt was curt.

"Okay, but I may keep badgering you. Which brings me back to the first question; are you doing a track tomorrow?" Tom stacked his arms behind his head and leaned back.

"Yes, the first thing in the morning," Matt told him.

"I heard that the coroner is releasing Amir's and Shara's bodies tomorrow. The burials will be tomorrow, before sundown." Tom stretched out his legs.

"Who told you?" Matt asked.

"Kaufman mentioned it as I was leaving the station."

"Will you be going to the services with me?" He would need to let Jessie know.

"If you're going, then yes, I'm going, too." Tom found the sports channel and paused his surfing.

"I figured you would be tagging along. I hope you don't get too bored playing my shadow." Matt placed the file on the table beside his chair. "Leave it here for a minute. I want to see today's scores."

Chapter 15

The team met in the woods early the next morning. With Radar's help, they found the next victim a short time later. Tied to an old broken fence, the young man's battered body hung limp. Matt thought for sure he was looking at the fourth fatality. He placed his fingers on the boy's head and ran them down the vein in his neck looking for some sign of life.

"Call an ambulance," Matt yelled out. His finger had found a weak pulse. "Help me get him down and covered. The sick bastards left him to die from exposure." Dylan helped Matt gently lift him, and they placed the young man on the ground. Each of them took off their jackets to cover his body. This crime scene was different. He had been tortured the same way the others had, but then had been brutally beaten and strapped to the fence to die. The derogatory word written across his chest led Matt to believe that this was Carlos.

"Do you think he'll make it?" Kip stared down at the battered body.

"I hope we found him in time." Matt squatted beside the young man, willing him to live. "Dylan, go wait for the ambulance. They won't be able to get back here. The Inn has a motorized garden cart. You can drive them back here with the stretcher in it."

"I can hear the siren. We'll get them here as soon

as possible." Dylan took off running.

For what seemed like an eternity, Matt watched his team do what they did best, work together. He was proud of this group. Kaufman had even commented on how well they worked together. Matt heard a soft moan come from the young man. He bent close to his mouth. There were no words, only groans of pain. "Hang in there, son. Help is on the way." The young man groaned several times, and Matt tried to comfort him the best he could. Words were powerful, but they failed him when he needed them most. Tom was watching the woods with an anxious expression. "Relax, Tom, I doubt they're still in the area. Take a look at Radar. He'd alert us if they were close by." Radar was chilling, stretched out by Frank's feet.

Matt was relieved to hear the sound of the cart headed toward them. The last time he had used the cart had been to carry Jessie after she had jumped out of the tree. He hated feeling powerless, and he knew every second counted when it came to this boy's care. Matt stood and moved out of the paramedics' way. They lifted the young man onto the stretcher and inserted a drip line. The medics wrapped him in a hypothermia wrap. After a few more checks, they were ready to make their way back to the ambulance to transport him.

Matt watched until they were out of sight. "What's next?" Tom stood beside him.

"I'm headed to the hospital. I want to see what the doctors say." Matt gave his team a few instructions and walked back to the car with Tom. Frank and Radar walked with them.

"You know, Frank, you have a damn fine dog here." Tom patted Radar's head. "He found the kid with minimal effort and probably saved his life." Tom stopped at the car while Frank put Radar in his crate. "I think every police department in the country should have access to a dog like this. It would make our work a whole lot easier, believe me."

"I've said the same thing myself, but with a shortage of funds and too many egos, it won't happen anytime soon." Frank got into his SUV. "I'll see you back at your place later, Matt."

"You know the protocol by now, Frank. Make yourself at home." Matt smiled at him. "Thanks again. If you can stay around, I think we should try to find the men who did this. Their scent should be all over our victim's clothes."

"I agree. I can stay for as long as you need me." Frank waved.

"His dog is one of the best." Tom nodded. "I know Frank his proud of him. He told me earlier that Radar's receiving a big award for his service."

"Frank trained him since he was a puppy. He should be proud of himself, too. The dog has a better track record for finding criminals and victims than most cops could dream of." Matt walked toward his car, followed closely by Tom.

****

Jessie knew Matt and his team would be checking the woods for the fourth victim, and she wished she could be there with them. Frank's car was parked near hers, so Radar was already busy tracking. Jessie was almost to town when the ambulance sped by her. Where were they headed? Could Carlos be alive? It was a nice thought anyway. No wonder she hadn't seen another ghost. His friends had kept her up most of the night with their wailing. Had they been trying to get help? Was it possible?

Jessie parked behind her store and unlocked the door, locking it again when she stepped inside. Matt would fill her in on the details soon enough. Right now, she had a store to open. She went about her morning routine.

Except for Larissa, who had chosen to hang in her shop, her latest ghostly sightings had been minimal. They chose to keep their distance, which was okay with her. Maybe they weren't aware she could see them or sense their presence. *Speculating again.* She straightened the counter, grabbing a stack of books to put on the table at the front of the store. It was enough that she saw them, and it didn't matter if they were conscious of her or not.

Jessie watched the clock. She was ready to open as soon as the clock said nine. The last few minutes took their sweet time. At nine, she opened the doors leading into the coffee shop, unlocked the front door, and opened it to wave at Audrey who was walking into the church. Jessie shook her head at Audrey's three unseen followers. Wow. First Community Church was becoming a gathering place for spirits.

"Do you have this book?" A customer walked in from the coffee shop. The pudgy middle-aged woman handed her a piece of paper with the title on it.

"I do." Jessie showed her where it was on the shelf. "Her other books are here as well."

"I have a friend who loves her stories. She told me I would enjoy them, too. I thought I would try it. I used to read all the time as a kid, but I haven't read any books for years now." She grabbed a book from the shelf, turning it over in her stubby hands.

"I think you'll find it enjoyable and relaxing."

"She said the same thing. I read about those kids' bodies found here, and I can't help but wonder what our world is coming too." She clucked disapprovingly and pushed a strand of her fading auburn hair back from her freckled face. "I could use an escape from reality, I think."

"A break from reality and all the bad news is something we can all use." Jessie left the woman to decide on her book. She went to the back room to get the bookmarks for her basket. She ordered them specially, with the store's name and phone number on them.

The bell over the door rang. "Hey, Blondie, I've come for another book. I'm starting to like this whole reading thing."

"I'm happy to hear it." Jessie noticed Melinda's glasses had slipped down her nose and she was looking over the top of them.

"I have some time to kill, and if it's okay with you, I'm going to get me some coffee. I want to sit in here and read. I'll leave these books here." Melinda placed them on the counter. "I'll be back to pay you in a few minutes. Do you want a cup?"

"No, thanks, I'm good." Jessie watched Melinda's lopsided ponytail begin to topple as she walked into the coffee shop. She pushed it back up. It looked more precarious than it had before. This was a first. Jessie smiled. Melinda often bought books but didn't stay and hang out. What was on her mind?

The woman brought her books to the counter. "I decided to start with the first book in her series. I have some catching up to do to get to the book my friend told me about. Three is a good beginning, I think."

"It will give you a chance to see if you like her writing. I think you should. Her books are quick, easy reads with lots of twists and turns. They're perfect books to get lost in." Jessie stuck one of her new bookmarks into the bag and handed it to the woman.

"Thank you. I'm sure I'll be back." The woman walked into the coffee shop.

"I'm back." Melinda bounced through the doors. "You should ring me up. I want to pay for them in case I spill my coffee on them or something." She put her coffee cup on the counter and began digging through her purse. "Here you go." Melinda handed Jessie her card.

"I'm glad you're staying to read your book. Besides liking your company, I was hoping people would enjoy spending time here. That's why I put in places to sit with tables close by to hold your coffee." Jessie handed Melinda her bag.

Melinda sat in the chair that Larissa had once claimed as her own. "It's kind of sad she's not here anymore."

"You think?" Jessie gave her an odd look. "I'm glad she's not throwing books at my customers or rearranging my store. Plus, you're sitting in the chair and not getting zapped."

"All true, but still I felt comfort in knowing she was around." Melinda took a quick glance around and motioned for Jessie to come over to her. Her voice softened. "She may be gone, but something strange is going on. The church has a different feel to it lately. I don't want to work in there at night or alone. I wait until I know there will be others in the building. You wouldn't happen to know anything about why it feels strange would you?" Melinda was serious.

"A few bodies have been found in Blue Cove. Maybe you're feeling concern about it." Jessie could see her shaking her head no.

"That's not it. The atmosphere is charged with something different. I don't know how to explain it, but I don't like working there right now."

"Anything is possible. As I said, the students' bodies were found near here. The girl was found in the woods behind the church." Jessie sat in the chair beside her. "They were kids. I can't imagine them being bad, though."

"All I'm saying is it's not the same as when Gina was there. That was a comforting feeling. Do you think the people who did this to them could be close by? Maybe that's why I'm so nervous."

"I have no idea. I guess they could be still in the area." Jessie frowned.

"You're not much help. I thought for sure I could count on you to know. This seems so different to me." Melinda's curls bounced up and down with her head. "It might be what you said. I've been reading about the death of those kids and the rise of hate crimes and protests across the country in the paper. The nightly news is filled with it." Melinda shuddered. "It has upset me more than usual. If you don't see any ghosts, then it must be that the people who tortured them are still around."

"Oh, I didn't say I haven't seen any ghosts. I simply have no idea if they are at the church or not."

"I knew they were around the area." Melinda

pointed her finger at Jessie. "You have to tell me where and when you saw them."

Jessie explained where she had seen the spirits and when. "It is strange because they don't seem to know what to do or what happened to them. They look lost somehow. I know that sounds weird, but that's how I feel about it."

"We need Reba. She could explain what's happening. Why don't they have a purpose?" Melinda seemed perplexed. "What if they are too shocked to have discovered their purpose for being here? Maybe we need to help them find it."

"We might have to." It made sense to Jessie. Who knew? Not her. How could she help them find the reason they were stuck here?

****

Matt walked into her store with Tom close behind him. "Hi, sweetheart, how's your morning going?"

"You're just the person I wanted to see." She walked toward him and reached for his hand.

"You listening, Tom? She wants to see me." He kissed her.

"I sure do," she whispered in his ear.

"I hear." Tom walked into the coffee shop. "I'll be watching."

He led her over to the table and pulled out her chair. "We found Carlos this morning. He was barely alive, but there was a pulse."

"I'm so happy. That must be why I didn't see a fourth ghost. The image of his friends wailing and flying through the trees was more than enough. They were agitated, and I didn't want to have a run in with them. Truthfully, I was overwhelmed." She squeezed his hand.

"The doctor told me the next forty-eight hours would be touch and go. If he makes it through, he might survive." Matt shook his head. "What happened to him was awful. If he survives, he'll need help for a long time to come." Matt told her how they had found Carlos. "I was happy you weren't there to see him. It's an image I will have a hard time forgetting."

"Why did they let him live?" Jessie shook her head. "These people don't make sense. They aren't following a pattern. It's as if they are making it up as they go along."

"I'm not sure they counted on him living. This was their way to disgrace him and torture him at the same time." Matt cracked his knuckles.

"Sick!" She frowned. "His friends were making a lot of noise last night. Melinda asked me earlier why their ghosts were still in the area. Maybe finding Carlos is one reason. I keep watching for a sign."

"I'm not much use to you there. I'm not sure I'd want to be, either." He leaned close to her. "You see enough for both of us." Out of the corner of his eye, Matt saw Tom point at his watch. "We have to go, but I wanted to let you know about Carlos. I love you, sweetheart." He gave her a long, delicious kiss that left her fanning her face.

"Hey." She tugged on his arm. "Why are you both in suits? I don't see you dressed like this often. You clean up nice by the way." Jessie straightened his tie.

"We're on our way to Shara and Amir's services. The bodies were released." Matt motioned for Tom. "I'll tell you what—if anything—I learn." Matt left, followed by Tom.

Would Amir or Shara be there? It was too much to think about. Thankfully, she didn't have to think for long. The bell rang, and her next customer walked in.

Chapter 16

On Saturday morning, Jessie waited for Matt to arrive. He was on time as usual. She waved and locked the door behind her.

Matt opened the car door for her. "How's your morning?

"So far so good." She smiled at him. "Hi, Tom," she said as she slipped into the backseat.

"Howdy, are you ready for the day?" Tom turned in his seat. "We'll be watching for someone who looks like they don't fit in."

"Sometimes a perp likes to attend the services of the victims." Matt latched his seat belt. "Are you ready?"

"Yes," she replied. "I did some research on Ryan Lucas. Did you know he played in a band and was considered to be an excellent musician?"

"I didn't know, and that's why I need you around to tell the rest of the story." Matt drove past the Inn.

"According to what I read, he was a terrific vocalist and played several instruments. Some of his music is on Internet social media sites. I listened to several songs last night."

"It ought to be an interesting crowd there today." Tom watched the traffic behind them in the side mirror as they drove through town.

"I've found whenever I do a human interest piece;

there are many layers to a person's life. Ryan didn't only study sports medicine, he played baseball for years. He loved music and his girlfriend, Emma. Ryan was popular on campus and well liked among the Foreign Students' Club members. Besides being a good student, he was considered to be a great friend to many."

"You need to put this in your story on him." Matt turned onto the highway.

"Did you know his memorial service today was planned by his friends? It isn't in a church. His friends, with his family approval, chose to hold it at one of the venues where he played his music. They're expecting a packed house with standing room only. It should be an eclectic mix of folks." Jessie smiled at Matt when she caught him watching her in the rearview mirror. He winked at her.

"The venue should make our job of blending in and mingling a whole lot easier." Tom checked the side mirror again. "I don't see a tail unless he's hanging back far in the pack."

"I haven't noticed one either, and I've been watching." He glanced back at Jessie. "You may as well relax, Jess; we have a drive ahead of us."

Leaning her head back against the seat, Jessie started thinking of the questions she wanted answers to. What piece of information would she learn about Ryan by listening to his friends? She planned to make herself as observant as possible today. That was her last coherent thought until Matt woke her up.

****

"Are you awake yet?" Matt put his arm around her waist to steady her when she got out of the car.

"I'm fine. I can't believe I fell asleep. I wasn't even tired." She chuckled. "I woke up a few hours ago after a good night's rest, for heaven's sake."

Tom walked a few steps behind them. He pointed to sign above the door. "The Watering Hole sounds like an interesting place. We've all hung out in a place like this back in the day."

"It wasn't that long ago." Jessie smiled at Tom. "You're not ancient, you know."

"Oh, I don't know. Some days it feels that way."

Jessie walked into the big open room. "Wow, it's a good thing we're early, or we wouldn't even have a place to stand." Jessie mentally counted the number of young people already there.

Near the front of the building on the screen above the stage, a video was playing. It showed Ryan in various stages of life. Jessie couldn't take her eyes off the smiling young man. She could feel those annoying tears filling her eyes. Matt handed her a tissue. "Thanks."

"I think we need to own stock in these when we get married." He waved the white tissue in front of her. "You'll keep the makers in business."

"Be nice, children." Tom stood behind them. "Being around all these young faces makes me feel ancient."

"I was thinking the same thing." Matt leaned back against the wall. "How about you, sweetheart, what's on your mind?"

"Unlike you two old men, I'm feeling young and happy to be alive." She smiled coquettishly at them.

"I want what you're drinking," Matt teased her.

Jessie handed him her bottle of water. "The

fountain of youth, take a drink."

He could see the excitement on her face. "Tell me what you see besides a large crowd."

"I believe I'm witnessing a remarkable way to celebrate a person's life. I'm glad on many levels we're here to see this." Jessie could barely move. She listened to the various groups talking around her. She fought back more tears when Ryan's girlfriend, Emma, shared stories of his life, followed by his parents. The band played his music as a finale. On the last song, the kids joined in and rocked out with the band.

Jessie tried hard to process the people, the conversations, and the genuine regard she could sense among the group. It was an amazing way to celebrate Ryan's life. The planned memorial was over, but the kids didn't want to leave.

"We should be going," Matt whispered in her ear.

She moved forward at a slow pace with Matt's hand on her elbow. There was an opening in the crowd. She made a quick move to the right and found herself staring at a familiar face. "He's here." She saw the man who had been in her store. He was talking with a group of men near the front door.

"Who's here, Jess, and where is he?" Matt kept up with her rapid pace.

"Darn, he must have seen us. The whole group left. We need to get out of here quickly." There were too many people near the door to go anywhere fast. Everyone seemed to have the same idea. By the time she made it outside, they were gone.

Matt stopped her. "You never answered my question. Who did you see?"

"The man who has been in my store, the one Misty

Carlson gave us the picture of." She frowned. "He was with a group of men near the door."

"Do you get a good look at any of them?" Matt folded his arms across his chest.

"I tried, but I didn't have a clear view of all their faces. He saw me and left as I started toward him." Jessie jumped when Tom grabbed her arm.

"Tell me before you take off like that again, would you?" Tom sounded breathless. "You left me behind, and I'm supposed to be watching him." He poked Matt in the chest with his finger.

"Sorry, Tom, we're used to working as a team. I forgot I needed to include you."

Matt explained what Jessie had seen. "They were gone by the time we got outside."

"Damn, why didn't you tell me? We could have gone out through the side door." Tom raked his hand through his hair. "From now on the three of us work together. You got it?"

"Aye, aye, Captain." Jessie saluted Tom.

"Take it easy, Tom. She's not on the payroll, and I don't want anything to mess up our working relationship. I'll keep you in the loop, but don't take it out on Jess."

Jessie patted Matt's arm. "I'm fine." She stopped listening to the argument brewing between Matt and Tom. Ryan Lucas was at his memorial service, and he was watching her. Their eyes locked on each other. He was aware that she could see him. The moment of recognition was electrifying as he moved around her. "We'll get them," she whispered. She rubbed her eyes not quite believing what else she saw. The image remained. Spellbound she watched, afraid to move lest she disturb the glorious light emanating from a creature moving in sync with Ryan, she couldn't take her eyes off them. Beauty and peace flowed between them to her. Tears flowed down her cheeks. How could she explain what she was seeing to anyone? She couldn't, and for now, she wouldn't try. "Angels unaware are among us," Sadie used to tell her when she had a bad dream. "They are here to watch over us even though we can't see them." But here she was all grown up and seeing one now.

Chapter 17

Matt hadn't taken his eyes off her. "Jess, are you okay, sweetheart?" She wasn't responding. "Jess, what's happening?"

Jessie turned into his arms. "Matt, please hold me."

"What is it, sweetheart?" Matt's hand stroked her back.

"I saw Ryan, and he knew I could see him. I can't explain how it felt. There are no words." She let the power of the moment wash over her, fighting back the gathering tears.

"Let's get you to the car." He maneuvered around people until they made it to the car.

"Is she okay?" Tom got in the car and closed the door. "I shouldn't have been so hard on her."

"Wait until she can explain it to you." Matt pulled out of the parking spot.

"I'm sorry. Don't worry, Tom. I'm overwhelmed right now." She had seen the existence of another world, and there were no words.

"We'll give you time, Jess, to pull yourself together. You can tell me when you're ready," Matt told her.

"Thank you." She wiped the tears running down her face. "I can't explain what happened to me back there. It was an overpowering emotional experience. Ryan's spirit was at his service. We saw each other.

The remarkable thing was that he was aware that I could see him. He came close to me, and a strange sense of electricity passed between us. The sorrow I saw in him was overwhelming, but it changed to peace. I need to think about it and talk to Reba. I've never had to process emotions like this before." She closed her eyes wanting to hold on to what she had seen. *An angel had wiped away his tears.*

"Whew, I didn't expect this. I thought you were upset with me for getting on you. I don't know how you handle this crap. If I didn't know you better, I think you were on the weird side." Tom shook his head. "I'm a blockhead, but even I could tell something had changed as we stood there. I found myself wanting to get as far away from there as I could."

"I'm glad we went," Jessie patted Matt's shoulder. "I won't forget this day. If ever I wonder again if a victim knows what has happened to them, I will remember the look on Ryan's face. I'll do everything I can to share his story so those who killed him can't snatch away his memory along with his life. Finding their murderers is important."

"We'll find them. As you've told me often enough, we have to bring justice and closure to the families." Matt smiled at her in the mirror.

"I remember reading an article about people who are adopting the victims of the Holocaust. They research the person by name and find out all they can about their lives to restore their memory and lineage. One by one, they are reclaiming them from the ashes. Murder shouldn't ever wipe out the memory of a person's life." Jessie took the tissue Tom handed her.

"Powerful." Tom shook his head. "Is that what you

do?"

"In a way." She paused. "Matt solves the murders, and I write to keep their memories alive."

"Heavy." Tom raised his brows.

"Not to change the subject, but I could use something to eat. My growling stomach is reminding me." Matt winked at her.

"I'm always ready to eat, as you know." Tom rubbed his stomach.

"How about you, Jessie? Do you think you're up for it?"

"I guess." She sniffed. "I can't let you boys go hungry because I'm crying like a girl, can I?"

****

Tom was getting on her nerves, asking her every few minutes if she was okay. It made her feel like some kind of freak. She had learned to accept what was happening in her life. There were times she'd rather go through life blind to what was happening around her, but for whatever reason, she was here, and she could see. Maybe she wasn't so unique. Reba was like her, and there might be others. People might be minding their own business, not looking for the unusual, and *bam* there it was in their lives—the unseen world suddenly coming into view, the invisible suddenly visible. She might have to get out some of her philosophy books from college. She wasn't going waste her life worrying about it. She would help anybody she could for as long as she could. Even if the methods weren't conventional, the look on Ryan's face told her she had to try. The main question she had now was what was Matt up against, and how could she keep him safe? He always tried to protect her, and now it was her turn.

He wouldn't want her to hover. She would have to devise a plan that would let her be close but not close enough to stifle him. Jessie needed a plan. She heard a soft knock on her door.

Jessie opened the door to Matt, after checking. "What are you doing here without Tom?'

"He's out in the car. I told him he could watch me from there. I need time alone with my girl." Matt stepped in, shut the door, and stepped into her arms.

"And he's okay with it?" Jessie lifted her head to see his face.

"Not at all. Tom complained and whined the whole way over here." He grinned. "What can I say? I'm giving him job security. I won't leave him out there for long."

"Why are you here?"

"I wanted to check on you." His hand moved up and down her back.

"I'm still processing." She pulled his head down and kissed him.

"I knew I wanted to see you tonight, and it couldn't wait." It was his turn to kiss her, and she let him.

She didn't want him to stop. He didn't. By the time he pulled away, they were both breathless. She gazed into his eyes. "You're good at this kissing stuff, Mr. Parker."

"I get even better as the night wears on. I have a lot of moves I could show you." He smiled at her.

"I bet you do, but not tonight, not with Tom waiting in the car for you."

"Don't remind me. I feel like my dad's waiting in the car for me while I walk my date to the door and try to steal a kiss. We could practice until we're perfect. I could tell Tom he'll have to wait a few more minutes. I still need to comfort you after today."

"This is only my opinion." She gave him a coy smile. "But you're perfect enough. Not that I would mind you showing me some of your other moves, but as far as your kisses go, I'd say you've mastered the art."

"Why thank you kindly, sweetheart. I'll be happy to show you my art any old day."

"I'll hold you to your promise." She hugged him tightly. "Promise me you'll let Tom watch your back. Don't get all macho; let him do his job."

"What's this?" He raised her head to see her face. "Are you worried about me?"

"Of course, I kind of like having you around."

"The feeling is mutual. I won't stray away from Tom." He kissed her. "I promise, sweetheart." He opened the door. "I like when you're concerned about me. It makes me feel loved."

"You are loved."

"I love you, too, Jess." He stepped out the door. "Remember to lock it."

"I will." She watched him until they drove away.

After he was gone, she flipped on her computer to check her e-mails. She opened the one from Jeremy. He had found out some information that might be helpful to the case. Jessie would give Matt time to make it home and then she would call. They needed to talk. She paced for ten and then called.

"You miss me already. I can have Tom drive me back over."

"Not necessary." She laughed.

"I'm wounded."

Jessie could picture him clutching his chest. "Would you be serious for a moment?

His voice sounded stern. "You want serious, I can be a grown-up."

She fought to keep from laughing. "Did you get the e-mail from Jeremy?"

"I did. Tom has sent the phone numbers to the agency to have them checked."

"I wanted to make sure you saw them."

"I think it's an excuse because you miss me already." He chuckled.

"Yeah, and that, too." She smiled

Chapter 18

"You need to get married. I get tired of watching you two go back and forth." Tom turned on the TV.

"We will, but we're not in a hurry. We're having a good time getting to know each other." Matt sat on the couch. Frank was nice and comfortable in the recliner. Radar was sleeping at his feet.

"All I'm saying is there are sparks flying in all directions around you two."

"Yeah, I know, and I like it." Matt pulled his glasses out of his pocket and slipped them on. "I hope this case is solved soon. Jessie's birthday is coming, and I have something special planned for her."

"If the case isn't solved by then, I'll be involved in whatever you do." Tom shook his head. "Not a good visual at all."

"No way. You're not invited. No offense, but you're not wanted." Matt glared at him.

"None was taken. I wouldn't want you on one of my dates either. I do my best work alone." Tom flipped back and forth between stations.

"I have it better than both of you. I've been with my wife long enough that we can fill in the words to each other's sentences. She's comfortable being with me and isn't shocked by my less than perfect habits. I like coming home to her at the end of the day."

"Don't you get tired of the same person day after

day?" Tom muted the TV.

"No, she's the love of my life. Why would I get tired of her?" Frank stroked Radar's head when he lifted it. "I used to think like you when I was young, too. There's something to be said about being with the person you love when you're past your prime. We all get there, you know, and it comes faster than you think."

"I guess you're right." Tom looked at the TV.

"With your mug, you'd better hurry; you're almost out of your prime." Matt slapped Tom on the back. "So am I. That's why I'm not taking any chances. I love Jessie, and I have a well-ordered plan when it comes to her. I'm not letting her slip through my fingers."

"The goal is to keep you alive long enough to see it to the finish line." Tom turned the sound back on. The sports scores were on.

****

Jessie was at the store early. She turned on her laptop and searched through the wanted posters of international criminals. Jeremy had taught her how to do it. After a while, the faces blurred together until a familiar face popped up. Interpol wanted him for various crimes. Matt needed to see this.

"Matt, where are you?" Jessie asked when he answered the phone.

"I'm on my way to the station, why?'

"Can you stop by the store for a minute? I have something you need to see."

"We'll be right there." She heard him tell Tom they had a quick change of plans.

Jessie stood at the door and watched for him. Excitement bubbled up inside of her. Another piece to the puzzle had fallen into place. She unlocked the door when Matt parked in front of the store. Tom got out of the car, too. "This won't take too long. I know you have to get to work," she called out when she opened the door.

"What do you have?" Tom stepped in the door.

"Don't mind him." Matt grinned at her. "Good morning, sweetheart."

"Jeremy taught me how to search wanted posters in the US and internationally, and look whose face showed up today." Jessie pointed at her computer screen.

"Well, I'll be damned. He's the guy who's been lurking at your store." Tom shook his head. "What's he wanted for?"

"He's wanted for racketeering, money laundering, and for torture, to name a few. He has several aliases, too." Jessie read from the list a few of his names. "All of which were names of real people whose ID's he stole after they were murdered."

"It's hard to believe the picture of the man you gave me and this guy are one and the same." Matt pulled up the photo on his phone.

"Looks can be deceiving. This man has a mean streak; I could see it in his eyes. Old Harry, here, would order a death in a heartbeat if someone crossed him. At least I thought so when I saw him, and now this confirms it for me." Jessie shivered, rubbing her arms.

"Harry, huh? Doesn't sound like the name of an international crime boss, does it?" Matt scrolled through the list of his names.

"I don't think he's the boss, only one of the minions. There's someone above him who doesn't want to get his hands dirty." Jessie's eyes lit up as she talked. "Jeremy can track his movements so we can learn how Harry operates and who he meets up with."

"You'd make a great FBI agent, Jessie. Any chance you'd consider a job with the Bureau?" The corner of Tom's lips curved up.

"No, I'm happy where I'm at. Matt and I make a good team."

"You've trained her well, Matt."

"She answers for herself, don't you, sweetheart? From the first day we met, she told me what she was going to do." Matt pulled her into his side. "Not one lecture I gave ever stopped her, and she was right most of the time."

"I'm a bit of a rebel when it comes to men telling me what I should do. I would rather rise or fall on my own actions and decisions." She turned her head to glance at Matt. He was smiling.

"Do you want to ask Jeremy to do the research?"

"Sure, I'll send him an e-mail right now while I'm thinking about it." She typed it as they talked about a trap for Harry.

"Great work, Jessie. I'll send this information on to the agency." Tom walked to the front of the store.

"Jess, if you see him around, let me know. There will be someone watching the store. If he comes in again, we want to follow him. Who knows where he might lead us?" Matt kissed her.

"He's Harry to me, although I wonder what his real name is. He'll be back. I've seen him several times already." She walked with Matt to the door. "Be careful, Matt. He may not look the part, but he's one tough customer."

"I will, and this is where I tell you to do the same. I have someone watching out for me, but you don't."

"I'll be careful. Only this time, I think I'm safe. The suspects are not after me." She kissed him goodbye.

"We don't know that yet. Be cautious. I'll send you my observations from Amir and Shara's services in an e-mail."

"Thanks." She waved.

****

Marshall had hit pay dirt getting up early to follow the cop today. He had no idea who the man with him was. He snapped a photo of the two men when they came out of the store. The boss could figure it out. Today he'd watch the store for a while. Marshall didn't want to go anywhere near the police station. The place was crawling with reporters. He couldn't risk anyone placing him in town or someone recognizing his mug. He had done a few interviews with reporters over the years. Marshall was tired of sitting in the car. What was the purpose? Yeah, he made money, but he had no idea what he had gotten himself into. This was a mean crowd. A few more pictures and he would tell them he was done.

Chapter 19

Matt stared at the open file on his desk willing something to jump out at him; even a small clue would be nice. The man casing Jessie's store was trouble; that much he knew. The tail following his car was still waiting when they came out of her store. Jessie was right. The guy wasn't good at it. How did he fit into the case? Matt saw no correlation between the man at the store, the person following him, and the murdered students. He had to find something to connect them or a least a way forward. Right now, he had pieces. How did they all fit together?

Tom walked into Matt's office. "I checked on Carlos, and he's showing signs of a slow but steady improvement. He's still in a drug-induced coma because of swelling in his brain. The hospital promised to let us know when we could talk with him." Tom sat in the chair in front the desk.

"I'm happy to hear about Carlos. It would be nice if he made it." Matt tapped his pen on the notepad.

"You look stumped." Tom placed his coffee cup on the corner of Matt's desk.

"I am. We have a lot of parts, but nothing that ties them all together. We're missing something significant: the link."

"You know how this works. Eventually, the sections come together to form a story. We'll figure it out."

"I want to work with Jessie. You see how her mind works. She thinks around the edges like the investigative reporter she is. One idea leads to another. We play off each other." Matt ran his hand through his hair. "Did you see the excitement in her eyes when she found Harry, as she likes to call him? She's good at this, and she makes me better. Her questions challenge me to think."

"You'll have to spend time with her then. Look, I, of all people, know the value of a good partner. They can save your life in a tight spot. We'll do what we have to do. Hell, I can babysit the both of you, or better yet, chaperone you." Tom laughed.

"Good. I wanted you to understand how important this is. When Jessie said we work well together, she meant it. So do I. Kaufman is skeptical, and the other agents wouldn't give her the time of day, except for her looks. I'm telling you, if something should happen to me, listen to her. She's not crazy. She knows and understands this better than we do."

"Nothing is going to happen to you." Tom frowned at Matt. "You know I have respect for Jessie, and I'd listen to her and make the others listen also."

"Thanks, Tom, this is a must for me. I knew you'd understand." Matt doodled on the paper in front of him. He looked up to see Tom watching him.

"Something is bothering you? What is it?"

"I'm not sure. I may be in for a tough time. I've had more people warn me to be careful than on any other case." Matt's jaw flexed.

"You can't go there. Don't invite trouble. You're good at what you do, and you've been in tight places before. Your instinct as a cop will kick in. Besides, I'm not letting you out of my sight. I know Jessie will be fighting for you every step of the way."

"I know you're right, but I don't want her to become the target. I couldn't take it if I lost her." Matt closed his eyes. "She means the world to me."

"There are risks that come with the job; we all know it. To minimize those dangers is the best we can do."

"I've had too much time on my hands waiting for something to break." Matt's phone buzzed.

"Chief, Jeremy is on line one."

"Thanks, Kenny." Matt pushed the button for the line. "Hey, Jeremy, do you have something for me?"

"You bet I do. The man's real name is Harry Roth. He's never been married and was bullied growing up for being a mama's boy. Roth is a front man of sorts. He schemes, plots, and makes sure the deals go right. The authorities want to question him regarding several crime rings overseas."

"Jessie calls him Harry. I guess she's right. I wonder why he's in the U.S."

"This is where it gets interesting. Interpol tracked him coming across the border but lost his trail. According to the open file on him, he may have joined a gang that crossed into the country from Mexico. The gang is new on the agency's radar, and the information is limited. There's an open investigation on them. The FBI should be able to get more information."

"Jeremy, this is Tom. How dangerous is Roth?"

"It's all speculation. Every witness the agency has found to testify against him ends up dead. His reach is long even when he's no longer in the area."

"He appears so unassuming." Matt scribbled down a note in the case file.

"He doesn't stand out. I guess you'd want that in a front man. But from what I've read, he's meaner than blazes."

"Jessie told me his eyes were angry. We'll have to keep our eyes out for him. It's possible he'll lead us to the others."

"I'd say you have another big case on your hands. Notify the authorities about the prize they have in your area."

"I'll contact the right people," Tom said. "What we don't need are more agents in the area."

"All right, I did my part. I'm going to try to find out more about the gang. Be careful. I'll call if I find out more."

"Thanks, Jeremy."

"Before I forget, I traced the numbers on Amir's phone, and I'm sending you a list. Most of them were to and from his friends, Darsha, and the embassy. There were several from untraceable numbers, probably throwaways."

"I'll watch for your e-mail, and we'll talk later." Matt hung up.

"I don't know what I was expecting, but it wasn't what I heard. Roth sounds like trouble to me. I'm going to make a few calls to the department and CIA working with Interpol. I think we might need to rethink this case." Tom stood. "Keep this quiet for a while. I want to hear what they say before we do anything."

"Sounds like a plan to me." Matt stood to stretch his legs. He took his coffee cup to refill while he was up.

****

Jessie finished showing a customer where to find the book she wanted. She ran to answer her ringing phone. "Idle Time Books, may I help you?"

"Hi, Jess, how's your day?"

"No complaints so far, Matt. How's yours?"

"I've convinced Tom that I have to be around you to solve this case. He even offered to chaperone us."

Jessie chuckled. "An interesting idea, but I think I'll pass."

"I figured you might because I told him no way. Have you seen Harry around today?"

"No, but I'm sure he's in the area." Jessie did a quick peek into the coffee shop to make sure he wasn't in there.

"His actual name is Harry Roth. You got the Harry right. What makes you think he's still in the area?"

"I'm not sure, but I sense that he is."

"I trust your feelings. Let me hear the minute you see Roth."

"I will. I figure since you have his real name, you probably learned a few things about him. You'll have to fill me in when you get a chance."

"Of course, I will. Just a minute, Jess." She could hear him talking in the background. "We'll be at your house to pick you up at six. We're making you dinner tonight at my place."

"Wow, sounds great. I've never had three men cook for me. I'd call it scary, but I happen to know you're a great cook. I'll be ready."

"See you soon, sweetheart." Jessie hung up after Matt did.

Jessie pulled up Harry's face on the screen. "What

is it with this guy?" she muttered.

"Jessie?" Molly walked through the open doors. "I've brought you a sweet delight for your afternoon." She placed the plate with a small chocolate raspberry tart and mini brownie on it.

"Oh, goodness, these are good. I can't make up my mind which one I like best. I do love German chocolate brownies, but the tart is yummy, too." She went back and forth with her fork. "Since I can't make up my mind, I'll take six of each. I'm going to Matt's for dinner, and he has other guests tonight."

"I'll box them for you, and you can pay me when you pick them up."

"Perfect, Molly. I'll be over before five."

Jessie enjoyed her afternoon. Two new customers from town came into her store. Meeting new town folks was always a treat. She planned to make Blue Cove her home for a long time to come. Jessie grabbed her box from Molly, did her closing routine, and was ready to leave for the day. She couldn't wait to see Matt's reaction when she told him that Reba had come into the store simply to say hello and grab a book. A book was the only reason she came. There was no message, no dire warning, it was a simple visit. Jessie was a tad perplexed by it. Reba rarely came for a visit without bringing a message. She must simply enjoy the moment. The smile lasted on her face the entire drive home.

Chapter 20

Jessie grabbed her jacket when Matt arrived but waited for him to come to the door. It would give her a few minutes alone with him. Those few minutes were priceless as far as she was concerned. She opened the door when he knocked.

"I see you waited for me to come to get you, which is a first." He smiled.

"Yes. I did. There is an important reason for me to wait today." She fluttered her lashes at him.

"Is that right? Do you mind letting me know what it is?" He leaned closer to her.

"We've had only a little time alone in the past few days. I wanted to make sure I thank you in advance for dinner tonight." She pulled his head down and kissed him. When she pulled away, they were both breathless.

"Maybe I should tell Tom to sit in the car for a while." He grinned at her. "I like this side of you. I'll have to make you feel grateful more often." He leaned closer and kissed her back. She gave him a funny look. "What?" Matt chuckled. "Call it one more for the road." He took her hand as they stepped outside.

She told him all about Reba's visit. "I hardly knew what to do without one of her warnings."

"I can imagine. Has she ever come to visit without one?" He glanced at her.

She shook her head. "Not when we're in the

middle of a case. I'll admit it was quite refreshing and yet strange at the same time."

"What was strange about it?" Matt's thumb stroked the palm of her hand.

"If you want an answer you'd better stop that," she said under her breath.

"Am I bothering you, sweetheart?" He did it again, his lips pressed tight together.

"You have no idea." She pinched his hand when he did it again. "Are you listening? I bet you can't remember anything I said."

"I'll stop." He gave her a lopsided grin. "Why was it strange? See, I was listening. You lose, and I get to claim a forfeit." He leaned in and pulled her close. She closed her eyes. He whispered in her ear, "Not now. I'll wait until you least expect it and no one's around." He pinched her cheek playfully.

"We'll see about that, Parker." She took his hand and pulled him along.

"Ah, the challenge. You know I'm going to win, sweetheart." He laced his fingers through hers. "What's in the box? I can carry it if you want." He reached for the box in her hand.

"I'm fine. It's a small taste of dessert heaven for you boys. Molly loves owning the coffee shop, and she's always searching for new items to put on the menu. Thankfully, she tries them out on me first. What's new today?"

Matt told her about the hospital's report on Carlos. "I'm hopeful he'll make it." He opened the car door for her.

"Hi, Tom," she said as she got into the back seat.

"It took you long enough. I was beginning to think

I needed to send out a rescue party."

"I tried to drag it out as long as possible. I knew you'd be thrilled by the wait." Jessie patted Tom's shoulder.

"Now, why doesn't that surprise me?" Tom laughed. "You were target practice while you were standing out there."

"Sorry, I forgot. Next time I'll keep him inside longer. See? I brought treats." Jessie pointed to the box. "It's a bribe to turn your head and get you to look the other way. A woman has to have some time alone with her man."

"You have it as bad as this guy. He can't think without you in the room." Tom winked at her.

"He brings out the best in me." She caught Matt's eye in the rearview mirror and saluted him.

"He said the same thing earlier. I might have to watch you two in action. I don't spend near enough time with my partner. Of course, he's not as pretty as you are."

"Yeah, and you haven't solved any major cases lately." Matt glanced at Tom.

"True. You two seem to have all the cases handed your way for some odd reason. I'm not jealous, mind you, but I wouldn't mind a bit of action occasionally."

"Feeling tired of your pencil-pushing paperwork?" Matt turned onto his property. "You could always move here, Tom." He pulled into the garage.

"Moving to Blue Cove isn't necessary. I seem to end up here helping you anyway. Besides, paperwork comes with your job, too." Tom stepped out of the car and closed the door.

"I can't get away from the mounds of paper." Matt

opened Jessie's door. "The City Council reminds me too often how important the reports are."

"I take it you don't enjoy filling out all the reports. Paperwork is the downside of your job, but every profession has its drawbacks." Jessie walked into the kitchen. She placed her box of goodies in the counter. "Hi, Frank," she called out to him. "Yum, something smells good."

"Hi. I'm watching the news. Come join me," Frank called from the living room.

"Sit down, sweetheart; we'll call you when dinner is ready." Matt turned her around and gave her a gentle push toward the living room.

Jessie could hear Matt and Tom talking in the kitchen. She settled on the couch and noticed that Frank was already dozing. Her mind turned to the facts she'd read earlier about Harry Roth. Why was he in Blue Cove? Did it have to do with the students or Matt? Unless some major information came to light, Harry was too big a player to be in the area for no reason. He had several agencies looking for him. Why now? What was about to go down?

She walked into the kitchen. "Frank is sleeping. Give me something to do, please."

"You can put this on the table." Matt handed her the basket of bread.

"I hope you're hungry." Tom tossed the salad with the dressing.

"I am. Can I help?" she asked. "There must be something I can do."

He nodded his head. "You can hand me those." He pointed to the stack of salad plates on the counter.

"Let me dish up the salad for you. It's an easy

enough job." She filled each plate, topping the greens with dried cranberries and candied pecans. "I'm convinced Roth is in Blue Cove because something major is about to go down."

Tom's head snapped around. "Okay, it's possible, but why?" he asked.

"Everything I've read about him tells me he's only seen when there is something big happening. Too many agencies are searching for him to risk him surfacing for a small job. I'm not sure he's even watching for Darsha."

"Why is he here then?" Matt stopped what he was doing and turned to her.

"When we know the answer to your question, I'd say we'll be close to solving the case. My preliminary idea on the subject is that it's bigger than you or those kids. But part of it is tied to you, Matt." Jessie touched his hand.

"Damn, my thought exactly, and that's why I'm here babysitting him. I want to hear how you came to your theory. Let's get this food on the table. We need to talk." Tom handed her a couple of salad plates to carry to the table.

"Why me?" Matt stopped her on her way back to Tom.

"There are some reasons I can think of, which are all speculation right now. You've solved so many major cases this past year. Roth had to be involved in one of those cases; I can sense it. We need to find out as much as we can about Harry. He's one of the major players and the link between you and the students. We know he met with Amir; the picture Misty gave us gives us the connection. He was at Ryan's funeral with a few other men who are probably involved too. Follow him, and you will find the others." She pursed her lips. "I still think it's bigger than you. You're not the reason he's in the states, but he does have a score to settle with you."

"Is it possible it's tied to your days at the agency?" Tom frowned.

"Anything is possible, I guess. We need to search through the cases that I was a part of for a link." Matt raked his hand through his hair.

Jessie held up her hand. "Whoa, back it up a minute. You were in the FBI and I'm just hearing about it now?"

"It never came up in conversation besides it was only for a short time. Remind me to tell you about it some time."

"Now would be perfect. She glared at him.

"Another time, it's not important."

"Not important, hell. He was in line to be promoted when he quit. His record gives a report of a damn good agent. Speaking of good, you're not half bad yourself, Jessie." He grabbed the carving knife out of the drawer." Tom caught Matt's frown and changed the subject. "The big question is who is the tail, and how does he fit into the picture?" Tom uncovered the standing roast and handed Matt the knife.

"He's so sloppy and easy to see it makes me wonder if he's been hired as a distraction. They want to keep Matt sidetracked so he won't see what's coming at him until it's too late." Jessie handed Tom a plate.

Matt placed a slice of prime rib on the platter. "Cooked to perfection," he smiled. "No more shop talk. I want you to enjoy this while it's hot."

"I'll get Frank." Jessie walked into the living room.

"Frank," Tom yelled, "soup's on." He cut a few more slices of beef.

Frank jumped out of the chair, rubbing his eyes. "I must have dozed off. It's this darn chair. Every time I sit down in it, I'm out." Jessie followed him to the table.

****

After dinner, they talked about the case over their coffee and dessert. Jessie fielded every question that Tom threw at her, and Matt couldn't have been more proud. She had thought this through and considered every angle. He could see that Tom was impressed, while Frank beamed at her like a pleased father. Jessie never ceased to amaze him. Tonight, she had him convinced Harry Roth was after him as some kind of retaliation. How would it go down? He wanted Jessie involved in this case. She was the only one with a working theory that made any sense right at the moment.

"Tell Molly the brownies were great." Matt reached for the tart to have a taste.

"Before I let him change the subject, how do we keep him safe?" Tom pointed at Matt.

"We need a plan." Jessie sat back in her chair.

"Jessie always has to have a plan." Matt smiled at her as he took her hand. "It's one of her most endearing qualities.

"If Harry Roth is the link, at some point you'll have to follow him. Matt will have to have a backup and a cover all the time. Does Kaufman or anyone else know about him?" Jessie stroked her thumb across the palm of his hand.

Matt smiled and leaned close to whisper in her ear.

"Your own form of payback, sweetheart? I don't mind."

"What are you two whispering about?" Tom frowned and grabbed a brownie from the plate.

"It's personal, Maxwell."

"To answer your question, Jessie, I haven't told Kaufman yet. We're waiting for the agent to arrive with information on Roth and Interpol. He'll tell us how to proceed."

"Tom, I know this will sound strange to you, but I have to say it. When it comes to the cases that come our way, it's for a reason. I heard Amir's cries, and we are connected. Many others can come to help and give their expert advice, but in the end, it will be us"—she pointed at Matt, Frank, and herself—"who solve it. They want us to."

"You're right, it sounds strange. I don't get it, but I saw it in your last case. I'm on your side."

"I know this much; it will take Matt's ingenuity to get through this, but he'll do fine."

Matt was glad she had confidence in him because as their conversation moved forward, he wasn't sure he had any left.

Chapter 21

Jessie couldn't believe the things she had said to Tom. What must he think of her? She knew she was right, though. Once again, the case had found them, and they had to be a part of solving the murders. A quick glance at the clock told her it was past time to get up. She stretched, threw off her covers, and sat on the edge of the mattress. If her instincts were right, they wouldn't have much longer to wait. Even if the ghosts didn't interact with her much, she knew when the time came, they would be on their side.

With her morning routine finished, Jessie decided to stop in the coffee shop for a breakfast sandwich and coffee before she opened the bookstore. She didn't want to cook or wash a single dish this morning. The guys had treated her to a great meal last night, something she could learn to live with on any occasion. Only once in a great while did get the urge to create a culinary experience. She wondered if marriage would change her.

When she was in the middle of a case, it consumed her thinking and her writing. Matt was rubbing off on her. She honked and waved as she drove by the Inn. Katie expected it every morning now and often commented if she forgot. Tradition was important to Katie,

Katie is getting married. She shook her head and

smiled. Her crazy friend was going to be Dylan's wife. Wedding plans were moving ahead, sort of, but it would help if the two of them would settle on a date. Katie was waiting to hear from Sally, their good friend from high school. Sally had to be in the wedding; Katie was adamant about it.

Jessie parked at the back of the store. She went through the interior doors into the coffee shop as soon as she was inside. "Hi, Molly, your place is hopping this morning." She pulled the door to the bookstore closed.

"Hey, Jessie, how did they like the dessert last night?" Molly handed a bag to the customer ahead of Jessie.

"They ate them all. Matt was a big fan of the brownies. The empty plate says it all."

"What do you want this morning? A scone perhaps?" Molly smiled at her.

"I want a coffee and the breakfast croissant." Jessie reached into her purse for her wallet.

"Have you ever had one before?" Molly asked. "I can't remember you ever ordering one."

"No, but everyone says how good they are, so I wanted to give it a try. If it's like everything else you make, it'll be great." Jessie put cream in the coffee Molly handed her.

"I think you have steered more customers my way by your comments about my food than anyone else. I should give you free food for a year." Molly took her money and gave her back her change.

"No, you shouldn't. You're building a business and a mighty good one. You get rave reviews from all the people I've talked to who have come in here. It's convenient for me to have you so close to where I work. You have great items on the menu." Jessie took the bag from Molly. "Besides, I didn't want to cook this morning, and this seems like the perfect alternative." Jessie put money in the tip jar. "I'm glad we share these open doors. It is good for both our businesses."

"I agree." Molly leaned close and lowered her voice. "You haven't seen Larissa's ghost again have you? I thought she left after the last case."

"No. Why?" Jessie studied Molly's face.

"Strange things have been happening around here again. I haven't seen anything, but it's either some kind of phenomenon or I'm flat out absentminded. I think I'm too young to be going there yet."

"You're not forgetful, Molly. You're the most organized person I know." Jessie paused at the door and added. "If you get a break later on, come over, and we'll talk. You have too many customers right now."

"I will because you know something about all this; it's written on your face." Molly moved on to help the next customer.

Yes, Jessie had an idea who might be in the coffee shop after hours. She often saw Amir's ghost sitting on the stool at the front window. Rarely did she see anyone else sit there. Who he was looking for? Maybe she should have Kaufman bring Darsha to the store. Amir might be keeping an eye out for her. It was possible he needed to know she was okay.

The few ghosts she had dealt with seemed to hang around until whatever they needed to finish in their lives was complete. She took a bite of her breakfast sandwich. Molly had another winner. Everything Molly made was good.

Patience wasn't one of her strongest attributes. It would be great if answers were immediate, but that never seemed to be the way of it. Why Amir and the others were still in Blue Cove was a mystery for her to discover. Walking to the front of the store to unlock the door she spied Melinda crossing the street and waving at her.

"Pastor John said you were here today. We have to talk." Melinda brushed past Jessie in the open door.

"Look around while I finish opening up, and I'd be happy to talk to you." Jessie finished her tasks and went to stand by Melinda. "What do you want to talk about?"

"What's going on in town? There's something strange happening around the church and the cemetery." Melinda scrunched her face. "I figure you'd have to know because you usually do."

"You've figured wrong. I have no idea. I was wondering the same thing myself this morning. I know there are spirits around, the atmosphere in town is charged, but I have no idea why they are still here. Unlike Larissa, I've had minimal interaction with them, but I feel a strong emotional tie."

"Believe me when I say that peculiar things are happening at the church. I don't want to be there alone at night. I've heard slamming doors, crying, and all sorts of strange sounds. I've noticed a car with a strange man in it in the parking lot a few times when I've arrived early. I move on and come back when I'm sure one of the pastors has arrived. I'm telling you, it's weird over there." Melinda pushed her glasses up to their rightful position on her nose only to have them slip down again.

"Have you talked to Reba?"

"That's the weirdest part of all, Reba has been quiet. She hasn't said one word. Not one."

Jessie shook her head, her mouth tight at the corners. "You're right. That is strange."

"I believe she knows something, but she's holding back for some reason." Melinda cradled her chin in her hand. "I only wished I knew why."

The light turned on in Jessie's head. "You know she was here the other day and didn't say a word. She didn't give me a warning or one of her cryptic messages. I thought it was unusual at the time, but kind of refreshing, too. I wonder if Reba is all right." She had to be. Jessie couldn't imagine doing any of this without Reba.

"No, she can't be. It's not like her to be quiet on a subject this important, ever." Melinda's eyes got misty. "We'd better check on her."

Jessie started to call Reba when she noticed her crossing the street. "You'll be able to check on her in a minute. She's crossing the street from the church."

Melinda jumped up and ran to hold the door open. "Are you all right? I'm worried about you." The words spilled out of Melinda's mouth in record time.

"Let's sit down girls, shall we?" Reba sounded breathless. "I'm fine, Melinda, dear."

"If you are, why have you've been so quiet?" Melinda grabbed her hand. "It's not like you, and you've had me quite worried." Her springy curls bounced with every word.

"It has been the strangest thing. I know something is going on, but I have no idea what is happening. Other than that, I know Matt must be careful. It has been the same for you, hasn't it, Jessie?" Reba reached in her purse for a tissue.

"Yes, I've been in a fog of sorts." Jessie touched Reba's hand.

"I now know why. This morning I understood why it has happened this way. This is Matt's time. He's about to come into his own. Matt has listened to us and trusted what we've said against his own better judgment. He will solve this case, and you, my darling girl, will be there to back him up but not in a conventional way."

"It's true Matt is a trouper when it comes to the strange things I've put him through. It would be only right for him to solve the case and do it the way he knows how." Jessie was relieved. She sat back her chair and took a deep breath.

"Don't get too comfortable. Matt will still need your help. I'm not sure how you'll help, but you'll be pulling for him, and he'll make it because of your love." Reba patted Jessie's hand. "Most important of all is your belief in him."

"Dang, I don't understand any of this, Reba. Should I be worried about the strange noises at the church or not?" Melinda pursed her lips, and frown lines appeared on her forehead.

"We do have active spirits about town. Maybe you shouldn't work there alone until after this storm blows over. I don't know whether they are friendly or not."

"My observation is that they are troubled and shocked. How long they'll remain that way, I have no idea." Jessie waved at Molly who came through the door.

"You ladies are deep in conversation." Molly sat across from Reba. "What's going on, Jessie? I know you know."

"I said the same thing, but I'm not sure you'll get much out of them." Melinda frowned again.

"I've seen Amir's spirit in your store. He sits at the front corner on a stool some days, looking out the window. I have no idea why he's there or what he's waiting for. The stool is usually empty when he's there. No one else sits on it." Jessie leaned forward in her chair and rested her elbows on the table.

"I don't know what answer I was expecting, but it wasn't that one. Will my shop always be plagued by ghosts?"

"You do own a shop across from the cemetery. What were you expecting?" Melinda slapped her leg and laughed.

"Molly, you wouldn't have known a ghost was there if Jessie hadn't told you. I don't think he means to harm anyone. He's stuck, dear. Until whatever needs to be completed is done, he's between worlds. I don't see him here for long. Other than a few odd things happening, I think you'll be fine. Leave him alone. He'll go soon enough."

"Believe me, I'll leave him alone. I don't want to make trouble, but I wanted to understand why strange things were happening again."

"I daresay he probably spent a lot of time in a coffee shop while he was alive. That's why he migrated to your business to wait." Reba smiled at Molly. "You could become a busy waiting spot being as more people drink coffee then read." Reba chuckled.

"Reba, you're brilliant. Molly, many folks spend their time in coffee shops reading. I think our businesses might invite wayfaring spirits who are passing through." Jessie laughed with Reba. Soon Melinda's cackle joined, and Molly gave in to the humor of their situation before long.

"I have no idea why I'm laughing." Melinda stood. "I need to get back to work. I'm happy you're okay, Reba." Jessie walked with her to the door.

"Please stop in anytime, Red. I love it when you do." Jessie held the door open.

"I'll be back, Blondie." Melinda waved and started across the street.

"I need to be on my way, too, dear." Reba stood at the door watching Melinda. "Laughter is the best medicine, as they say. I don't have any more answers than when I came, but I'm happy." Jessie watched until Reba was safe across the street near the church.

"I'm with Reba." Molly laughed. "I have few answers, but I'm feeling better than when I walked in here, too. See you later, Jessie. A tour bus pulled in across the street. I think our day is about to get busy."

Chapter 22

Matt received an envelope with no return address in a stack of mail. He took the letter opener and slit it open. The paper was dirty and the penmanship messy.

Parker, I've waited to give you what you deserve. You messed in my business, and you'll pay for it. I'm your worst nightmare, and I'm waiting around the next corner.

Matt found Tom and tossed the letter onto his pile of papers. "You might want to check this for fingerprints. It looks like whoever wrote it might have spilled his dinner on it. I guess if there was any doubt about how I'm connected, this proves someone is after me."

"We already knew as much. I'll run this by our tech." Tom put on a rubber glove to handle the note. "You'll have to accept my tagging along for now."

"I'll accept it, but I don't have to like it."

"I never thought for a moment you would."

"Chief, the hospital is on line one." Gary stood beside Matt in the officer's lounge where Tom was working.

"I'll answer it here." Matt picked up the phone. "This is Parker. Great, we'll be right there."

"Tell me." Tom stood. "Carlos is awake." He began stuffing his files into his briefcase.

Matt nodded. "Carlos is ready to talk." Matt

walked with Tom out of the station. "The nurse said he was groggy but lucid."

"Perfect. Let's hope we'll make some progress in the case. I'll drive." Tom got into his car, and Matt slid in the passenger's side. "We have press following us."

"The hospital is out of bounds for reporters except in the main waiting room. I know they're doing their job, but sometimes they get on my nerves. I'm wound tight when I wait for a break in a case, and it worries me that I might deck one of them. Jessie calls me a tyrant, and she's close to the truth."

"Only sometimes? Hell, they get on my nerves all the time." Tom chuckled. "None of us are good at the waiting game. I have my superiors breathing down my neck for results. I know Kaufman is up to his eyeballs in questions from the head of the FBI. When you're talking about a diplomat's son, people want answers yesterday. The problem is the breaks come when they come. Everyone knows it, but the heat comes from the highest in command because that's what they do."

Matt and Tom stopped to talk to the officer standing guard at the door before they walked into Carlos's hospital room. There had been no trouble so far. Always good news to hear.

"Mrs. Huerta, I'm Chief Parker, and this is FBI Agent Tom Maxwell."

"The nurse told me about you both." Her smile lit her coffee brown eyes as she stood to greet them. "It's nice to meet the men who saved my son's life. He's doing much better, and the doctor said he's out of the woods." She grabbed Matt's hand and held it tightly in her tiny one. "Please, sit." She motioned toward the chairs.

"It's good to hear Carlos is doing better, Mrs. Huerta." Matt sat in a chair by his bed.

"Please call me Bernice." She kissed her son's cheek. "You're safe, *mijo*. You must talk to these good men. They are the ones who saved your life." Carlos opened his eyes, and his mother raised the head of the bed. "I will leave you to talk. I know he's in good hands, and my heart can't bear to hear of his suffering yet."

"Thank you, ma'am." Tom sat in the chair she'd vacated.

"Bernice," she said over her shoulder as she left the room.

"Carlos, do you need anything?" Matt heard his soft no. "We would appreciate whatever help you can give us in catching the people who did this to you. You can start when you're ready."

Carlos reached for his glass of water, which was too far away. Matt handed it to him, and he took a drink. "There were five of them. Four who tortured us and killed my friends. We saw their faces daily. I keep thinking that one of the men seemed familiar to me, but I can't place where I saw him before. One of the men never showed his face. We feared his voice, though." Tears spilled from Carlos's eyes. "You could hear him in the background saying 'turn up the current.' My body would tense knowing what would happen next. The most excruciating pain I've ever experienced. If you weren't the one on the receiving end, you got to hear the awful screams of the others." Carlos wept. "It was the hardest for me to hear Shara's cries. It made me think of my sister and my mother. I thought I would never see them again."

"Do you remember the day you were abducted?" Tom handed him a tissue.

"We were on our way to the coffee shop for a meeting. Amir wanted us to read the letter he had received a few days before." Carlos sniffed. "The day was a warm one and we decided to sit in the park after we got our coffee. We had just crossed the street in front of the park when a van pulled up beside us. Several men jumped out with guns and ordered us into the van. They tied our hands behind our backs and put bags over our heads."

"Did you hear anything while you were in the van?" Matt pulled out his small tape recorder and placed it on the stand beside the bed. "Is it okay with you if I record your testimony?"

Carlos nodded. "They spoke a different language. I didn't understand their words nor did the others. I speak Spanish, and it wasn't what I know." He paused, wiping the sweat forming on his brows. When he shifted to his side he grimaced in pain. "We were on the road for a while. When the van finally stopped, they led us inside and removed the bags from our heads. None of us had any idea where we were or why we were there. The men yelled at each other constantly, and I was afraid they would turn that anger on us. The first day and night they left us alone. I was relieved, but I knew it probably wouldn't last long. We could talk to each other, and we tried to figure out why this was happening. Amir was quiet at first." Carlos sobbed.

"Take your time, son. We know this has to be hard for you." Matt patted his shoulder.

"Amir told us he had received a letter. Our names were all in it and the names of our families. The next day a man called him threatening to kill his father and each of us if he didn't do exactly what the man told him. When Amir questioned the caller about what he wanted him to do, the man said he would know soon enough. Amir believed it was probably pushing drugs, but he didn't know."

Matt remembered the conversation Darsha had overheard. "Did he share why he thought it might be to push drugs?"

"No, Amir said he was only speculating. He wasn't sure if they were even the same people. One thing Amir did say was the note had made it clear they were angry that the five of us were friends. It was an insult to their religion." Carlos closed his eyes. "We couldn't talk anymore. The next morning, they came for Amir. They taped the rest of our mouths. Then the nightmare began." His body shuddered. "Amir's screams still haunt my dreams. They never brought Amir back. Ryan was next and then Shara. The men left me alone for two days with the screams ringing in my ears. I hoped they would forget me, but I was to have my turn." Carlos took a sip of his water. "What I saw in the room where they took me, I'll never forget. My friends were tied to chairs, and their bodies had burn marks all over them. The man's voice ordered them to open their eyes and watch what would happen to me. After they had begun to torture me, the man told Amir he knew how to stop it. Before he answered, I passed out. When I awakened next, I was here."

"Can you remember what any of your abductors looked like?" Tom asked.

"I will never forget them!" Carlos wiped his eyes. "I see their faces every time I close my eyes." He shuddered.

"I'll send for a sketch artist and let you work together." Matt turned off his recorder and stuck it in his shirt pocket.

"It's time for his medication," the nurse said as she walked in the room.

"Jared will be here to see you later today or sometime tomorrow. We need to get their faces before the public." Matt patted his hand. "You rest. I'm going to double the guards outside the door. I don't want you to worry."

"Thank you," he murmured. "If I remember anything else, I will let you know. Things are still jumbled in my mind."

"You've helped a lot." Matt walked toward the door.

"Here you go, young man. The doctor wants you to sleep until dinner." The nurse attended to Carlos as they left the room.

"Damn, those kids went through hell." Tom's hand fisted at his side.

"I wonder what Amir was asked to do? It had to be something easy for him to have access to." Matt pushed the down button on the elevator. "If they find out Carlos is alive, he's a sitting target. Carlos can ID them." Matt called the station and doubled the security on the hospital floor. He added a third officer across from the elevator and another by the stairway.

"Smart call. Once they see their ugly mugs on the front pages of the newspapers and on every TV news channel, they'll know Carlos lived." As Tom got off the elevator, a waiting reporter started shouting questions at him.

"What's going on? You owe us." He stuck the mic in front of Tom's face.

"No news here. We were visiting a sick friend. Aren't you missing a scheduled police update? If you hurry, you'll make it on time."

"Quick thinking." Matt watched the two reporters scurry to their cars.

"I feel sick for those kids. And how do you tell their parents about the hell those kids went through?" Tom kicked at the dirt as he walked outside.

"We can't keep it from them. It will come out at trial if nothing else. The best we can do is to tell the parents the story of their children's bravery."

"It won't be easy. It would devastate me. Times like this make me hate my job, but when we nab these perps, I'll love it all over again." Tom unlocked the car.

"Love, hate, lose some and win a few, it comes with the territory." Matt fastened his seat belt. "We are closer now to solving this case than we were a few hours ago." Matt placed the bag the hospital had given him on the floor. "With some help from this scent item from Carlos, I hope Radar can find this gang—if they're anywhere in the area."

"Carlos's life is in danger if they're still in the area, and yours is, too." Tom started his car and glanced over at Matt. "My job just got a lot harder."

Matt's chin lifted. "I'll be damned if I let this guy keep me from doing my job out of fear." Matt pulled out of the parking space.

"What's that?" Tom pointed to his chin. "I know a girl whose chin does the very same thing when she goes off on one of her stubborn streaks. She's rubbing off on you, man." Tom chuckled.

Matt smiled. "You're right. Her chin does lift when I've struck a chord she doesn't like."

"Lift, hell, it becomes like a block of granite, and you looked the same way a moment ago. Would you please make it easy for me? I'll take anything you give me."

"I'll try." Matt turned to look out the window. If he were honest, he was troubled and afraid. Yes, fear might be a good word to use. The men who had tortured the students were brutal, and he didn't relish a run-in with them.

Chapter 23

Jessie was happy her store had several customers in it when a strange man walked through the door. He was tall, with dark, unruly, curly hair and a dark beard, which was normal enough, but his eyes sent shivers down her back as if tiny spiders were racing up and down her spine. Grams used to tell her she'd always know the person's soul by their eyes, and his made him appear evil. Jessie turned her head away but kept a watchful eye on his actions. He pulled a book from the shelf, turning it over in his hand. The man moved from one shelf to another and then made his way to the coffee shop. Jessie hoped he would leave. He didn't. He bought a coffee and sat in a chair where he could see her store. With a storage bag in hand, she moved out of the line of his menacing glare to the front of the store where he had first grabbed the book. He had shoved it back on the shelf the wrong way. With a tissue, she pulled it from the shelf and placed it in a bag, then tucked the bag under the counter and out of his sight.

Her instinct told her this was no ordinary man. He was involved in something sinister, and if she were careful, they might be able to pull a fingerprint off the book. Next, she called Molly.

"Hey, Jessie, what do you need?"

"Do you see the guy with dark hair sitting at the table against the wall?"

Molly took a quick glance. "Yes, why?"

"When he leaves, save his coffee cup and bring it to me. Use a plastic glove or a bag to handle it. Don't let anyone wash it or handle it if you can."

"Sure, what's this all about?"

"I might be presumptuous, but there is something off about the man. His eyes are disturbing, and I'm wondering if he is involved in Matt's murder case. They might be able to gather DNA or a fingerprint from the cup that could ID the man." Jessie smiled at the customer who had just placed her purchase on the counter.

"Intriguing, I'll take care of it. It's strange—I thought the same thing about his eyes."

"I have to go; I have a customer waiting. Talk to you later, Molly."

"Did you find everything you were looking for?" Jessie asked the woman.

"Yes, I did. You have a lovely store." The woman signed the receipt that Jessie handed her.

"Thank you, I love it. It has been my dream since I was a kid to own a bookstore. Although, I think I told my mother I wanted to own the library so I could read any time I wanted." Jessie put the woman's books in a bag and handed it to her. Out of the corner of her eye, she saw the man stand, slamming his chair against the wall. Jessie walked the woman to the door to make sure he had left the coffee shop. He had crossed the street and was walking down Main Street.

Matt needed to know. Jessie called him and left a voice message. "Thank you," she said as Molly handed her his bagged cup. There was still a trace amount of coffee in it.

"Did you see how the chair hit the wall? I'll have to touch it up." Molly shook her head. "You wonder about some people."

"I know. I'm glad he left. I didn't want him to come back into my store. He scared me." Jessie put the mug on the shelf next to the book he'd handled.

"The ghost lady, afraid? I never thought I hear you say that." Molly clasped her hands behind her back.

"Well, I was." Jessie saw Tom's car pull up in front of the store. "Thank heavens they're here." Jessie waved at Molly as she turned to leave.

"I need to get back to work. Matt will sort it out."

The bell rang above the door when the two men walked in. "I saw you called." Matt moved to where she stood.

"A man came in the store earlier, and there was something off about him." She explained about his eyes and what she had felt as he had moved around the store and coffee shop. "I think he's involved in those murders. I can't tell you why I think it, but his eyes were evil. They were emotionless and dead. Anyway, he touched a book and drank a cup of coffee." She handed him the bag with the book in it and the baggie. "I hope this will help you ID this guy. I know he's involved somehow."

"Way to think on your feet, Jessie." Tom smiled at her. "I'll get these to the lab. Maybe they'll give us another name, and we'll be able to identify the gang he belongs to."

"Jess, you're something." Matt grabbed her hand. "We were at the hospital visiting Carlos. He's awake and improving."

"Oh, that is good news. Was he able to tell you

anything?"

"He told us a lot." Tom frowned. "I don't know how he survived what they did to him."

"If the man who was here earlier is involved, I could see him torturing another person with no remorse at all." Jessie pointed to the items she had given him. "I hope it signals a break in the case."

"Me too, sweetheart. I want to put them away. Did you see where the man went when he left Java Joe's?" Matt turned to Tom. "Why don't you order yourself a sandwich, and I'll be right in."

"I will go when you do," Tom shot back. "You know, the whole watching your back thing."

"The guy crossed the street and headed south on Main Street." Jessie gave him a playful shove. "I'll hold these for you until you go get your lunch." She placed the bag behind the counter again.

She was helping a customer when Tom and Matt brought their lunch over and sat at the table in the middle of the store. She stopped by Matt's chair when she was finished ringing up her customer.

"I think you like your sandwich, Tom. You can stop to breathe." Jessie chuckled.

"I was hungry, and this was good." Tom took a swig of his iced tea.

Jessie sat beside Matt. "Is there someone who can talk to Carlos? He'll need help for a while to get over this."

"I've already requested a victim's advocate to talk to him and his parents. I imagine he'll need therapy for a long while." He frowned as he held her hand. "What those kids went through is unspeakable."

"Come on, lover boy, we need to get back to the

station. I have several calls to return." Tom gathered his trash and shoved it in the wastebasket.

Matt kissed her on the cheek. "If you see the man around here again, or Harry Roth, call right away. If you're alone in the store when he comes in, go over to Joe's. Don't stay alone in the store with him."

"I won't." She lifted her head, and he kissed her forehead.

"Promise me," Matt called over his shoulder to her.

"I promise. Wait a minute. You almost forgot to take these." Jessie went to the counter to get the bags.

"Thanks, sweetheart." He waved as they left. She watched until they drove away.

Jessie hoped she'd never have to see the man again. Roth was bad enough, but the guy who had been in her store earlier made her fear for Matt's life. How could he deal with a ruthless murderer who had no feelings? "Keep him safe," she whispered.

Jessie kept busy the rest of the day. The man never came back, and she'd be happy not to ever see him again. She wrapped her sweater around her, shoving her hands in the pockets. What caused a man to become a cold-blooded murderer without feelings or remorse? All the criminals she had dealt with over the past year had been different. From the white-collar crime of the organ harvest club and a senator making money off human trafficking to the bank president involved in illegal weapons trade, what made them do what they did? What turned a drama student into a serial killer, or a religious group leader into a mass murderer? Jessie wasn't sure if she would ever understand.

Hate was a powerful emotion. She straightened the books on the table. Greed and the promise of wealth were strong enticements. Ultimately, it was about power and control. Jessie frowned. The world seemed ripe for it at the moment, and Jessie saw no way to stop it. All she could do was her own small part to make the world a better place. She closed the store and headed for home.

Chapter 24

Matt was happy to be home. He had spent most of the day on the phone. Roth had been the subject of several conversations. Agent Dickerson had come to Blue Cove to help and stay in touch with Interpol. Harry had been one busy fella and was wanted in several nations. The more Matt learned about Roth, the better he understood why he found himself connected to what was happening. The kids' bodies showing up in his jurisdiction wasn't an accident. There were still a lot of unanswered questions, but clues were coming together. He placed his case files on the counter.

"I made dinner," Frank told Matt. "I thought both of you could use a night off."

"Thanks, Frank. I thought it smelled good in here." Matt went to the sink to wash his hands.

"I made my famous lasagna. I have a few good meals I can cook, and this is one of my best. Add a little salad and garlic bread… I think you can see where I'm going."

"Count me in." Tom went down the hall to put his briefcase in the room.

"I bought a bottle of wine that I serve with it when I make this meal at home. Do you have any wine glasses?"

"I sure do." Matt placed the wine glasses on the table.

Frank placed everything on the counter, and they served themselves. "How did your day go?" Frank asked after they sat at the table.

"We learned a lot, almost too much. We talked to Carlos, who is improving each day. I have to say it messed with my head. Those kids suffered." Tom took a bite of the lasagna. "Frank, this is great."

"Frank, the hospital gave me the clothes Carlos was wearing when he was brought in. In the next couple of days, I want to see if Radar can track anything. The gang might still be in the area." Matt took a sip of his wine then told Frank about the man who had come into Jessie's store. "She had the presence of mind to preserve his fingerprint on the cover of a book and possible DNA evidence in a cup he drank from."

"If they're around, Radar will find them." Frank smiled. "I'm not surprised Jessie would get the man's fingerprints. She's good. I'm prejudiced though because I saw her in action as an investigative reporter. She always did a top notch job." Frank took a bite of his garlic bread.

"She is good; the more I talk to her, the more impressed I am. I think she'd make a great agent. She could live in the city and get away from this small town. Her talent is being wasted here." Tom glanced at Matt's face and grinned. "My good buddy over there would never let it happen. He knows a good thing when he sees it." Tom went into the kitchen. "I could use some more of your lasagna."

"Thanks for a great meal." Matt carried his dish into the kitchen, rinsed it, and put it in the dishwasher.

"I have dessert. Do you want it now or later" Frank

had followed Matt in. He covered the salad and put it in the fridge.

"I'll take mine later, Frank, I'm stuffed." Matt carried his files and wine into the living room. He sat on the sofa and, slipping his glasses from his pocket, he began to read. He wanted to find a link between his cases and those kids. Kaufman was learning more each day about the students. Somewhere in one of these files there had to be answers. He pulled out the first file and started to read.

Tom followed, plopping down in the overstuffed chair. "Do you mind?" Tom waved the remote in the air. "You know, man, all work and no play will make Matt a dull boy. I'm just saying ease up. It will come to you when you least expect it."

"Go ahead. I know you're right, but it's my life these guys are after, and I want to know everything I can about how their minds work. The idea is to study your enemy so you can't be taken by surprise."

"You tell me when you want Radar to track. We'll be ready when you call." Frank sat back in the recliner. He sighed blissfully. "Coming to town to help is worth it for the chance to sit in this chair alone. I've done a lot of napping since I've arrived here. I'm out in a few minutes every time I sit here."

"It's a good one." Matt nodded. He'd taken many pleasant naps reclining in his favorite chair.

"I might have to buy me one when I go home. It's the best I've ever sat in." Frank settled back in the chair and put his feet up. "The problem is if I had one, I'd never get any work done. My wife might want to chuck the thing out the door."

****

Marshall didn't know why the boss wanted him to follow the cop to his home. He followed instructions, and here he sat. They were probably eating a hot meal in there, and he was in the car again with another dry peanut butter sandwich and a thermos of coffee.

The cop wasn't alone; he never was. The tall man followed him everywhere. Both of them were taller than he was. Marshall had always been on the short side. His dad called him Bruiser because he was short, stout, and strong. He could wrestle anyone to the ground when he was younger. Of course, those days were long gone, but he didn't mind. He was getting close to retiring somewhere warm soon. He took out one of his many brochures from the glove compartment. The blue water and white sand called to him. Marshall had dreamed of this for the past five years. It kept him sane as he went to work every day with the same people, hearing the same gossip over and over until he thought his mind would explode from the tedium.

Being a beach bum appealed to him. He liked the idea of seeing the scantily clad women sunning themselves. They'd never give him the time of day, but what the hell did he care? He could enjoy the sights. He wasn't dead yet. Anything had to be better than walking in the cold wind, sliding on icy streets in the winter, and dealing with the lowlife of the city. He was done with it. He'd put in his time for over thirty-five years driving the same neighborhood beat with a lousy chief out to get him, and enough was enough. He was happy to have had all the saved vacation days to do this side job. He'd made more here in a few days than in a whole year working for the PD. He should have started doing side jobs years ago.

Marshall followed the cop, did what he was told, and kept his mouth shut. He still wondered why, though. Marshall wasn't privy to any other information than what the man on the phone had told him. The cop seemed like a nice enough guy. His girl was a pretty one. He'd shove this job right now, but what they were paying him would put him on easy street. Marshall couldn't let himself think about it. He kept his mouth shut, snapped a few photos, and collected a check. Any day now, he'd be on the flight to this little island paradise. The brochure in his hand waved in the air. With any luck, he'd never know what they did to the cop. It was best to keep it that way.

Chapter 25

Jessie typed at her computer. She paused, tapping her fingers on the desk. She found a certain comfort every time she worked on an article. Placing words on paper and working with them until a sentence sounded right was a cheap form of therapy. Tonight, though, her mind was on the students. Each of their faces as she had first seen them was vivid in her mind. She wanted to take her experiences of the past few weeks and make sense of them on paper—and without talking about ghosts or spirits, which would leave her readers thinking she had lost her mind. She sighed. How could she explain the emotion of watching Amir's body coming ashore or of Ryan's memorial service? She had found hope in all the young people gathered to honor him in the way that made sense to them. It had been an eye-opening moment for her—a love fest of sorts as love and life often took many forms.

Life didn't come neatly packaged in the way people thought that it should. Riddled with unwanted change, life had a way of messing with the best laid plans. Change was the one constant in life as Grams had always said. Life took a tragic turn for the students. Somehow, Jessie had to find a way to tell the story of Amir's, Shara's, and Ryan's lives through the window of their deaths. The more she thought about Ryan's service, the more her own life came into view. She had connected with him. Maybe she was a mystic like Sadie, aware of the many facets of life that went unnoticed by others. From now on, Jessie would no longer feel like a victim of circumstances. This was her purpose for this time in her life. It was a part of her person, and she wouldn't make excuses for it anymore.

The phone rang. "Hi, Matt." Jessie had given him his own special ringtone.

"What you doing?" He drew out the word *doing* in a sing-song kind of way.

"I'm writing about the students. It's cathartic for me."

"My English teacher in school would have loved you. You would have been her ideal student. Writing makes me need therapy." He chuckled. "I could write a whole page without ever putting in one comma or period. Then I would go back and throw them in randomly here and there. She found it a great challenge to make a writer out me. I think it devastated her when she got nowhere. She quit teaching the next year."

Jessie laughed. "You're exaggerating, I'm sure."

"Honest, it's the absolute truth. Her name is Mrs. Draper, and she still lives in town. All you have to do is say my name, and she shakes her head. Of course, I did make it through college, and I had to write quite a few papers, which I managed with the help of spell check and a grammar program. Thank heavens for computers."

"Computers are nice, easier than the typewriter. I'm still not sure whether to believe you or not." Jessie laughed.

"Believe me, sweetheart, I'll take you to meet her. Wait a minute." Matt tried to muffle the sound. "Pipe down." She could hear Tom laughing in the background. "I'm back. Tom's a royal pain."

"Did you have a reason for calling?" Jessie looked at her e-mails while she talked.

"Do I need a reason to talk to my girl?"

"No, but you usually have one."

"You're right, and I have one now, too."

She smiled. "I figured you might."

"As soon as we get some info on the prints and DNA, I want Frank and Radar to try doing another track to see if the guy is still in the area. I thought you'd like to go along for the ride. I wanted to give you the heads up in case you need to make arrangements at the store.

"You bet I do. I'll get someone to stand in for me, or I'll close the store for a few hours." Jessie stood in her excitement.

"I don't know if I told you or not, but I got a threatening note today. I guess I'm happy to have Tom around after all."

"No, you didn't tell me. I'm glad he's there, too." Jessie sighed. "How could you forget to mention such an important detail?"

"I'm in denial, as Tom likes to say. Carlos gave us a lot of information today, you gave us more, and my tail followed me home. He really isn't good at it. Tom wants to go out and have a chat with him. I think we should wait a few more days. Your idea of him being a decoy makes sense to me. He's too sloppy to be the real deal."

"Whatever you do, be careful. I kind of like having you around. You're easy on the eyes."

"I could say the same thing about you." She heard

him take a deep breath. "Frank made us dinner tonight. He made a great meal. I'm impressed."

"Speaking of Frank, what's he doing?" Jessie grinned at Matt's attempt at small talk. She was fascinated.

"Right this minute?" He mumbled something, which she couldn't hear.

"Yeah, right now."

"He's sleeping in my favorite chair with Radar sleeping at his feet. I may never get to sit in that chair again while he's here."

"I thought he might be sleeping. He must like your chair." She laughed.

"He does. It seems to put him to sleep every time he sits in it. I'll see you tomorrow."

Jessie smiled. Frank had been sleeping in the chair the other evening when she was at Matt's house for dinner. He must need it.

Jessie decided she wanted to meet Carlos and his mother. She would go after work tomorrow. Carlos might be able to give her a bigger picture of his friends. Jessie wanted to do justice to their story. She needed another point of view to go with Darsha's observations. Her fingers flew over the keyboard, typing her beginning ideas.

A phone call from Katie interrupted her. "I'm glad you're still awake. Dylan and I argued, and I'm depressed." Katie sniffed and blew her nose.

"What happened?" Jessie could imagine Katie's facial expression. She was pouting.

"I'm still not sure. We were talking wedding plans, and Dylan blew up at me." There was a long pause. "Okay, I might have said something to upset him. The next thing I knew, he was heading out the door with only a small peck on my cheek."

"Knowing you, my dear friend, you have left out a lot of details. None of which is my business anyway. Did you try apologizing?"

"Why should I?" Katie sniffed again. "He was totally unfair about it all."

"Well, I might be wrong, but if you said something which upset him, you should talk about it with him, don't you think? After he tells you why it bothered him, you might want to apologize."

"I don't see how you can take his side. I'm your friend, after all."

"Yes, and it's because I'm your friend I won't let you ruin the best thing that's ever happened to you. I've seen how happy Dylan makes you. Call him and tell him you're sorry; you didn't mean to upset him."

"Okay. Never mind, he's back. Maybe he'll apologize to me."

"Katie Donovan!" Jessie tried to sound like Katie's mother.

"I know, I know, I'll take care of it. Wish me luck."

Forget writing; it wasn't going to happen now. Jessie went to the kitchen for a glass of water, shut off her computer, and grabbed the book she had been reading. A few minutes later, propped up against the headboard and her pillows, she began reading where she had left off last night. It didn't take long for her mind to drift to other thoughts. She closed her eyes and leaned her head back. Jessie didn't want those guys anywhere near Matt.

Chapter 26

Jessie walked into the hospital room after checking with the two officers outside the door of Carlos's room. A tiny woman, her dark hair streaked with gray, came to greet her.

"My name is Jessie Reynolds. I brought you a treat." She handed her a box with assorted pastries from the coffee shop.

"Thank you. Everyone has been kind to us here. I am Carlos's mama, Bernice Huerta. He still is sleeping a lot, but he is much better than the first day I saw him. Sleep is healing as they say." She wiped the tears from her eyes. "I wasn't sure my son would make it. Today is a better day."

"I'm happy to hear the good news. I work with Chief Parker, and my friend's dog is the one who found Carlos. I would like to do a story about him and the life of his friends, but I don't want to bother him while he's resting. I should leave."

"Please don't hurry off; it gets a little lonely sitting here all day watching him sleep." Bernice looked wistfully at her son.

"Would you like to go walk around? I can sit here and watch him for you."

"You wouldn't mind?" Bernice stood and stretched her hands over her head. "I could use a walk. I've been sitting too much the past few days."

"Of course not, I'd be happy to stay and let you take a break. It's a beautiful day. Go out in the sunshine for a while." Jessie smiled at Bernice as she walked out the door.

Jessie sat in the chair next to Carlos's bed. The only movement was the steady rise and fall of his chest. The blood pressure and pulse on the monitor above his bed stayed constant with only an occasional dip. His random snores and the ticking of clock sounded loud in the otherwise silent room. A hospital worker delivered his lunch, but he slept on until the nurse came in and roused him. She grabbed his arm to put a blood pressure cuff on him, and his eyes opened wide. Jessie stepped out of the room while the nurse checked his wounds.

"You can go back in now, hon, the police are sending over a sketch artist, so we need to keep him awake for a while. Keep talking to him."

"I'll give it my best shot." Jessie walked back into his room.

She introduced herself to Carlos and explained why she was there. "The nurse told me a sketch artist is coming to work with you today. I'll talk to you about your friends another day if you wish." She pushed his lunch tray closer so he could reach his food and raised his bed so he could sit up. "I also brought you and your mom a few sweet treats if you can have them."

"I want to talk about my friends." He gave her a weak smile. "I'm glad you're going to write about them. They accepted me as I am. Not many people do. You can come back anytime." Carlos pushed the button to raise his head a bit more, as his mom walked into the room followed by Jared. His mom rushed to help him position his pillow behind his head.

"I'll be back to see you another day. You'll need all your strength to give Jared the best descriptions of your abductors. He'll work you hard." Jessie gave his hand a squeeze. "I'm happy you're feeling better. I wasn't there the day they found you, but I've heard how bad you were. My goodness, you've come a long way."

"My mama says the same thing."

"Bernice, it was nice to meet you. I hope you enjoy the treats from Java Joe's Coffee Shop. Molly makes some of the best food around."

"I'm sure I will, and so will Carlos," Bernice said.

"Carlos, work hard with Jared. We want to get the men who did this to you and your friends." Jessie moved so Jared could set up his sketchbook.

"I will. It was nice to meet you." He smiled, and she waved at him as she left the room.

Jessie walked out into the sunshine. It was good to see Carlos so much better than when they had found him. Matt hadn't been sure he would make it. Jessie drove back to the store. She had a good feeling about the young man. He would do something purposeful with his life when this was all over.

****

Matt and Tom looked at the sketches that Jared brought to the station. Kip went through the mug shots at the station, agents poured through the ones at the Bureau, and Agent Dickerson sent copies to Interpol. This was the biggest break they'd had yet. The tension was building in the department. They were one step closer to solving the case. The fingerprint on the book was a match for the one on Shara's body. Tom was running the prints through the computer now.

"I want to take these by Jessie's and have her check them out. I want to know if one of these sketches is the man who showed up in her store." Matt grabbed the keys to his cruiser.

"You're not going anywhere without me." Tom put a hand on his shoulder.

"Then get with it, man, we've got things to do." Matt walked out of his office with Tom hot on his heels.

They pulled up in front of Jessie's store a few minutes later. Matt carried the sketches into the store and over to the table. "Hey, sweetheart, do you have a minute to look at something for me."

"Yeah." Jessie walked over to where he stood.

"You look good enough to eat," he whispered in her ear. "What have you've been up to today?" He pulled out Jared's handiwork and laid them on the table.

"I went to see Carlos and met his mother." She looked at the sketches. "This is the man who came into the store. I'll never forget those eyes." She shivered. "Jared captured them perfectly."

"Are you sure?" He studied her face as she nodded.

"I'm positive." She glanced at each one again. "I don't see Harry in this group."

"I don't believe the kids ever saw him, although they might have heard him. These men are the ones who tortured them. Carlos was adamant that he could remember each one."

"He did a good job of describing this guy. The eyes are perfect—cold and dead." Jessie shuddered as she studied the sketch again. "He's capable of great evil, I think. What's next?" She rubbed her arms and walked over to Matt's side.

"We find them before they can do any more damage." Tom picked up one of the sketches. "These are some mean-looking dudes."

"I want some names and background checks. It helps to know what we're up against." Matt studied the sketches.

"We should have those soon." Tom walked into the coffee shop. "I'll be back. I need coffee."

Matt grabbed Jessie's hand as she twisted a lock of hair around her finger. "One day you're going to twist your hair into a knot you can't get out."

"It's a nervous habit." She slapped his hand away.

"I've noticed. There's nothing to be nervous about at the moment."

"The thought of him being in my store makes me panicky." She glanced at Matt. "He was here handling my books and watching my store. Just thinking about it makes me uncomfortable."

"Well, he's not here now, so you can relax." He massaged her shoulders. "Damn, Jess, your shoulders are tight."

"It's this town. Oops, I almost forgot." She slapped her hand across her mouth.

"Forgot what?" Matt gave her an odd look.

"I'm not going to blame what's happened in my life since moving here on anything. I've come to accept it as part of who I am. No, more blame games for me." She shrugged.

"That's extremely gracious and mature of you." Matt grabbed her hand again, smirking.

"Not really, I'm finally accepting that I might be the reason for all these happenings, and it has nothing to do with the town." She squeezed his hand in hers.

"Sadie has always been a bit of a mystic when it comes to life, and she might have rubbed off on me. Whether it's true or not, I want to stop complaining and accept the fact, peculiar is who I am for now. The future could change it all again."

"I'll like you either way." He kissed her knuckles. "You're perfect as far as I'm concerned."

"I hope you don't live to regret it." She turned to face him. "How are we going to get these guys? We can't leave anything to chance. We need a foolproof plan. Having seen their handiwork up close and personal, I don't want them anywhere near you."

"I'd prefer it that way, myself, but nothing is fail-safe. I've been thinking about Reba's words and your dream. I doubt I need to worry, but I'll be smart about it too. You see, Tom over there doesn't leave my side, and right this minute, I can guarantee you he's watching all the action including the people ready to come into your store." Matt pointed to where Tom was sitting.

"I know Tom is good at what he does. But as you've told me in every case we've been involved in, you can plan for everything, and there's still a risk that something could go wrong. It happens, but I don't want it to happen to you."

"Jess, you're worrying before it's necessary. No wonder your muscles are all in knots. I'll be okay. You need to stop fretting about me." His head turned when the bell above the door rang. "You should get back to work." He put the sketches into the case file folder.

"Wait a minute." She went to check on the customer and then came back. "Did you or did you not worry about me in all the cases where I was the target?"

"Yes, I did. I get the message." He grinned at her.

"I'm glad you can see where I'm coming from. I've learned from the best. I might even come up with a lecture or two for you while I'm at it." She made a face at him and laughed. "I could be wrong, but love and concern go hand in hand." She waved at him when he went to join Tom.

Chapter 27

Dylan met Matt by his office door. "I'm glad you're back. I was getting ready to text you. We have identities on each of the four perps. I thought you'd want to know." He handed Matt the files.

"What have you learned so far?" Matt sat in his chair and opened the first file.

"Each of the men comes from a different ethnic background and country. This man"—Dylan handed Matt the sketch—"is an American citizen. He grew up in Trenton, New Jersey. The FBI is interviewing his family and friends as we speak. They confiscated his computer, and they're monitoring his social media sites. The other men first showed up on the agency's radar in crimes involving Americans traveling south of the border." Dylan leaned back in the chair waiting for Matt to react to the sketch in front of him.

Matt studied the drawing, a frown spreading across his face. "The one element all of them have in common is a connection to Harry Roth and a strong anti-American sentiment, except for him." Matt held up the sketch Dylan had shown him. "How did a kid raised in New Jersey with no ties overseas get involved in a group of terrorists?"

"Someone recruited him." Dylan said.

Matt nodded at Tom when he sat in the chair next to Dylan. "What is this group doing in the States?"

"I was asking myself the same question. It's possible their operation in Mexico was only a training mission for a bigger undertaking." Tom drummed his fingers on the chair. "It's possible they have a larger objective in mind."

"Now there's a scary thought, but Jessie mentioned the idea the other night." Matt frowned.

"What does any of this have to do with those kids?" Dylan asked.

"Beats me. I think we'd better take a closer look at their parents while we're at it." Matt glanced at the open file again. "Could this group be a small part of a larger group?"

"I sure as hell hope not," Tom growled. "If there's a bigger picture, let the agency work on it. I want to concentrate on these five. Have either of you seen Kaufman around?"

"I saw him right before you two got back. He was headed for the door." Dylan stood.

"I can't understand why he's not meeting with us on a regular basis. Dickerson meets with me every morning." Matt scowled. "If you see Kaufman again, tell him I want to see him."

"I will." Dylan walked out of Matt's office.

"Kaufman is an all right guy, but he's on the fast track, climbing the ladder. I can't abide it when agents withhold information. We all get different details and work from a different premise, and then we collaborate. We all work together—no Lone Rangers. He's given me no updates for a few days. Have you gotten any?" Tom's hand drummed on the chair.

"No, and I've had words with him over it. It started with him calling you to watch my back, and he never told me he was doing it or gave me a reason for it." Matt scrolled through the texts on his phone. "I've not had one text or update for several days now."

"I'll find him and have a few words with him." Tom pointed at Matt. "Don't you go anywhere outside this building without me."

"I'll be here." Matt glowered after him. "You're not my damn wife," he muttered under his breath.

"I heard you, Parker. We'll get a divorce as soon as we catch our perps." Tom chuckled on his way out the door.

He read more of the files. This was a dangerous group of men. Matt didn't like the idea of two of them having been in Jessie's store. She was right; concern and love seemed to go hand in hand. He turned his chair to look at the window. Right now, all they had was a gang of four killers, Roth, and his inept tail. When and how did the American come into the group? Timing was important. Was it possible he knew the movements of the students? Misty talked about the hate groups at the school. Were any or all of them somehow connected? Matt hated chasing rabbit trails; he needed something concrete to go on. They were getting closer though. He could feel it in his gut.

Matt arranged to get Jessie after work. Frank and Tom would have to come along. He needed to run all this by her and get her perspective.

****

When the last customer checked out, Jessie locked the front door behind him. Closing the store was routine. The rag in her hand swished across the tabletops. Chairs were rearranged, the book table straightened, and money taken from the register. Doing the work now meant less work in the morning. With the money bag in the safe, she closed the heavy door, spinning the dial. Walking past the switch, her hand reached out and flipped off the lights at the front of the store. *Dream* or no dream, *I won't stand idly by and let anything happen to Matt.* The blast of chilly night air hit her face; the shiver followed close on its heels. "Come on heat. Work your magic." She started the car, turning the heat on full blast.

Dylan's car was at the Inn. Sweet, they must have made up. She pulled into the parking space, shifted into park, and shoved her hand into her purse to reach her phone as it rang.

"Jessie, it's me, Sally."

"How are you?" Jessie was happy to hear her voice.

"I'm great, especially since my divorce is final. The jury found Bruce guilty of assault today. He'll receive his sentence next week, and then I'll be free to come to Blue Cove."

"Oh, Sally, that's good news." Jessie could hear the excitement in her voice.

"I think it might only be for a visit. A new job opportunity has come my way since I've been here. I want to talk it over with you girls when I come to see you. I don't know what to think about it. I'm both nervous and excited at the same time."

"Where would you live?" Jessie asked her.

"In Rocky Pointe, which would be close enough to come see you from time to time. I'm not sure I want the job, but I'm excited about life for the first time in a long time, and I'm looking forward to Katie's wedding. Who knew she'd get married before you?"

"I did. Katie has wanted this ever since I can remember. Dylan is a super great guy."

"What about you and Matt? Any date yet?'

"No, we're getting to know each other and working our way toward engagement. We aren't in a hurry. Seeing what happened to you reminded me to take it easy. I do love my hunky cop, though."

"I'll call Katie when we're through talking. I'm looking forward to hanging out and spending some time with you gals."

"Call us with the date, so we'll know when to expect you."

"I will, Jessie. See you soon. Remember you promised to help me get my life back on track." The phone clicked off before Jessie could reply.

Sally sounded excited. Jessie couldn't help wonder what the job opportunity was. Sally could use a break and some good things to come her way.

****

Matt's car pulled in next to hers. She waved, leaned in the open window, and gave him a kiss. "Hi, all." She slipped into the backseat and latched her seat belt. "I see Matt was able to get you out of the recliner tonight, Frank."

"He had to work at it." Frank laughed.

"You seem to like it and feel right at home there." She patted his hand. "You'll be happy to get back in it after your next track."

"I need to do some work and get outside for a while. I've been idle the past few days. I sleep more when I'm bored." He smiled at her. "I could find things to do, I guess, but I'll have enough work to keep me busy when I get home. I'll enjoy the quiet times when I get them."

"Where are you taking us?" She caught Matt looking at her in the rearview mirror.

"Tom has never been to the diner. I thought we should take him to meet Franny." Matt winked at her. He drove down Main Street toward the turn onto the highway.

"You'll love it, Tom. It's a trip back in time and great food." Jessie's eye lit up.

"I agree," Frank said.

"We were ordered out tonight by the chief here. It seems one night away from you is one night too many." Tom turned to glance at Jessie. "I was afraid I'd have a mutiny on my hands if I didn't give in."

"You won't regret it." Jessie listened to Matt's banter with Tom over his last remark.

"I wanted to bring you up to date on the case and hear what you think." Matt explained the new details they had learned about the perps.

"You got all the info after you left my store earlier?" Jessie saw Matt nod. "It seems strange they would come here to murder four college students. The murders must be only the tip of the iceberg. What's going on?"

"I believe we are all in agreement this is a part of something bigger." Matt turned on Old Homestead Road. "We are waiting for some intel from Interpol. I want to know what they were involved in overseas. Mexico seemed to be a training exercise for them. At least that's Tom's take on it, and I agree." Matt parked the car. He unhooked his seat belt and turned to look at her. "Tell me what you think."

"My first instinct is to ask whether they're a small

part of a larger group or operating alone. Having thrown the question out there, I'd say, either way, we have our work cut out for us."

"You've got that right." Tom unlatched his seat belt.

"You should get Jeremy involved with the research on them and see if they have ties to any other organization."

"I sent him the names and mug shots this afternoon."

She smiled at Matt. "Of course you did."

"I hope he'll have something for us soon." Matt opened his door.

"I've read through the intel on Harry Roth, and he's up to his eyeballs in criminal activity around the world, including organ and human trafficking. He also has ties to a few terrorist groups."

"I wonder how he keeps it all straight. Some of the groups he's involved with are at odds with each other. He has to keep one step ahead of them all to stay alive."

Matt stepped out of the car. "Let's eat."

Chapter 28

Jessie shut off the light and laid her head back against the pillows. She could still see the look on Tom's face when Franny had called him son. He'd chuckled all the way back to town. He couldn't get over Franny's fifties hairstyle, heavy blue eyeshadow, and her poodle skirt. Every time she licked her pencil tip and stuck it in her hair, he had smiled. Tom described the evening as a flashback in time to some of the old reruns he had watched on TV as a kid.

The meal was enjoyable and good as always. Of course, the wonderful pie was the way to top off the evening. She'd had a slice of pecan pie with a scoop of vanilla ice cream. The evening had been a small reprieve for a few hours. The sense of impending trouble was never far away. It had lurked beneath the surface of their conversation all night.

Blue Cove was the epicenter for now. Why? Had Matt's cases somehow crossed with Harry's criminal involvement somewhere? Or had they been drawn into it when Amir's body came ashore? Either way, they were in it. If she were a gambling person, she'd say it had to be the first. Matt and Harry were somehow linked.

She had seen each of their ghosts for a reason. It was time to get them involved in helping to solve the case if they were still in the area. She had no idea where to begin to look. Would the angel be nearby? She could only hope.

****

"I enjoyed the evening, Matt. I haven't been called son in years." Tom headed down the hall. "I'm turning in."

Frank followed Tom. "I am, too. I'll just go take Radar out, and we'll be ready for the track when you call."

"Sounds good. See you in the morning." Matt sat in his recliner with his laptop in his hands. He began reading an e-mail from Jeremy. He glanced at his watch. It wasn't too late. Matt called.

"I was reading your e-mail. I wanted to hear what you thought as you read the information on these men."

"They're each dangerous for different reasons. I wrote beside each name what his field of expertise seemed to be and what they did on each of the jobs they had been involved in."

"I can see that. Their skills range from munitions to chemistry. This has the potential to be a disaster. What was the first thought that struck you as you read all of this?" Matt asked him.

"It scared the hell out of me. You can add torture to the list. The first question that came to my mind was why is the group here? It has to be more than the Foreign Students' Club. I want to know how their paths crossed. I'm trying to find a link now."

"We had the same question here," Matt told him.

"Why were the students' bodies in your jurisdiction? I think it might have been engineered that way."

"To suck me in. Bait. We're in agreement, so far."

199

Matt ran his hand through his hair.

"I believe Blue Cove may be a side story to why these men are in the country, though. I think it's a personal vendetta before they finish a larger mission."

"I agree, which is why we have to stop them." Matt clenched his jaw.

"Did you notice the one suspect's expertise in bomb making?" Jeremy asked.

"I noticed. His rap sheet involving those skills is unnerving, to say the least."

"I'll work at finding the link; you take them out before they can do what they came here to do."

"I'm going to give it my best shot, along with all the agents working with us."

"One word of warning, which is free—these men are dangerous. Don't be a hero alone." Jeremy told him.

"I don't plan on it. Thanks, Jeremy, call me anytime. I think you ought to move here and be a part of the team."

"Believe me, I've considered it." He ended the call.

Matt turned the TV on and turned the volume down. He laid his head back and put his feet up.

****

Matt jerked upright as Tom grabbed the remote. Daylight seeped through the blinds and the voice of the morning news anchor rambled on about the weather.

"Did you sleep here all night?" Tom shut off the TV, cutting off the man's cheery voice.

"I guess I must have." Matt rubbed his eyes.

"Why didn't you go to bed? Couldn't you sleep?" Tom walked into the kitchen to put the coffee on.

Matt followed him. "I received an e-mail from Jeremy. He had some information on our perp's activities overseas. I wanted to hear what he thought, so I called."

Tom filled the filter basket with coffee. "Something tells me we need it strong this morning. What was his take?"

"The same as ours." Matt paused. "Jeremy thinks Blue Cove is a payback, and they're here for something bigger."

"Damn, this is one time I don't want to be right. I'm calling my superiors." Tom added the water. "Go take a shower, sleeping beauty; I'll make breakfast. We need to get out to the station early this morning."

Matt walked down the hall to his room. He turned the shower on and stepped under the warm spray. Another fine mess he found himself in again. He poured some shampoo into his hand, rubbing it into his hair. He had better come up with a damn good plan fast. Everyone knew it, even if Tom and the others avoided saying it to him. Roth wanted him taken care of before he finished the mission he was being paid to do.

"Something smells good." Matt joined Frank and Tom in the kitchen.

"I can't do much in the kitchen, but I do make a killer omelet." Tom flipped the omelet in the pan. "Grab a plate. Frank has his, and this one is yours."

Matt handed him a plate. "Looks good."

"Try it with some salsa." Tom stuck a piece of toast on Matt's plate. "Don't forget the coffee; it's nice and strong. It will get you through all the meetings I have set up for today."

Matt poured a cup of coffee and sat at the counter next to Frank. "Did you sleep well?"

"I did." Frank took a bite of the omelet. "Good

eats, Tom."

"I told you I make a great omelet. Do you like it with the hot peppers?"

"I do, but I like most food with a little heat." Frank drank his coffee.

"Me too, everything is better when it's hotter." Tom joined them at the counter. He dumped hot sauce all over his omelet. "I had a chat with my superiors, and let's say things are moving along. You'll be in meetings all morning. I think Kaufman might have been downplaying the significance of the evidence, but I gave them an earful. Believe me, heads are going to roll."

"Does that mean we'll be tripping over more agents?" Matt spread jelly on his toast and took a bite.

"I would imagine. We are going to get some of the top experts in the field. A few of the field agents here now will be leaving. I hope Kaufman will be among the first out of here. He didn't handle this case well, and he didn't work with the locals. That's a no-no with our superiors. We're trying to right our image among the locals, you know." Tom gulped down his food. "We need to get a move on."

"Can I finish this in peace?" Matt drank a sip of his coffee.

"Of course, if you can finish it in the next five minutes." Tom took his plate to the sink. He rinsed it and placed in the dishwasher.

"I'll take care of the kitchen." Frank carried his dish over.

"Thanks, Frank. You'll need to bring Radar by to a meeting at one this afternoon. I've been talking about you with Dickerson and the lead agent assigned to this case. They want to meet you." Tom handed Frank the sponge.

"I'll be there."

"Okay, Matt, put your coffee in a mug and let's get out of here."

"You're getting damn pushy for a guest." Matt stood and carried his plate to the sink. "Thanks, Frank; we'll see you at one." Matt poured his coffee into a travel mug and followed Tom to the garage. Within a few minutes, they were on their way to the station. Matt wasn't a big fan of meetings, but he didn't have much say in the matter. Tom saw how serious the situation was and Matt knew he needed all the help he could get.

"Look who spent the night last night." Matt honked as he passed the car with its sleeping driver.

"At least he knows that we know he's there. Is the guy really that dumb?" Tom chuckled and waved at the bleary face peering at them through the car's windows.

****

"Damnation." Marshall hit the steering wheel. His cover was blown. How could he have been so dumb as to fall asleep on the job? The cop had seen him. Hell, the whole neighborhood had probably seen his car parked there. He was lucky no one had called the cops. Marshall shook his head. The last drink must have put him over his limit. He had passed out again. Double damnation, the cop had seen his car. He was done. What excuse could he give his boss?

Chapter 29

Jessie was heading into the church when she saw the first ghost. Amir was near the gate to the cemetery. She walked toward the graveyard, and that's when she saw Ryan and Shara near the bench by Gina's grave. Amir was watching her. She stopped in front of him. "We're getting closer to solving your murders; please help in any way you can. I thought I should tell you. If you are waiting for Carlos, he's alive. He made it." Jessie heard her name.

"Jessie, what are you doing over there?" Pastor Kevin had a puzzled look on his face.

"I thought I saw something, but it was nothing." She walked toward Kevin. "I was giving myself a pep talk about the things I have to get done today. It helps if I say them out loud to myself." She walked in the door he held open for her.

"I'm the same way. My mom said she used to hear me saying my spelling words in my sleep the night before a big test." He chuckled. "I don't remember doing it though."

"I guess we all have small quirks that help us get by. I'm notorious for planning and writing notes. I stick them everywhere so I won't forget." She unlocked the office door.

"I don't know if Melinda has told you, but we've had some strange things going on here at the church. I almost believe her story about a church ghost." He flipped on the lights behind her. "Ever since the students' bodies showed up in the area, it's been intense around here."

"Melinda did tell me she had heard strange noises in the church. She said that she didn't want to work when no one else was in the building." Jessie started making coffee. "Unsolved murders make everyone a little edgy, don't you think?"

"You're probably right. Still, I've heard things myself and seen a few things I can't explain." Kevin leaned his hip against the counter.

"Like what?" She pushed the brew button on the coffee maker.

"Like strange looking apparitions floating in and around the cemetery." He cleaned his glasses on his shirt as he talked. "I'm a realist, but I felt myself panicking when I saw whatever it was. I ran to my car and didn't look back. Now I'm wondering if I made it all up."

"I understand, but then you already know that I've seen Gina's ghost."

"Yes, and truthfully, I thought you were weird until I got to know you. This is all too strange. What is going on? Can you tell me?"

"You're asking the wrong person. I'm no theologian, but I do see and hear some strange things. I've made peace with it. I've always been sensitive to people and their hurts. I don't know if that has anything to with it or not."

"I want to understand. Explain what you've had happen to you." Kevin sat in the chair in front of her desk.

Jessie told him about some of what had happened with the students. "The connection I felt was strange. I could share the pain and shock they were feeling."

"I guess none of us know all of the answers to the questions of life and death, do we?"

"No, I'm sure we don't. To me, not knowing all the answers is the main reason why we should treat each other with compassion and kindness. Life is hard enough. We shouldn't make it harder on each other."

"You're right. Put a few scriptures with it, and that would preach well, I think." Kevin stood. "Would you like a cup of coffee?"

"No, I'm fine."

"Do you mind if I ask you another question?" Kevin sat, placing his coffee on the edge of her desk.

"I don't mind." She smiled at him.

"How do you deal with it? Doesn't it scare you?"

"At first, I was scared. Matt told me I looked as if I had seen a ghost." Jessie chuckled. "Later, Reba explained to me how Gina needed my help, and that's why I could see her." Jessie straightened in her chair. "I know this might sound strange, but I want to help people, and for some reason, this is how I can. I tell their stories, so they're not forgotten. It doesn't scare me anymore."

"You'd make an interesting case study." Kevin laughed.

"I can only imagine. If telling their stories helps to solve the crimes against them, then it's worth it to me."

"Great attitude." Kevin stood. "I'll let you get to work. I may have more questions for you if this stuff keeps happening."

"You know where to find me if you do," Jessie

206

answered the ringing phone. Her morning was off and running.

****

Jessie crossed the street from the church to her store. She took a quick glance toward the cemetery. They were no longer visible to her.

Audrey held the door open for Jessie. "How was your morning?"

"I had a nice talk with Pastor Kevin. Pastor John was out for the morning. I was busy answering the phone. With the church dinner coming up, everyone had questions. I know you gave the congregation a flyer with the information in the Sunday bulletin, but I'm convinced people never read them. Melinda told me once they made good bookmarks."

"I hope you weren't too busy." Audrey grabbed her purse from under the counter. "It's my turn this afternoon."

"I like to be busy." She smiled. "It makes time seem to go faster." Jessie walked with her to the door.

"Before I forget to ask, did Pastor Kevin talk to you about all the strange things happening at the church?" Audrey stood in the open door.

"He mentioned a few things to me. Have you noticed anything?" Jessie asked.

"No, thank goodness. I don't believe much of the stuff Melinda tells me, but Pastor Kevin seemed genuinely troubled by some things. I heard him talking with Pastor John one morning. Anyway, I'm glad he talked to you about it." Audrey waved as she closed the door.

Jessie watched her cross the street. A confrontation must be getting close. She looked at the cemetery. What had Pastor Kevin seen? Jessie knew it bothered him whatever it was.

****

Matt's head was spinning. He couldn't believe how efficient Sanders was in comparison to Kaufman. He brought a completely new range of ideas with him. Sanders filled in a lot of holes in the investigation for Matt. The FBI had been watching Roth and three of the four men for some time. The American was new to the group, but agents were digging into his background. Details crammed the files on each man. Facts which Matt had needed to see at this time. A theory was starting to come together in his mind. When Jessie and he had shut down the Harvest Club, he had unknowingly crossed paths with Roth. It had happened again in Palm Springs. Roth was the front man for a terrorist group ready to buy weapons. He could understand why Roth was angry. His well had dried up, and Roth had lost millions of dollars. How the kids fit in the picture was still an unknown, but with all the dedicated agents working on the case he was confident they would discover the link. One fact they all agreed on was that this was a terrorist group here to attack a major event. They wanted to take out as many people as they could. It had to be sensational enough to cause people to panic.

Usually, a terrorist group remained in the shadows, not wanting to tip the authorities to their presence. These perps had made several bad moves, which didn't make sense. Why would Roth, who was meticulous and elusive, be careless and stupid? Unless, of course, it was all a part of his plan. Damn, what was their game? Matt read over the files and the notes he had made.

Somewhere in all this paperwork, there had to be an answer.

Think, Matt. His mind worked through several scenarios. Each one seemed more improbable than the one before it, but then again, maybe not. He stood and went to find Tom. He had stumbled on something. He knew he was getting close.

Chapter 30

After work, Jessie visited Carlos. He gave her some great material on his friends for her articles. He had mentioned something in passing that was still troubling her. Matt would need to know the details if he didn't already. Jessie drove by the station on her way home to see if Matt was still there. She parked her car in the lot. At least a few of the reporters had gone home for the night. There was no way she wanted one of them to shove a mic in her face and ask a question.

"Hey, sweetheart, I was going to call you later. What's up?" He stood to give her a hug.

"I was at the hospital visiting Carlos. We had a great conversation. He said something in passing that's bothering me, and I wanted to run it by you. I took a gamble and came to see if you were still here."

"Sit." He pointed to the chair. "Tell me what's troubling you." He sat on the corner of his desk.

Jessie sat and crossed her legs. She took her notes out of her purse. "I wrote it down, and I want to tell you the way he said it. He was talking about Amir and Darsha's relationship being in trouble. Not that they weren't in love; they were. Darsha's parents were trying to break them up. Her parents had arranged a marriage for her years ago. They had many arguments about her dating Amir. The young man she was to marry had recently arrived in America from India. He was not happy that Amir was dating her. They had several intense arguments. When I talked with Darsha, she made it sound like Amir's family was angry. Carlos made it sound more as if it was Darsha's family. There was plenty of drama in the lives of these kids."

"Wow, I didn't know they still had arranged marriages anymore." Matt shook his head.

"Some countries still do. It must be hard for families who immigrate here and discover our free lifestyle when it comes to dating. I imagine her parents were exasperated by her defiance."

"Attraction and love are strange emotions. Look at us. We fought it so hard, and yet here we are."

"True, but we were raised in this culture. Darsha, on the other hand, was not. She must have had strong feelings for Amir to go against her parents and everything they taught her. I have no idea if this has anything to do with his death, but I find it strange that she was not there on the day they were abducted, and now I wonder why. I also wonder about the young man she was supposed to marry. You might need to have a chat with him."

"You think? Have I told you lately that I like how your mind works?" He nodded, his expression thoughtful. "No one else got that out of Carlos when he was interviewed. Of course, Maxwell or Dickerson aren't half as pretty as you are. Carlos was out of his league when it comes to you, and I know just how he feels."

"Oh, you do, and how does he feel? I'd like to know. For research, of course." She poised her pencil to write.

"Well, if it's for research, I'll be happy to answer. I

know when I look at you I have a hard time keeping my thoughts in order in my head. I see the light in your eyes and those dimples of yours, and I want to do anything I can to make you smile so I can see them again. I've even run off at the mouth to keep you standing near me for a few minutes more. Yep, Carlos was mesmerized."

Jessie laughed. "Knowing Carlos, I'm not his style, but you made a great attempt at being romantic, and I'm touched."

"You've only seen a small side to my romantic possibilities." He leaned close to her, so close her breath fluttered across his face. "I know what I want, and I'm going to use every weapon in my arsenal to win your hand." He smiled at her intake of breath. "When it comes to you, I plan to pull out all the stops." He straightened back on the corner of the desk. "Dickerson wants to meet you. He left earlier for the day, which is his loss. I suppose I'll have to bring him to the store tomorrow."

This side of Matt interested Jessie. "You don't sound so happy about it." She chuckled.

"What can I say? He's a single male, he's an agent, and some would say he's good-looking in some off-beat kind of way, and you're *you*. I don't like the idea of him being within twenty miles of you." Matt folded his arms over his chest.

She stood and kissed his cheek. "You're a dear, and you can stop teasing me. I'll meet your agent whenever you bring him by. As for you," she poked her finger in his chest, "I'll have to spend more time reassuring you and stroking your ego." He grabbed her pointing finger, and Jessie found herself wrapped in his arms.

"You do that, sweetheart." He kissed her soundly and nibbled on her ear. "I'll be doing my own convincing. I think it will work out well for both of us."

Jessie wiggled out of his arms and took a big step toward the door. "You're at work for heaven sakes, and there are people around." She heard voices out in the hall.

"I know where I am. I don't want to kiss them, Jess. Besides, they all know we're an item and that I have it bad when it comes to you." His lips crinkled at the corners. "The guys rib me every chance they get."

"I know all about male banter because of growing up near Liam and Connor. I'm sorry, it can be rough." She moved toward him and ruffled his hair.

He took her hand in his. "Dylan's the one they're the hardest on. They still think of me as their boss."

"Speaking of Dylan, I'm headed to the Inn for dinner. Katie has been pouting and telling me I haven't spent any time with her lately. We talk almost every night, but only in person counts in her mind." She kissed him. "Call me later." She walked out of the room and looked over her shoulder at him. There was a goofy grin on his face.

"I'm going to win," he whispered.

"Only if I let you." She mouthed the words back at him,

Chapter 31

Jessie made it to the car, rubbery legs, and all. Gosh, his crooked grin pulled at her heartstrings. She had no doubt he would win because she would let him. It was her choice, and he definitely was her choice. He almost made her forget about what Carlos told her. She needed to talk to Darsha without her aunt in the same room.

She started her car. Was Darsha's family involved? Had they hired someone? They seemed like a nice enough family, but nice people were capable of murder under the right circumstances. She had seen it often enough in years covering the news. Still, it was a stretch.

Walking up the steps to the Inn, she could hear Liam and Connor laughing. She hesitated, but opened the door knowing they would probably tease her; anything to see her blush.

"Jessie, where's your cop boyfriend?" Connor placed her hand on his waiting arm.

"I left him still working at the station." She tried to pull her hand away, but he held tight. "You both have an evening off?" Jessie looked from Liam to Connor's laughing face.

"No. We're taking a little time off for dinner and trying out a new guy at the pub under the watchful eye of a friend."

"Sweet." She tried to pull her hand away again.

"I'm not letting go. Matt should be here soon. Katie called right after you left and invited him to dinner. I don't want Matt to get complacent when it comes to you. There's nothing like a well-placed kick to jump-start a man's heart." Connor chuckled.

"More like his wrath," Jessie mumbled under her breath. "His heart is in fine shape when it comes to me. You can stop meddling if you don't mind." She yanked her hand free and walked away. She wanted to stuff a sock in Connor's mouth to stop his hooting.

Jessie almost made it as far as the kitchen when Connor came up on one side of her and Liam on the other. Liam threw his arm around her. "Jessie, we want to help your slow-moving guy along. If he doesn't hurry, one of us might have to steal you right out from under his nose."

"Like that would ever happen. He's moving fast enough. I'm the one dragging my feet."

"Matt hasn't convinced you yet. Is that what you're saying?" Liam ducked just in time to avoid her slapping hand.

"No, you've got it all wrong. You're putting words in my mouth." Jessie lifted her hand again.

"I should hope they have it all wrong." Matt's voice came from behind her. "I thought for sure my campaign was working the way it was supposed to." His lips curved into a smile.

Great! Jessie bristled and pushed Liam's arm off her. "They're wrong as usual. Your campaign is fine, and if they had given me time to finish my response, they would know I'm happy with...ouch." She rubbed the place where Liam had pinched her.

Liam interrupted. "If it's not Matt who needs a nudge, then Connor and I are maybe going about this all wrong. We need to throw some girls at Matt. I think Jessie might be too sure of herself."

"Jess is fine, and we don't want you two clowns to help us at all." Matt winked at Jess. "We've got it all figured out, don't we, sweetheart?" Matt pulled her into his side. "We're enjoying the ride."

Jessie's face warmed to a rosy blush. "We sure are."

Liam looked at her. "Our Jessie is blushing. I think Matt can handle this all by himself."

"Dang, but I think you're right, bro," Connor chimed in. "Jessie was always a blusher; it makes teasing her all the more fun."

Jessie laughed. "Matt, I think you and I need to do a little matchmaking and torment these two for a while."

"I'm in, sign me up." Liam chuckled. "You can throw the women my way."

"I'm in, too," Connor added. "I'll give you my wish list."

"You're incorrigible." Jessie tousled Connor's hair. She knew he hated it when his hair was messy. "That's what you get for teasing me."

"Ah, Jessie, you make it so easy, sweetheart." Connor chuckled. "I know I can get a rise out of you every time."

Matt smiled. "She walks right into it with her eyes wide open. Ouch." He winced when she poked his ribs with her elbow. "You know you do, sweetheart."

"Never side with them against me." She smiled as she poked him again. "What is this, gang up on Jessie night to watch her blush?" She tossed her hair over her shoulder and left the three of them standing in the entryway grinning like idiots. "Men are such pains," she muttered under her breath as she walked into the kitchen. "Pleasant, but royal pains."

"Who are royal pains?" Katie was tossing the salad with dressing.

"Men, especially Connor and your brother." Jessie stood beside Katie, watching her dice green onions. Katie tossed them into the salad.

"I'm not sure you could call them men. Liam's more like a man-child." Katie gave her a puzzled look. "I guess most of them are, at some point. Anyway, I'm glad they're picking on you and finally leaving me alone. Those two can be brats." Katie handed her the bowl of salad. "Put this on the table. You know where I like it."

"I'd be happy to, unless one of those guys decides to tease me again and then I might throw it at him." Jessie grabbed the salad bowl from Katie and walked into the dining room.

"Throw the salad tongs please; I don't want to make another salad," Katie called after her.

"Don't worry; I'll make the next one. It'd be worth it just to see the look on one of their faces."

"Whose face?" Matt walked up behind her, wrapping his arms around her waist.

"Yours if you're not careful." She laughed.

"Who me? I'm always careful." He turned her around and kissed her cheek. "You bring out the kid in me. What can I say?" He kissed her on the lips.

"Would you look at this, Liam? I think the cop might know his way around our girl after all."

"Give it up, Connor." Matt waved him off.

Jessie slipped out of Matt's embrace. "I need to help Katie bring in the food."

"Did I embarrass you, sweetheart?" Matt followed her into the kitchen,

"Not really, but guests will be coming into the dining room to eat soon." Her blush gave her away. "Where's your shadow?"

"You mean Tom?" Matt carried the meat platter out for her. She nodded. "He dropped me off and went to pick up Frank. He didn't think I'd get into too much trouble if I were inside with you. Little does he know, huh, sweetheart?"

"You're trouble with a capital T for me." She fluttered her lashes at him and strutted toward the kitchen.

"Am I? That's good to know. You're all I can handle and then some." Matt followed her. "Why, Miss Reynolds, I think you're flirting with me."

She grinned. "You could be right." Jessie would have said more, but there were guests in the kitchen and the dining room. She placed the last bowl on the table just as Dylan, Tom, and Frank walked in.

The night was fun and relaxing. Katie's meal was perfect, and Liam and Connor entertained everyone with their crazy stories. With the stress of the case looming in front of them, it was what Jessie needed. In the back of her mind, she knew this was a moment of calm before the storm, and she meant to take advantage of it in every way she could. She had no idea what the next few days would bring, but she was sure it would be trying for Matt. What affected him had the power to break her heart.

Chapter 32

The kiss seemed awkward with Tom standing a few feet away. Thank heavens it was too dark to see the blush she knew that was staining her cheek. She struggled with her self-conscious feelings.

"It's hard having an audience. It takes all the romance out of it," Matt whispered in her ear. "I promise you won't have to endure this much longer."

"I hate to intrude on your romantic interlude, but you need to wind this up. You're a sitting duck out here, remember." Tom folded his arms across his chest.

Jessie pulled out of Matt's arms. "He's right, of course, we have to be careful." She nudged his shoulder.

Tom grabbed Matt's arm. "Come on, lover boy. Let's get you out of sight."

Jessie stood in the open door until he was out of her view. A sense of foreboding careened through her. What if this were the last time she ever saw him? She shook her head to banish the depressing thoughts and fragments of the dream that swirled through her mind. "Stop it!" she cried, "You have to believe he'll be okay." Leaning against the door, she locked it. He was gone and the room seemed suddenly empty. What was happening to her? Grasping for an element of control, she closed her eyes, taking deep breaths. It wasn't working. Several short, rapid breaths came one on top of the other, followed by fear. Lost in a dark vision, only the sudden, persistent knocks at the door brought her back to reality.

"Jess, open up." Matt's voice reached her.

"What's wrong?" She yanked the door open.

Matt frowned. "Are you okay? I knocked for quite a while."

"I'm fine." She reached for his hand. "Did you forget something?"

"Are you sure you're okay?" He laced his finger through hers. "We think it's best if you stay at the house." Matt pointed at Tom. "You explain it to her. It's your idea."

"The thing is, Jessie, a couple of the suspects have been in your store, and they have to know you're connected to him." Tom pointed at Matt. "Neither one of you hide your feelings well. The air crackles between you two when you're in the same room, and I don't want them to use you to get at him. I want you both where I can keep an eye on you." Tom leaned against the door with his chin jutted out. He appeared unmovable to Jessie.

"You already have a full house, and you don't need me to add to it." Jessie glanced at Matt. He showed no reaction on his face.

"I insist. You have no choice. Pack some things for tomorrow, and we'll work out all the details later." Tom gave Matt a slight push. "Help her."

"I don't think this is necessary. I would rather stay here," she told Matt as she pulled out her overnight bag and placed several items it.

"But you're going to do it anyway, aren't you?" He leaned against the doorframe. "We have no option. This case is about to break open. I want my wits about me, and I don't want to be worried about you." Matt reached for her and pulled her into his arms. "I'm sorry this will be an inconvenience for you, but if it keeps you alive, it's worth it, don't you think?" His chin rested on the top of her head.

"Of course, and I know you're right. I'm sure it won't be long before they make a move. I've made it work before, and I wasn't happy about it then, either." She grabbed his hand. "I'm not upset with you. I don't want you to worry."

"That's my girl." Matt released his hold on her and let her get back to packing. "You seem a little shaken. Are you sure something isn't wrong?"

"I'm all right," she answered tersely. Jessie folded a few more items neatly into her case, and she was done. "Oh, I need my computer." She flipped off the light in her bedroom and went to her desk. She packed her computer and the book she was currently reading. "Let's go, I'm ready." At least she hoped she had all she needed. It wasn't as if she was leaving town. She went out the door Tom held open, and Matt locked it behind them.

"You'll have to leave the driving to us for now. No car," Tom sounded like a drill sergeant again. "We'll be nice and cozy, you'll see." He smiled at her muttered response. Tom carried her suitcase. "You both get in the car, and I'll put this in the trunk. I want you both out of sight."

"Whatever." Jessie opened the car door and got in. She latched her seat belt, and her chin tilted upwards.

"You okay?" Matt turned to look at her.

"Of course, why wouldn't I be?" Her voice had a

slight edge to it.

"I know you well enough to know you don't like any man including me telling you what to do. I might be wrong about it, though." Matt grinned at her.

"I'm here, aren't I? I did what I was told to do." She emphasized the word *told*, dragging it out.

"All I know is when that beautiful chin of yours goes up, someone has crossed the line with you. I'm hoping it wasn't me."

"Like I told you before, I'm not upset with you. I need a little time, and I'll work through it." She gave him a tentative smile. "You know me well." Her frown lines deepened. She turned her head and stared out the window. "Let's go."

****

Matt caught the look she gave to Tom when he got in the car. Tom had no idea he had issued a challenge to Jess, and she was no pushover. She was miffed. If Tom were smart, he'd lighten up a little on the drill sergeant routine. "Are we good to go?" His eyes met Jessie's in the mirror. "Thank you," he said.

"For what?" she asked.

"For coming, I know this is inconvenient for you. It will give me peace of mind having you where I can see you." He saw her lips turn up at the corners. She knew he was trying to placate her.

"It'll make my job a whole lot easier, too." Tom turned in his seat. "I won't have to traipse all over town following this guy so he can talk to you."

Tom had gone and ruined it. Matt knew what was coming and tried in vain to stop it. "Jess is a good sport, aren't you, sweetheart?" He winced at the fire in her eyes.

"You know, Tom, I'm glad I could make your job easier. It would have been a lot nicer if you had asked me and not told me to do it, though. I'm not one of your agents, I'm just saying. You see, when a man thinks he can insist I do something because he told me to, well, something rises inside of me, and I want to rip his lips off." Her voice was slow and terse. "I restrain myself when the feeling arises, but it's there nonetheless."

"Oh, I get it. You're one of those." Tom's hand went to his forehead.

"If by *one of those*, you mean a woman who thinks you should *ask* her and not *tell* her, out of respect for her as an equal, then yes, I guess I'm *one of those*."

"Hell, I didn't know you were so touchy." Tom frowned.

"I'm not, Tom. I've worked hard to get where I am. I don't think it's asking too much for you to treat me with the same respect I would give to you in the same situation. I would have done what you wanted without any response if you had asked me."

"I'm sorry, Jessie, I'm used to barking out orders and having them obeyed." Tom actually sounded contrite, and Matt had to swallow a grin.

"Apology accepted. Most men are used to giving orders or lecturing a woman. I've worked with many men in my profession over the years. It was incumbent on me to tell them when they had crossed the line and treated me like a subordinate instead of an equal."

"Including me, eh, sweetheart?" Matt chuckled.

"Yes, including you. You do love to lecture me." She smiled at Matt in the mirror.

"You'll have to remind me," Tom said. "Old habits die hard. I've been doing it for years."

"Sadie used to say to me that men like to tell women what to do because it makes them feel in control. On the other hand, women think by nagging a man they'll get him to do what they want. Neither method works, and in the end, it will separate them." Jessie touched Tom's arm. "I'd rather be honest and not lose you as a friend. I'm awful touchy when I'm ordered to do something. It started in kindergarten actually."

"I can see your point of view. I'll try to remember it in the future, unless of course, your life depends on my commands. Then you'll have to move when I say to."

"I can live with that." She smiled at Tom.

"We dodged one bullet, now we need to do the same with this case." Matt started the car and headed for home.

Their conversation turned to the case, but Jessie was too quiet for Matt's liking. She stared out the side passenger window. He never caught her glance in the mirror all the way home. Matt didn't think she was still upset. What was she thinking?

Chapter 33

Her anger toward Tom had been a huge overreaction on her part. Jessie thought she had this area of her life under control. Matt always treated her like an equal, and her response to Tom had been both ridiculous and extreme for the request. Why? She tossed her hair over her shoulder and frowned at her reflection in the mirror. Disturbing thoughts had infiltrated her mind earlier and only Matt's persistent knocks on the door had interrupted them. She had been out of control and afraid.

Her normal assurance and confidence were failing her. Whoever their suspects were, they were dangerous, and the case could get a lot worse before they solved it. For the first time, Jessie wasn't sure if it would all turn out okay. There were no ghostly impressions, no premonitions of all being well, only a sinking feeling in the pit of her stomach.

The knock on the door grew louder. "Are you okay in there?" Matt called.

"I'm fine. Come in," she told him.

Matt leaned against the doorframe. "I haven't seen you react this way in a while. What's going on?"

"I asked myself the same thing a moment ago. It's this case. Three young people are dead. I have no idea how to respond to their spirits. They aren't like the others I've dealt with." She shook her head. "I'm concerned about you, too. These people are serious. The hell they put those kids through is too much to think about without losing it."

"I understand, but what else is bothering you." Matt pushed away from the door and sat on the bed beside her.

"Have you listened to the news lately? I've been feeling melancholy most of the day. When I was young, my grandmother took me to several protest marches. She wanted me to learn to stand up for not only my rights but also the rights of others. Sadie wanted me to be proud of who I was, but never forget others along the way. She would tell me, 'Jessie, don't get it in your head that you're better than other folks are because you're not. Everyone has to work hard at being a nice person and making the world a better place.'"

"Did your mom ever go with you?" Matt asked.

"She did at first, but my dad would make fun of her, so she gave up her ideas. She always walked on eggshells around my dad. She never knew what would set him off. Over the years, I watched her change into a different person trying to please him. He loves her in his own way, but he tends to be heavy-handed."

"I know there are a lot of men like him, but I'm not one of them," Matt reassured her.

"You're getting better." She patted his hand. "Those were special times with Sadie. She taught me so much. I don't think I can ever repay her."

"I bet you already have. You have a great relationship with her."

Jessie smiled. "I do. She's the best." She folded her hands in her lap. "Have you ever noticed how life seems to push us to move on and ignore all that is happening?"

"I call it survival."

"Is surviving all that it's about? What about caring?" She folded and unfolded her hands. "Every day I go to work like nothing is happening around me. I have to make decisions about what I should wear and what to eat for dinner. I make plans for the future as if I have all the time in the world, but in reality, it could all be over in a moment. None of us knows for sure." She glanced at him. "All the while, three kids are dead. There's nothing I can do to change it."

"You're right; it's a mess. The best we can do is be grateful to survive." Matt grabbed her hand in the act of twisting her hair. "Still, in the middle of the chaos, life hands you a few moments to remind you it's a joy to be alive. I'm not good with words, but given a chance, I would fight to stay alive with all my strength. I still have things I want to do and see." Matt tightened his hand around hers. "Look at how hard Carlos fought. No, life isn't perfect, but it's all we've got."

"What's the purpose of it all?" She felt hope rise in her heart with his words. He would fight to live. She had needed to hear it.

"I have no idea, and that's the truth. Greater minds than mine have tried to figure it out—with little success, if my philosophy class was any indication. For me, it's a no-brainer. I grab the high moments when they come around and go with them." His hand touched her cheek. "Don't worry. Survive is what we have to do if we are going to bring closure to these families."

"I know you're right. My thoughts have led me down a crazy rabbit trail today. I don't get why people do the things they do."

"I doubt you ever will, sweetheart. I've heard all the answers from many sources, and it always comes back to personal choices." He stood. "Frank told me to tell you soup's on," he called on his way out the door.

****

Jessie had escaped to her room again right after dinner. Matt checked in on her once, saw that she was busy writing, and left her to her work. The blues had colored his day, too. Matt tried hard not to give in to the depressing thoughts, but he hadn't done a good job of it. The public wanted answers, the families needed them, too, and he had more questions than answers right now. He sat in his recliner, put on his glasses, and began to look over the case file. There had to be something hidden in all the information that Dickerson and Sanders had given him.

Tom walked into the living room. "I've checked all the doors. Are you going to be up much longer?"

"I want to look over this file again. I need to familiarize myself with these suspects. I've never come up against anyone like them in my years on the force."

"Not many cops would have. You can see from their rap sheets that this is a way of life for them." Tom sat on the couch.

"What are we facing? What are your sources telling you?" Matt looked over the top of his glasses at Tom.

"These men are ruthless, which is easy to figure out. There are links between Roth and Amir. We know Roth had business ties in Kuwait. Slowly a picture is coming together. It could be he was hired by someone politically opposed to Amir's father."

"When did all these political factions make their

way to our soil? It seems strange. The world used to seem like such a big place, and now it's small, with all the anger spilling across borders and oceans." Matt took off his glasses and rubbed his forehead.

"We've known it was coming. The Internet makes communication with people from around the world easy. People you'll never meet in life can chat with you on social media. It's a recruiting tool for terrorists and political ideologues. Fake news and real news bombard us twenty-four-seven. People tend to believe everything they hear or read on the Internet. They don't check sources or fact check. This information age is a great boon but can be bad at the same time. You can see the results of how it can work for you with Jeremy, but it can work against you just as well."

"It's a damn mine field. You never know where to step." Matt twirled his glasses in his hands.

"I'm going to call it a night. If you need anything, you know where to find me. Don't stay up too long. I'll be awake because technically, I'm not supposed to sleep while you're awake." Tom stood.

"Look, the house is buttoned up tight, and Radar should warn us if he hears anything. Go ahead; I'm fine. I won't be up much longer. Sanders gave us a lot of new information. Something is bothering me, and I can't put my finger on it." He motioned him to go ahead.

"Like I said, you know where to find me." Tom headed down the hall.

Finally, the house was quiet, and he could concentrate. Matt scanned the pages, looking for the piece of information that would tie the facts together. He read a paragraph at the bottom of the page, paused, and read it again. "Bingo! There it is." He slapped the chair arm. There was the connection, a motive, and the perfect means to cover their crime. Roth wouldn't let a couple of kids stand in his way.

Matt closed the file and placed it on the end table. He shut off the light and went to the kitchen for a glass of water.

There was a faint rustling sound coming from the garage. He turned toward it. There it was again. The darn raccoon must have slipped through the dog door again, digging in the trash and making a mess of his garage. Matt set his glass on the counter, flipped on the light, and opened the door. He stepped into the garage, and someone grabbed him from behind. Something wet and pungent covered his face, and he gasped, his head swimming instantly. One chance... He slammed backward with his elbow, heard a grunt of pain, and yanked the cloth free as he started to turn.

Then, darkness exploded in his head, and he fell down into it...

Chapter 34

Jessie flew out of her room. Radar was going crazy. Tom was in the garage yelling for someone to call an ambulance. Her heart beat rapidly, and her stomach was churning as she raced through the kitchen.

Matt lay on the floor of the garage, his blood shockingly bright against the gray concrete.

Oh, God… She froze in the doorway.

"Stay with him!" Tom yelled at her. He took off running after Frank and Radar.

Jessie dropped to her knees beside Matt's sprawled body, almost afraid to look at him. Her shaking hand reached for his, searching for a pulse. Thank God, he still had one. He was out cold. Not dead.

Not dead. *Thank you, God.*

Jessie knelt beside Matt and lifted his head onto her lap. She stroked his cheek. "I love you, damn it," she whispered. "Don't you dare die on me now. You hear me?" Tires squealed on the asphalt as a car sped away. Radar's insistent baying and sirens filled the night air, but Jessie didn't move. She held him, never taking her eyes off the steady rise and fall of his chest.

Tom ran back to the garage. "Damn, they got away." He looked at Frank who was right behind him. "How did they get in here?"

"Beats me. Is he okay?" Frank placed his hand on Jessie's shoulder.

"His breathing seems to be fine." She turned her head to look at Frank. "There's a huge bump and a gash on the back of his head." She used her sleeve to wipe away the sticky blood.

"If we had taken a few minutes more to react, he wouldn't be here. Radar's barking saved his life. They were carrying him to the van and dropped him when we all came charging out here. I can't believe they had the audacity to waltz in here." Tom paced. "This changes the stakes. Damn, I wanted to get that van." Tom slammed the side door and locked it. He opened the garage door as the ambulance pulled up.

The medics went to work checking Matt's vitals. He stirred, groaned, and tried to sit up. "Sir, you need to lie back for a minute. Let us finish checking you out," the sandy-haired paramedic said firmly.

Matt groaned and reached for his head. "What happened?"

"I was about to ask you the same thing!" Tom swore under his breath. "Why did you go into the garage? Can you remember?"

Matt struggled to sit again. This time the medic helped him. "It's a little foggy, and my head feels like it's cracking open." He frowned. "I heard something and thought maybe the pesky raccoon I've been fighting with had found a way back into the garage and was getting in the trash." Matt rubbed his forehead. "I walked out the door, and a cloth was slapped over my nose. When I tried to pull it off, I was hit from behind."

"Damn." Tom paced. "They wanted you alive."

Jessie watched Matt's face pale. "Is he going to be okay?" Jessie asked.

"Yes, he'll have a big headache for a while," the

young medic told her. "The cut is bloody but pretty shallow. You might want to come in and get it stitched up." He shrugged as Matt shook his head. "My theory is, somebody put a cloth doused in an anesthetic over his nose—old fashioned ether by the smell of it—and he was hit with a blunt instrument from behind. There's a bump to prove it. He didn't stand a chance. The ether takes the legs right out from under you." He cleaned the wound. "I'd put some ice on that knot. It's minor, with no sign of a concussion, but it'll bother him."

"All I know is, I turned on the light, opened the door, and then everything went to hell," Matt mumbled.

"We're damn lucky. They meant to take you. You'd be another statistic had Radar not gone crazy and alerted us." Tom crossed his arms over his chest as he leaned against the wall.

"Let's get him inside." The two medics helped Matt inside to his recliner. The medic gave him a pill with a glass of water and handed Jessie a list of concussion symptoms to watch for. "He should be fine in a few hours, but if you see any of these things take him to the ER."

"I will and thank you." Jessie filled a bag with ice and wrapped it in a towel. "I know that headache all too well and, believe me, rest will help." She took hold of his hand. "I'm not going anywhere, so you can relax." She handed him the ice bag and started reading the paper the medic had given her.

"Thanks, sweetheart." He settled into his chair, adjusting the ice bag behind his head. Wincing, he closed his eyes.

"That was too close. They almost got him." Frank stood beside Matt's chair, his voice quiet.

"You're telling me." Jessie found herself often glancing at Matt to make sure he was doing all right.

"Now what?" Frank asked.

"I'll tell you what. We're going to secure the perimeter of this property. I want to make it as hard to break into as Fort Knox." Tom raked his hand through his hair. "Too damn close for my comfort. I'm on watch now. You catch some sleep, Jessie."

"I'm staying with him." She lifted her chin. "I told him I would, and I want to be here if he wants to talk." She glanced at Matt's peaceful face. "This isn't over. They won't give up without a fight."

"I know. They want Matt, and they won't stop trying until they're dead or in custody. Truthfully, I prefer the first," he said grimly. "It's the only sure-fire way to stop a group like this." Tom grabbed the file Matt had left on the table, plopped down in one of the chairs, and began to read it. "I know we haven't seen the end of them, and the next time we'll be ready."

"I don't know about you both, but I have too much adrenaline pumping through me to sleep. I thought Radar would rip my arm off as I tried to hold him back." Frank sat on the couch next to Jessie. Radar lay down at his feet.

Jessie glanced at Matt as she stood. "I could use a cold drink. Can I get either of you one?"

"I'll help you." Frank jumped up. "Tom?"

"I'll come with you. I feel like I could punch a few faces, but I might have to settle for a wall." Tom followed them into the kitchen.

"Tom, you know the guy following us, the one I wrote off for his inept ability? I bet he led them here." Jessie grabbed a glass from the cupboard.

"He probably did. I wish now I would have taken him in for questioning. Matt wanted to watch him for a few days." Tom pulled a beer out of the fridge. "How did you know about the headache? Will he be okay?"

"On our last case, Rose used some kind of drug on me. My head felt like it was cracking open. The only thing I could do was sleep it off. It does go away, but it's no fun until it does."

Frank filled his glass with iced tea. "How did they get into the garage?

"The lock was professionally picked, which tells me we'll have to be alert. The suspects know about the dog now, which changes how they'll go about it next time."

"I believe they'll draw Matt out the next time. I hope that doesn't mean someone else will be murdered." Jessie walked toward the living room to check on Matt.

"It's a possibility we'll have to consider." Tom opened his beer and poured it into a glass. "I've already talked to Sanders. He's sending a couple of agents over to watch the house tonight. I don't want to give them any opportunity to find us asleep on the job again."

Jessie picked up her glass. "Roth has an extensive record, and he wants Matt. He'll stop at nothing to get him, but in the end, Matt will be the one to stop him."

"You sound sure." Frank looked at her.

"Last week I wasn't. Nothing has changed in the circumstances, but I know he'll figure this one out. I'm sure of it." Jessie walked into the living room followed by the men.

"Where did everyone go?" Matt kept his eyes closed as he talked.

"We went into the kitchen for something to drink." Jessie grabbed his hand. "How's your head?"

"I've felt better." Matt grimaced. "Tom, I've been thinking, and we need to talk."

"We'll talk in the morning." Tom stood. "You're going to bed, my orders."

"One question; how did they get in?" Matt swayed as he stood.

Tom reached out to steady him. "One of them picked the lock. It's easy enough if you know what you're doing, and one of them did."

"I didn't think they would come to my house. I won't underestimate them again. Read the file that Sanders gave us. I want to see if you come to the same conclusion that I did. I have a theory that ties it all together."

"I'll read, and you sleep. We'll talk in the morning."

"Say goodnight, Jessie." Tom grinned at her.

Jessie kissed Matt goodnight. She walked behind them down the hall. "If you need anything, Matt, call me."

"I will."

Jessie walked back into the living room. They had been lucky this time.

Chapter 35

Jessie was typing on her laptop when Tom walked into the living room. "Matt was out when his head hit the pillow."

"He'll sleep it off and feel better in the morning." Jessie glanced over at Tom.

"Can I ask you a question?" Tom picked up the file Matt had told him to read.

"Sure." Jessie stopped typing.

"Does anything ever get you down?" Tom stroked his chin. "You seem to take all this in stride."

"Are you kidding?" She rolled her eyes.

"No, I'm serious. How do you do it?" He leaned forward in the chair.

"I try to make the best of a bad situation." She frowned. "But, don't be fooled, I've done my fair share of complaining through all of this. I can't say I've handled it well at all. I'm like anyone—I have my good and bad moments. Life can be dark at times, and you have to suck it up and find a way to survive. Sorry, I got mad at you earlier. I was struggling with my own doubts and fears about all of this."

Tom waved it off. "We're all tense; it's this damn waiting. All I'm saying is that you're a positive person."

"Thanks, but if you knew how many times I've trembled in my shoes since moving here, you wouldn't say that." She gave him a lopsided grin. "If I have one person to thank for any positivity, I'd have to say it's my grandmother. She's a trouper." Jessie glanced at her computer. "And Reba Thomas. I would have never made through all these crazy events without her."

"I'd like to go on the record as saying I don't know how you do it. I can't imagine any woman I know jumping out of a tree onto a hitman ready to fire his weapon. You're unique and a tad strange." He chuckled.

"Now you're talking more like the Tom I know. The truth is I've made peace with it all. I see it as a way to work with Matt and solve some tough crimes." She smiled and patted his shoulder. "It is what it is. Goodnight."

****

Matt jolted awake, his head jerking side to side. The house was quiet, too quiet. Silence filled the dark room. The dog wasn't barking, which was a good thing. He might have to get another dog after this. Radar's barking had saved his life. At least the fog had lifted from his head and he could think clearly again. Damn, he groaned when his hand brushed against the tender spot on the back of his head. What had they hit him with?

He rose to his feet and made his way down the hall. The light was still on in the living room. "What are you doing still up?"

"Some fascinating reading." Tom waved the file in the air. "Not of the light variety, but the kind that gives you nightmares. I should ask you the same question."

"I woke up and needed a glass of water. I have no idea what time it is. I never looked at the clock." Matt sat on the edge of his recliner.

"The sun will be coming up soon." Tom glanced at his watch.

"Shouldn't you get some sleep?" Matt stood up to get his glass of water.

"I'll sleep later. Dickerson is going to watch Jessie's store today, and Sanders has assigned a couple of agents to shadow you today while I catch some z's. He wants to keep an eye on the both of you. We're both convinced they will use something to draw you out after their failed attempt. Jessie is the likely candidate."

"I'm glad they'll be watching her. Was it someone's idea of a cruel joke to put the handsome single guy on duty as the one to watch her?" Matt ran his hand through his rumpled hair, wincing when he inadvertently touched the bump. At least the cut had scabbed over.

"I thought you would appreciate our attention to detail." Tom chuckled. "I doubt Sanders even gave it a second thought. It's possible that Dickerson was the first to volunteer for the job. I mean, what's not to like about a cushy assignment watching a beautiful woman all day."

"Well, that makes me feel a hell of a lot better." Matt's brows creased.

"You don't have to worry about her. She's rock solid when it comes to you."

"It's not her I'm worried about." Matt leaned back in the recliner.

"No, I guess it wouldn't be." Tom tugged at his shirt collar and unbuttoned the top button. "How's your noggin?"

"Better now. At least the fog is gone. What do you

think about what you've read so far?" Matt took a swig of his water.

"From your notes in the file, I'm beginning to see where you're going in your thought process. I'm following on your heels. You made some great connections. Our task is to keep you alive and catch these dudes before they can do what they came here to do. Should be a piece of cake, right?"

Matt shook his head. "I'm holding out for lots of luck, too." The squeal of the bedroom door opening reminded Matt he needed to oil the hinge. He smiled at Jessie when she walked into the room. "I hope we didn't wake you." He touched her hand as she walked by the chair.

"I thought I heard your voice, and we need to talk. I'm glad you're awake, too." Jessie looked at Tom as she sat on the edge of the couch.

"What's up," Tom asked her.

"To make a long story short, you're about to find another body." She leaned back and closed her eyes.

Chapter 36

Tom's jaw dropped open. "How do you know?"

"She saw it, didn't you, sweetheart?" Matt grinned at Tom's ridiculous expression. "Tell us what you saw."

Jessie described the scene. "The man was tied to a tree. He seemed to be in a place where he'd be easy to see. They want you to find him."

"Damn. Of course, they do. The perps were bold enough to walk into this house. What's to stop them from putting a body where someone will find it?" Tom slapped the file down on the table.

"What, if any, details did you see?" Matt rested his head back against the chair.

"He seemed to be older, but I didn't notice much else about his appearance. I couldn't get past the look of shock on his face. He was taken by surprise, which makes me wonder..." She hunched forward, propping her chin on her hands.

"What, Jess? I can see the wheels spinning. Tell us what you're thinking." Matt leaned forward.

"I wonder if he's the man who has been following you. He might have gone there to meet them thinking he would be paid and wound up dead instead."

"Good theory, and you could be right." Tom stretched out his legs. "Is she always like this?"

"Most of the time." Matt beamed at her. "Did you recognize the area?"

"I haven't had time to explore this area much since I've moved here. The main thing I noticed was there was a well-worn path like a hiking trail. The tree was near the trailhead, so he should be easy for someone to find. Who knows? Maybe they'll have another method of telling us where he's at." She straightened.

"I need coffee. Something tells me I won't get much sleep today. Anyone else want some?" Tom stood and walked toward the kitchen. "Jessie, Agent Dickerson is taking you to work today and will watch your store in case someone shows up there."

"Okay, I'd better get ready." She paused by Matt's chair. "Where will you be?"

He motioned for her to move closer then pulled her onto his lap. "I'll be at the station. If you need anything, or if Dickerson gets on your nerves, call me. I'll make Tom drive me to the store. Dickerson tends to talk a lot, and I don't want him bothering you while you work." He kissed her good morning.

She smiled at him. "I'm sure he'll be fine. I have enough work to keep me busy, and I'm sure he'll stay out of the way. I doubt he'll pay any attention to me."

"He's a man, and I'm sure he will." He buried his hands in her hair and kissed her again.

"I'll handle him." She stood. "I'll call if he pays too much attention." She laughed as she went down the hall.

****

Dickerson opened the car door for her. "How long have you known Matt?"

"Almost a year." Jessie fastened her seat belt.

"He seems like an okay guy. I've been reading about some of your cases. Your little town seems to have more than its share of big cases. It used to be small town America was a safe place to live and raise a family." He started the car and pulled out of Matt's driveway.

"True, but we are close to New York, and I think crime has a way of spilling out of the cities. By the way, Matt is a *great* guy. He's one of the best cops around. Blue Cove is lucky to have him as their chief." She waved at Matt who was standing at the window.

"You don't have to sell me. I've watched Matt at work with his officers. They all respect him, and that says it all to me."

"How long have you worked for the Bureau?" Jessie fidgeted with her seat belt, which had pulled too tight when he stopped.

"Six years."

"Do you like it?" she asked.

"Yeah, it's all right." He nodded. "I wanted to work there for as long as I can remember. Working in the international crime division can keep you awake at night, though." He pulled into the spot behind Jessie's store.

"Why is that?" Jessie took off the seat belt and grabbed the keys from her purse.

"I've seen first-hand how dangerous our world is." He opened his door.

"What's your first name? I can't call you Dickerson all day." She unlocked the door.

"You can call me Cliff." He smiled and held the door open for her. He followed her like a shadow as she did her money routine. "Nice place you have here." He looked around her shop. "You have some great art pieces. I like the vibe of the exposed brick and the modern look. Cool."

"Thanks, I like it, too. This was my dream as far back as I can remember." Jessie unlocked the doors between the store and coffee shop and waved at Molly. "You should go have a cup of coffee and one of her great treats. Molly is the owner, and she makes the best stuff ever. You can see my store from there, and you won't have to hang out here doing nothing. She has the newspaper to read, and you can come back later and grab a book off the shelf to keep you busy."

"Good idea. The coffee smells good," he said as he headed into Joe's.

Cliff was nice, but it would be a long day for both of them if he didn't have something to keep him busy. Jessie's day got off to a quick start. She had several customers early on, and as the morning progressed, the mystery book club arrived for their meeting. They were a high-energy group. The store's noise volume went up a notch every time they met. Jessie loved it. Moments like this reminded her of all the reasons she loved her store.

Glancing out the window she could see Pastor Kevin walking into the church. The store was getting busier. She missed the people, and working at the church would always hold a special place in heart. Tossing her hair over her shoulder, she turned to help a customer.

The book club was primed with coffee and busy arguing their theories when a young man in his late teens or early twenties walked in. He went to the counter and waited. "I'll be right with you," Jessie called to him. She was introducing a new customer to the recently released titles.

"I'm in no hurry." He glanced at the door often.

"If it's okay with you," Jessie said to the woman, "I'll leave you to browse and be back to check on you in a few minutes." She handed the customer the book she had been showing her.

"Thank you. Please go, take care of the young man." The gray-haired woman gave her a smile. "I'll be looking for a while, I'm sure."

"May I help you?" Jessie approached the young man.

He looked around the store, shifting from one foot to the next. "Are you the owner?"

"Yes, I am. Is there something you need?" Jessie's pulse quickened.

"I've never done this before, and I'm not sure if I should. A man outside stopped me on the street. He told me to come into this store and give this to the owner." He pulled the envelope from his jacket and handed it to her.

"Can you describe this man?" Jessie caught Cliff's eye and motioned for him to come.

"All I know is he was scary. That's the only reason I took the envelope in the first place. I was afraid not to. I hope I'm not in trouble." He looked away from her, tugging on his jacket sleeve.

"Can you remember anything else about him?" Cliff's deep voice startled the young man.

"He had curly hair and looked like he'd just got out of bed. His eyes had a crazy, mean look. I took the envelope and walked in here as fast as I could."

"You did the right thing, and you're not in trouble." Cliff gave his shoulder a light squeeze. "Let me buy you something to drink. I'd like to ask you a few more questions." Cliff showed him his badge.

"Sure, okay. What's going on?" He chewed on his lip.

"I want you to tell me anything you remember about the man. What was he wearing? Did he have any nervous habits? Think about it," Cliff told him.

Jessie opened the envelope. "Would you look at this? I think we've been given a clue." She handed the crude map to the agent. "I guess nobody has found the body yet."

"Do you have a large plastic bag? I want to protect any evidence they might have left on this," he asked her.

"I do. I have a box of gallon size double seal bags in the back room. Will that work?" Jessie went back to her storage area and got the box of bags. She handed it to Cliff.

"Perfect." He slipped the envelope and map into the bag in such a way that Sanders and the others could see it. He sealed it and looked it over. "You're right about the clue," Cliff called back as he ushered the man into the coffee shop.

They were leaving nothing to chance. They wanted the body found. Jessie had to admit a map to lead them to the body was a strange twist on the crime scene, but proof enough to her that they wanted to draw Matt out. He would go; it was his job, which gave her an unsettled feeling in the pit of her stomach as she went to check on her customer.

The club's discussion level was rising as several police cars pulled up outside her store. Dickerson and the young man walked out to meet with them. Jessie watched them pass the map around. The young man shook hands with Cliff and walked down the street. The officers got back in the cars along with Dickerson and drove away.

"Alone at last." But she couldn't help a nervous glance outside. They were right. She'd be very effective bait to lure Matt to them.

Absently, she listened to the each of the club members making their pronouncements about who they thought the murderer in the story was while she wondered why Dickerson hadn't called for a replacement.

"Hey, Jessie, I'm here. I'll be keeping tabs on you and your place." Kip stood in the open doors into Joe's.

"Okay, Kip." She breathed a sigh of relief. She should have known there was no way Matt would leave her alone. He was always watching out for her.

Chapter 37

When they got to the area shown on the crude drawing, Matt was the first to jump out of the car. Tom followed on his heels. "Wait up, I'm watching you, remember," Tom called after him.

"He's here." Matt pulled on his gloves. His killer had tied him to the tree with his arm pointing to a well-worn path off to the side of the main trail. The scene was as Jessie had described.

"Well, I'll be damned. Jessie nailed it, didn't she?" Tom took in the details Jessie had described so exactly. "He looks like a damn arrow pointing the way." Tom shook his head.

"I'm telling you, she blows my mind all the time." Matt noticed the same marks on the visible parts of the man's body that he had seen on Amir and the others. They had tortured him. He had died from a single gunshot wound to the head. Matt found a driver's license in his pocket.

"What are we looking at?" Sanders squatted down beside Matt as he looked through his wallet.

"His name is Owen Marshall. He has a badge number we need to run."

"He's a cop?" Sanders stood. "What are those marks?" He pointed to the burn marks on his arms.

"All of our victims have had them. At least we know he was murdered by the same group. The only difference is that he was shot."

"You've seen the crime scene. Let the team take over. I want Tom to get you out of the area. We'll work the scene and get the evidence to the lab."

"I'll leave for now, but tomorrow we're coming back to the area with the dog, and we're going to search for this group. They're in this area somewhere, and we need to find them."

"Are you asking me or telling me?" Sanders' brows arched.

"I'm telling you. This is still my jurisdiction, my town, and as far as I can tell, my life. I'm not sitting on the sidelines and waiting for them to come to me."

"I like your gumption, son. Today it's my way, tomorrow it's yours." He shook Matt's hand. "Now get out of here."

Tom slapped Matt on the back. "Do you have a death wish?"

"No, I have a lot of reasons I want to live, but I'm not sitting on the sidelines." He gave Tom a hard stare. "You wouldn't either, and you know it."

"You're right." Tom got in the car. "But I wouldn't get in Sander's face, either. He's in charge of the operation."

"I'm not sitting this one out, and that's final." Matt started the car.

"Calm down, I get it." Tom tapped the armrest. "We should go see Jessie. She needs to know you're all right."

Matt's eyes narrowed. "What's this?"

"I'm impressed, that's all. Jessie needs to know her description was accurate." Tom closed his eyes.

"I told you she was something special, didn't I?"

Matt glanced sideways at him.

"No wonder you've solved so many big cases. Unfair advantage, if you ask me, and you're damn lucky she can tolerate you." Tom's lips turned up at the corner, his eyes still closed. "It doesn't hurt that she's great to look at either."

"I couldn't agree with you more."

****

Roth had hoped they could grab Parker today and be done with it. No such luck! The trees shielded his hiding place. Harry had waited for almost a year. He could wait another day or two. Damn, the place was crawling with cops, all looking at the drunken, dead slug. Marshall was a greedy, lazy man, but he'd served his purpose. The task of killing Parker wasn't a job for his minions. He had a plan to take out Parker and few others with him. There was no money in this side trip for him, and his boss wouldn't be happy when he found out about it. Soon enough he—along with the rest of world—would know of their successful mission. Roth's slow smile bared his teeth. Now was for his pleasure alone.

Roth had wasted several days trying to work with the kids. Amir didn't want to play, and they all paid. Harry hit the tree with his fist.

The big job was waiting. Roth couldn't afford to mess this one up, or it would mean the ruin of his reputation. Jobs were getting harder to come by since his last fiasco—all thanks to Baz and Parker. Your track record counted, and they had wrecked his.

Time to pay, copper. He bared his teeth again.

With a little luck, he should be able to get the job done and be out of the country in the allotted time. The one thing people should never do was to underestimate him. He always paid back. No one got the best of Harry Roth. He would make them regret the day they thought they had.

He knew how to make it all happen in a big way.

Chapter 38

Matt parked the car in front of Jessie's store. She must have seen him pull up because she opened the door the minute he got out of the car.

Tom walked into the store first. "The crime scene was just as you described it."

"He's impressed," Matt said as he walked in the door. "Tom said we needed to come by and tell you."

"You nailed it." Tom plopped down in one of the chairs. He watched several people chatting as they packed up their belongings. Each one took a book stacked on the corner of the table and headed for the counter. He mouthed the words. "Who are they?"

"They're a book club that meets here monthly." Jessie went over to the counter. "You'll like this one. It's the author's newest book in the series."

"I hope we're not too noisy. We do get into our discussions with gusto," one of the women said to Jessie.

"I love it when you're here. Every bookstore should be so lucky as to have a group like yours." She placed the last club member's book in a bag and went to stand beside the chair Matt was sitting in. "What's next?"

"We'll take Radar back tomorrow and see if he can pick up their scent. They're still in the area. I'm sure of it."

"Oh, they're here all right, waiting to get their hands on you. And you'll be within their reach," Tom mumbled under his breath. "I can't talk this idiot out of doing his job."

"I'm going, too." Jessie made eye contact with Tom.

"I'm not sure that's a good idea, Jessie." Tom frowned. "I'd have to worry about both of you."

She stood straighter, planting her hands were on her hips. "I'm going."

"That's my girl. You tell him." Matt grinned at her. "You may as well give up, Tom. She'll be there if she has to follow you on the sly. Besides, I want her there."

"Thank you." She smiled at him.

"You're welcome, sweetheart. I mean it." He took hold of her hand. "Where's Kip? I thought I told him to watch you."

"He is. He's watching us now." She waved at Kip who was waving at them.

Tom stood. "I'm getting a cup of coffee and heading back to the station, which means you are, too." He walked into the coffee shop.

"Do you have your computer on?" Matt asked.

"Of course, what do you need?"

"While I go order, look up some info on this name and badge number." He handed her a piece of paper with Marshall's information. "I'll be right back."

****

Jessie looked up Owen's badge and precinct number. The poor man didn't know what he was getting into. The more she read about him, the worse she felt. How did he end up here?

"What did you find?" Matt stood at the counter.

She hadn't heard him come in. "He was close to retirement. The duty roaster lists him on vacation."

"Where's his precinct and station?" Tom asked.

"In Jersey City. I wrote them down for you." She passed the paper toward Matt.

"How did he get tied in with these guys at the end of his career?" Tom frowned. "A few months left to go and now he's dead."

"A lot of cops look for extra work. Our pension plan is adequate but isn't a lot of money." Matt folded the paper and put it in his shirt pocket. "He may have taken up tailing me as a side job, if this is the same guy."

"I'd put money on it. This is the same guy." Tom shifted his weight to the other foot.

"I agree with Tom. What I can't figure out is why he was sloppy about it. He must have followed others over the course of his career. Surely he knew how." Jessie wrote Marshall's address down on a sticky note along with the precinct phone number and captain's name. "Here." She handed it to him. "You will probably need this, too."

"He was sloppy, for sure. Maybe he didn't care if we saw him. It's possible he wanted to be caught."

"I'd like to hear your reasoning on that one." Tom reached for the bag Molly had just brought into the bookstore.

"Thanks, Molly. I'm only considering it as a possibility." Matt said. "Jess, see what else you can find. We'll be back to get you around five." Matt pointed to the bag in Tom's hand. I had to have brownies to go with the coffee. He grinned at her. "You know how it is."

"That's why I run." She smiled back at him. "See you later."

Owen Marshall must have had a drinking problem. Jessie had seen it often enough—people losing it at the end of a promising vocation. Everything they'd spent years building tumbled down around them because of their own actions. It was a scary perspective. The bell over the door rang and interrupted her thoughts.

"Hello, Jessie girl." Reba walked in. "Do you have time for tea and a chat?"

"There's nothing I'd like more." Jessie smiled at her.

"I called ahead, and Molly said she'd bring the tea and a lovely surprise when I walked in. Sit down, girl, and we'll be served." Reba waved at Molly as she carried in a tray with two steaming mugs of tea and a plate of lemon bars. "This looks delightful." Reba handed her a twenty and told her to keep the change.

Jessie wrapped her hands around the warm mug. "It feels good to sit for a moment. It's been an unusual morning around here."

"I'm sure it was. You must taste these lemon bars, dear, they are divine. Molly gets them perfect. Light, flaky, and full of lemon flavor."

Jessie took a bite. Reba was right; they were wonderful. "These are yummy." Jessie closed her eyes, savoring the flavors in her mouth.

"You look exactly how I feel when I eat them." Reba crossed her ankles. "I need to say what I've come to tell you."

Butterflies fluttered to life in her stomach. She placed her cup down on the table. "I'm ready."

"This case will be coming to a close soon. Matt

will survive, dear, so take a deep breath. It will be touch and go for a while. There are several surprises that are not easy to account for. The stress of it all will bring back something from his past. Buried deep in his heart, it will bubble to the surface. He won't be ready to share it with anyone. In time, he must face it if he is to love you as his heart wants to. When the time is right, you'll help him face it, but not until then."

"How will I know?" Jessie rested her chin in the palm of her hands.

"All I can say is, you'll know, and you won't ask the question of him until you know."

"I never know how to react to what you tell me." Jessie pursed her lips.

"It may start with this case, but it will end in another one. I'm not even sure if Matt will recognize it for what it is or try to bury it again. For now, don't worry about it. Be who you are, Jessie girl. Your love will bring him home to you, and in time, his whole heart will be yours."

They talked on a lighter note for a few minutes, and then Reba had to leave. What could she mean by *start here and end in another one?* One case at a time was enough to think about. Jessie decided to tuck it in her mind for a later day to dwell on. She forgot it altogether when she saw Darsha get out of a car across the street. Swirling around her were the ghosts of her three dead friends.

Chapter 39

"I'm surprised to see you," Jessie held the door open for Darsha. "Where's the agent who's watching you?"

"She's waiting for me in the car. I told her I needed talk with you alone for a few minutes. She is giving me ten minutes before she comes in."

"We'd better not waste any time then." Jessie motioned for her to sit. "What's up?" Jessie could see Darsha's dead friends all watching her intently.

Tears filled her eyes. "I haven't been completely honest with you. You've been so nice to me, and I am embarrassed that I lied to you. At the least, I've withheld important facts from you. I want to tell you everything first, and then you can call the police. I let you believe that our families were the problem. It's not true."

"What is the truth?" Jessie sat forward in her chair, making eye contact with her.

"I'm alive because I chose to be late that day. Amir and I had a fight and I was trying to make him pay. I saw him talking to another girl." Darsha closed her eyes. "I'm so ashamed."

"When I met Amir's family, it was easy to see that you had won their approval. They were against your relationship with their son in the beginning. But you won them over, didn't you?" Jessie smiled at her.

"Yes, I did. It makes me ashamed I led you to believe otherwise." Darsha looked away from Jessie. "Where I lived in India, there was an area of town where my parents told us never to go. I had a friend who lived there, and I didn't understand why they wouldn't let me visit her. One day after school, I went to visit my friend without their knowledge. We were sitting outside when my friend jumped up and yelled for me to get inside. I'll never forget the fear on her face. She locked up the house and closed the curtains. My friend kept peeking out the window. I asked her why she was acting so strange. She told me this story. Every few months a black limousine would drive through their neighborhood. Someone would jump out and talk to anybody they saw outside. When the car left the area several days later, there were stories of missing persons and dead bodies. The man I saw on campus recently was the same man I had seen that day when I peeked out the window at her house. I couldn't believe he was here."

"Do you know who the person in the car was?" Jessie asked.

"No, but I do know whoever it was had to be wealthy. Each time the car showed up, people received lots of cash. According to my friend, they were buying people, but I don't know why. The poor families sold relatives. Neighbors sold neighbors. It's awful to think about. I went home and never returned to the area again. A few weeks before Amir went missing there was a black limousine on campus." Darsha shuddered. "It could be nothing, but I saw a man get out of the car to talk with some young men from the group of protestors. One of those men got in his car."

"Could you describe what he looks like?"

"Yes, he's memorable, rumpled, and scary. I saw him a couple of times after that."

Jessie showed her the copies of the sketches of the suspects. "Do any of these men look familiar to you?"

"Yes." She picked out two of men in the photos.

"You need to talk to Matt. He will have more questions for you." Jessie pulled out her phone and texted Matt.

"I should have done more. My friends might still be alive."

Jessie watched Amir moving close to Darsha. She shivered. "Are you cold?"

"No, I can't explain it. I feel close to Amir at this moment and better than I have since he died. I hope this helps you solve the case."

****

Matt grabbed his coat and motioned for Tom. "Come on, babysitter. Jessie asked me to get to the store quickly. Darsha is there."

"Right behind you." Tom scrambled to his feet. "Why is she there?"

"It seems she's been holding out on us." Matt clicked his seatbelt. "Jessie befriended her, and she's willing to talk to Jessie."

"Where's the agent watching her?"

"Jessie said she's waiting in the car. She gave her ten minutes to talk to Jessie before she joins them." Tom looked at the passenger window. "I wonder what the new info is."

"We're about to find out." Matt pulled into the space in front of Jessie's store.

Darsha was waiting with the agent assigned to her.

She retold the story to Matt and Tom. "I saw a black limousine in India and now again on campus." Darsha rubbed her clammy palms with a tissue.

"Let me see if I understand you. You recognize both of these men and you saw them on campus." Matt pointed at the two pictures.

"Yes." She bit her lip.

"Do you know who the man in the limousine was?" Matt asked.

"No one did. He had to be rich, though," Darsha replied.

"My guess is that it was organ harvesting that brought this suspect to India," Tom said. "The guy in the limo was probably the one who bankrolled the operation. It's odd that a black limo would be on campus right before Amir went missing."

"It's noteworthy, but I'm still not sure how Amir's family fits into it though." Matt looked down at his notepad.

"Nothing surprises me anymore." Tom stood. "It looks like we need to question a few family members."

"My parents had no idea that I went to my friend's neighborhood, but I often wondered if they had heard the stories and that's why they wouldn't let me go there."

"We can ask to speak to Amir's father. He has diplomatic immunity. We can only go where he's willing to let us."

"Darsha, we need you to come with us. I have a few people who will want to ask you more questions," Matt told her.

"I figured you might. I want to help in any way that I can." Darsha stood.

"You two go ahead. I'll be right there," Matt said to Tom. "This may be the break we've been waiting for. With what I read the other night, I'm starting to connect the dots." He walked with Jessie to the door. "We'll talk later. I'll be back to get you in a while, sweetheart." He hugged her, rubbing his chin on the top of her head. He loved the feel of her silky hair against his skin.

"Be careful, Matt. I know these guys are closing in. They are watching for any chance to get to you."

"I'll do my best. If I can't beat them, I might have to outsmart them."

Chapter 40

Matt called the embassy and Amir's father was willing to talk. He didn't know Roth personally, but he knew someone in his country that Roth had approached about a weapons deal. The story he heard from Mr. Baz assured Matt that he was heading in the right direction. The light turned on for Matt. He knew why Roth was out to get him and now all he had to do was figure out how to trap him. Amir's father had heard through monitored chatter that Roth was searching for a group willing to do something big. He knew it was in the U.S., but he had no specifics on the job. Matt learned enough to know he was a small fish in the pond, and so were the kids. He learned more than he wanted to know. There was something to be said about being naïve about the real nature of the world around you.

Tom walked into the office and sat in the chair in front of Matt's desk. "Have we decided on the track for tomorrow for sure?"

"Yes, unless Sanders or the CIA agent has something else in mind. I've been thinking…" Matt sat forward resting his arms on his desk.

"About what?"

"It's risky, but I can't hang around waiting for them to make their next move. I think I should not only be the bait to draw our suspects out, but I should let them catch me." Matt studied the incredulous expression on Tom's face. He waited for the eruption.

"Not going to happen," Tom thundered. "Have you lost your freaking mind? I'm not stupid enough to let you go there, and neither is Sanders."

"Listen to me, if we play this right, we can trap them. They're coming for me no matter what. I may not like it, but after talking to Mr. Baz, I get it. I would prefer to have the element of surprise on our side and not theirs. Our suspects are the bottom feeders. This goes way up the food chain and far out of my jurisdiction. It's the agency's chance to stop something major from going down. Roth and his gang have apparently stopped here before going on to accomplish what they were hired to carry out."

"I get it, but it's brought all the agents who have been searching for him to Blue Cove. It seems like a risky proposition to me."

"Risky, unless you feel you control the situation, and Harry does. Look, I know I'm personal to Roth, but I don't think the kids were—except for maybe Amir. The file I was reading the other night led me to connect the dots. He was after me because of our earlier cases. The Palm Springs case led me to Amir's father and my time at the FBI. Darsha handed me another piece to the puzzle today. Mr. Baz confirmed my thoughts with some intel resource from chatter surveillance. This is big. If we can find the man in the limousine, we've found the man who can lead us to the top and reveal what Roth is in our country to do."

"I can't believe I'm saying this but tell me what you're thinking." Tom's hand drummed on the arm of the chair.

Matt told Tom what he had learned in his

conversation with the diplomat. "I think the murders of those kids and the attempt to kill me is a revenge side-story, which is chancy at best for them. I think they're making it up as they go. We're small fish, as I said before, and yes, it has alerted authorities to the fact this group is in the country. Maybe Roth wants us all here, but who knows why. He had to know killing a diplomat's son would have this effect. It's possible that killing the kids was a mistake and he's in too deep now. We need to talk to Sanders. The intel is big, and the investigation will take his department to people in high places.

"How high?" Tom asked.

"High enough." Matt wrote a few names on a paper and shoved it toward him.

Tom whistled. "Damn. Let's see how much of this Sanders already knows."

Matt spent the afternoon talking to Dickerson and Sanders. Mr. Baz had given Matt several pieces of information, which filled in a few holes in their investigation.

"The agency hasn't been able to identify the man in the limousine." Sanders wrote a note on the side of the page. "Our agents and the CIA working the case know that whenever he shows up in an area, bad things happen, and Intelligence puts him in the area. You're right, Parker, we have to do all we can to stop Roth. Let's get down to business. My big question is why does Roth want us all here?"

Matt spent the rest of the day planning and requesting more help from the county and state. Their plan was to send personnel out tonight and get them in place. They would cover the entrances and exits of the area and look for a place where the group might be staying. Matt would arrive in the morning with Tom to check the murder site. Frank and Jessie would show in time to track him. The trap was ready to set. All he could do for now was wait.

Matt and Tom left the station. The press ranks had thinned out, but even at this hour, there were still some hoping to get a jump on a headline. Tomorrow could be a big news day for them. Matt started the car as soon as Tom closed his door.

"You know, I didn't see this coming. I've been an agent with the Bureau for ten years, and I never thought I'd hear the things I heard at the meeting today. What's happening in our country? Has it always been like this, and I never saw it before? Maybe I've been sleepwalking through life." Tom rubbed his temple.

"Once I left the agency, I put it all the threats out of my mind. I no longer paid attention, I guess. I have my own world and don't think about what happens outside of it. It's too much to think of all the awful possibilities, never mind the people out to destroy what you love." Matt turned onto Main Street. "All I know is that was a sobering conversation."

"You've got that right," Tom said.

"I'm a small-town cop who fell into some big cases. I knew about some of the groups on Sanders' list from my days at the Bureau, but I had no idea there were so many. With what Mr. Baz and Sanders told me, it's downright scary."

"You heard Sanders. This could break it wide open. How many other groups are poised to take this one's place? We live in a dangerous world. Terrorists coming from the outside are hard enough to fight, but the homegrown variety coming from within are just as hard. The attacks against our institutions that have stood through the years—the Constitution, and democracy itself—pose an even greater threat to the freedoms we cherish."

"It becomes worse when those who are supposed to keep you safe are a part of the corruption." Matt pulled into the space in front of Jessie's store. "My job is hard enough." He shook his head. "I wouldn't want to work as an agent. Not after what I just heard."

"Hell, I don't want to either." Tom unhooked his seat belt. "How much of this are you going to tell her?" Tom asked as he opened the car door.

"Only what's on tap for tomorrow. That will be more than enough for Jessie to think about without getting overwhelmed." Matt followed Tom into Jessie's store.

****

Jessie was checking out her final customer when they walked in. Matt looked tired. The case and the personal danger were starting to take a toll on him. "Hard day?" Jessie placed her hand on his shoulder when he sat.

"You could say that." Matt reached for her hand.

"I could use something to eat. We forgot to eat lunch earlier." Tom paced like a caged animal ready to pounce.

"What is up with you two?" Jessie leaned her hip against the arm of Matt's chair.

"I've got a lot on my mind." Tom walked into the coffee shop.

"Is he okay?" Jessie couldn't take her eyes off Tom's jerky gait.

"I'll explain later." Matt got to his feet. "Are you about ready to leave?"

"I will be in a few minutes." Jessie got busy with her closing routine. She couldn't help but notice Tom pacing back and forth between the two businesses. What was wrong with him? She locked the money in the safe, closed the storeroom door, and shut off the lights. "I'm ready." She pulled the doors shut as soon as Tom popped back in.

"Let's eat." Tom held the door open for her.

"Frank made us dinner." Matt locked the store for her.

"I don't care where we eat, just so there's food."

"Tom, I have to admit that you've got me worried. I've never seen you like this." Jessie got in the back seat and clicked her seat belt.

"You're not going to like what Matt has to tell you. Hell, I don't like it, and I can't believe we all agreed it was the thing to do. I think we've all lost our damn minds. I'll leave it to you to talk some sense into us."

"Well, if I wasn't worried before, I am now." Jessie caught Matt's eye in the mirror. "Matt, what's this all about?"

"I'm not going to rush into it, now. We'll talk after dinner and go over the case like we normally do."

"Good call. Put it off as long as you can because there's no way she will see your point on this one." Tom's fist curled in his lap.

"Jess is more courageous than you give her credit for, Tom. If you remember, she was the bait in our last case. You even encouraged her to do it. I'm willing to listen to her, and I know she will know what the right thing to do is."

"I'm still here. I can hear your conversation." Jessie rolled her eyes at them. "What you're not telling me is that Matt is going set a trap for the suspects using himself as the bait."

"Well, I'll be damned." Tom turned in his seat to look at her.

"Do I like the idea? Of course not." She saw Tom direct a sly *I told you so* look at Matt. "He didn't like the many times I suggested I do it, either. Matt's thinking like the great cop that he is. He sees it as his chance to take these dangerous criminals out, and I'll do all I can to support him, even if I'm worried."

"Jess, I appreciate your faith in me. I'll give you all the details and answer any questions you might have."

"Do I get to lecture you about the risk and all the things that could go wrong while we're talking?" She caught the upturn of his lips in the mirror. "It's only fair."

"Sure, sweetheart, you can lecture all you want. It's your turn." He winked at her.

Chapter 41

Jessie's heart wasn't into lecturing him. A queasy feeling came over her just thinking about what Matt had told her. It was a risky plan, and plenty could go wrong, but she understood why Matt wanted to do it. The atmosphere was charged. Tom was detailing every worst-case scenario his mind could conjure up while Frank observed. His eyes traveled back and forth between the two men as if he was watching a tennis match. Jessie knew the feeling. She didn't know who to watch as the argument escalated. From past cases, she understood this was Matt's way of working off the tension.

"Jessie, are you going to sit there and say nothing? You of all people should care what happens to him." Tom stopped his angry pacing and finally plopped down in a chair. He stretched his long frame out, staring at her with a frown on his face.

"First of all, can I say I find it strange you were willing to send me out as bait to get the serial killer, but you're resisting Matt's similar reasoning. It has me wondering why." Jessie waited for his reaction."

"That was different." Tom jumped to his feet, his face reddening.

"How?" she quietly asked him.

"You aren't making any sense, and you know it," Matt snapped. "I'm a cop, she's a citizen. It was far more dangerous for her." Tom moved toward Matt, his fist clenched.

Jessie stepped between them. "I may be wrong, but I think you're both acting foolish. I get it—you're tense, but you're both smarter than this. You have a chance to solve the murder of those kids and give their families closure. You're doing your job. Besides, I think it will be okay." She pivoted to look at Tom, pointing her finger at his chest. "You're a team." She'd have plenty of time to worry later.

"That's good enough for me. I trust your instinct. If you're okay with it, then so am I, sweetheart." Matt turned her to face him. "Sorry." He kissed her forehead.

"Yeah, I'm sorry, too." Tom relaxed his stance.

"I know how he gets," Jessie told him, pointing at Matt, "but it's definitely more intense with two of you in the room at one time."

"I thought the neighbors might call the police," Frank joked with them. "If you've calmed down, I'd like to go over the plans again. I want to make sure I know what you want from us."

Matt went over the plans with Frank and Jessie. Radar was a critical part of getting him out of this alive. "That about covers it. Any questions?"

"I'm good." Frank stood. "I need to turn in early, so I'll be fresh for tomorrow. Come on, Radar, you need to go out one more time." The dog stretched and followed Frank out the front door.

Tom grabbed the remote and turned on the TV. "Do you mind? I have to keep busy or I'll be in your face again."

Matt shook his head. "Not me." He led Jessie into the kitchen. "Are you okay with all of this?"

"I am." She noticed his skeptical look. "Of course I'm nervous. I know there's always a risk, as you've told me often enough." The knot was getting bigger in her stomach.

"We owe it to those kids to do all we can to bring their killers to justice." Matt reached for her hand. "And we don't know what their next target is after this. Something big, the D.C. crowd thinks." He frowned. "A lot of lives could be at stake."

"I agree, but I wish we could do it without putting your life in jeopardy."

"I can't sit by and do nothing. Roth's men are coming after me anyway. I may as well give them all the trouble they can handle." He handed her two glasses filled with ice. "There's some tea in the fridge."

Jessie filled the glasses. "I keep thinking I'm missing something. Maybe they're in the woods where Marshall was found, or maybe they moved on. Then what?"

"They'll come to us. I'm sure of it. Roth will not leave the area without trying to get me."

Her apprehension level went up a notch. "Tom, do you want some iced tea?" Jessie asked.

"Yeah, sounds good."

Jessie gave Matt a gentle nudge. "Go watch your scores and take your mind off this stuff."

"I'll go if you'll join me for a while." He carried the glass of tea with him and handed it to Tom.

She nodded. "I'll be right there." Jessie put the tea in the fridge. Why couldn't she shake this apprehension? She twisted a lock of her hair. Something was up. She walked into the living room.

Matt grabbed her when she walked by and pulled

her onto his lap. "I want you close," he whispered in her ear.

"Fine with me." She snuggled against his chest.

When Jessie finally went to bed, she left Matt sitting in his recliner talking to Tom. Reluctant to leave him, she stopped in the hall to listen to the sound of his voice. Taking her time, she walked toward the room. He would be okay. He had to be. There was no doubt in her mind that he would survive, and the police would capture the suspects. Was she naïve? The big question was at what cost for Matt? She looked upward. "Please, keep him safe."

A cool, clammy feeling washed over her. The ghosts were here in the house. They had never ventured inside before, at least not that she knew of. Her uneasiness grew as Amir appeared outside the door to her room. The time had to be getting close. She forced herself to remain where she was and not retreat back to the living room. A cool mist swirled around her. All three of them were watching her. She shivered and rubbed her arms

"Are you here to help? He'll need you." She moved closer. Amir shifted in front of the door, his ghostly arms in front of his chest. "I hope you realize we are the good guys," she muttered under her breath. "Carlos is alive. Matt saved his life. It was touch and go for a while, but he's going to make it." She rambled on, making no sense even to herself.

"Who are you talking to, Jess?" Matt called out to her.

"Only myself. Goodnight, Matt." She walked into the room, followed by her three spirit friends.

"Goodnight, sweetheart," Matt called after her.

Jessie closed the door and sat on the edge of the bed. She couldn't see them, but she knew they were still there. "Are you friendly?" Jessie fought the desire to climb into bed and pull the covers over her head. "You have to watch him for me. I saw you in my dreams. You were with him in the woods. You must be here to help him. At least I hope you are," she whispered. Instead of cowering, she pulled out her laptop. Jessie concentrated on the next segment of their story. The end would come with the capture of the suspects.

It seemed as if only moments had passed when she lifted her head and realized that the house was nighttime silent. How long had she been typing? A quick glance at the clock told her it was after ten. She stretched her arms, wiggling her fingers. Still dressed, she pulled back the covers, leaned her back against the headboard, and closed her eyes. It seemed as if no time had passed when she opened them again and sat up. Something wasn't right—it was—all wrong! She forced herself to stay still.

****

If he were honest, his mind was giving him more than he could handle. Jessie had gone to bed a while ago, and here he was, wide awake. Arms stacked behind his head, Matt leaned against the smooth leather of the recliner. She had reassured him several times during the evening that he would get through this fine. Still, he was concerned about what he'd face before he got to the fine part. Having seen those kids, Matt knew it wouldn't be a picnic if Roth had any say in the matter. Their plan had to work like a well-oiled machine, which didn't often happen in his line of work. How many times had he almost lost Jess? *Consider all*

the possibilities and try to anticipate the surprises.
What surprises could Roth have at his disposal?

He couldn't let it be Jessie. His heart was only beginning to open to love again. One of his greatest fears was his job would come back to haunt him or his loved ones.

He needed sleep. Tomorrow could be a long day. Matt closed his eyes, his body relaxed, and finally, his mind was quiet. He dozed.

"Don't move." A chilling voice whispered in his ear as he struggled out of sleep. The cold steel pressed against his head. A rag covered his mouth and nose. He fought to pull it away. Radar wasn't barking. His consciousness was slipping away. Why hadn't the others heard? Had they killed them all?

Chapter 42

Jessie jumped out of bed glancing at the clock on her way to the door. Twelve-thirty; she hadn't slept long. The house was too quiet, panic rising like bile in her throat. Rushing across the hall, she knocked on Matt's door, pushing it open when he didn't answer. He wasn't in his bed. She ran to the living room, her heart racing. His chair was empty. "Matt," she yelled. The room was dark and silent.

"What the hell?" Tom came out of the room rubbing his eyes. Light flooded the hallway. "Jessie, what's wrong?"

"Matt's gone." She raced down the hall to Frank's room.

"What do you mean gone?" Tom shouted. He followed, hot on her heels.

"You know what I mean. Gone, Matt's gone, they've kidnapped him." Jessie banged on Frank's door. She heard Frank stir. "Frank, wake up."

"Gone? How in the hell did they get in here without us hearing them? Radar should have heard something." Tom reached for her hand before she could hit the door again. "Get a hold of yourself. We can't lose our heads."

"What's the matter?" Frank sounded groggy when he opened the door.

"They've got Matt." Jessie gulped back the scream

rising in her throat.

"No way. Radar would have heard it." Frank looked at the sleeping dog.

"He's not rousing, even with me banging on the door. Could he have been drugged?"

"You're right, he's too quiet." Frank squatted next to Radar. "He's alive, but he's not stirring."

"Damn, we need him, too." Tom phoned Sanders.

"How?" Jessie asked Frank.

"He must have found some drugged food outside when I took him out earlier." Frank rubbed Radar's fur and talked to him. Jessie was the first one to see his tail thump against the floor when he heard Frank's voice. "Are you okay, fella?" He placed some water in front of him, and the drowsy dog lapped a small amount.

"That's the only way they could get past Radar." Jessie paced. "How will we ever find Matt without the dog's help?" She brushed away the tears that were starting to gather. "I knew when I awakened that something was wrong."

"We'll find him." Tom stood behind her and placed his arm around her shoulder. "Sanders phoned the local veterinarian on call. I received a text that the vet is on the way to check on Radar. Get dressed and ready to go. As soon as the dog is able, we're heading out."

Happy that Tom was taking charge, Jessie changed into clothes and ran a brush through hair. Grabbing the gun off the dresser along with her badge, she shoved them into her jacket. The vet was in with Radar as she passed by the open door. He had to be okay. They'd never find Matt without him. Hands fisted at her side she walked into the kitchen and went through the motions of making a pot of coffee, "Darn," She fumbled with the lid on the canister. Suddenly coffee grounds flew in all directions and the tears streamed down her cheeks. Pouring coffee into the filter, she didn't bother to measure. Had she added enough water? The coffee seemed way too dark to her as it dripped down into the pot. Matt was in danger, and they were wasting time. He was probably being tortured right at this moment, the way the kids had been. Her dream was coming true. He needed help, and she couldn't get to him. She curled her hand into a fist and spun around as Tom's voice startled her.

"Radar is going to be fine." Tom came into the kitchen. "The doc thinks they placed a sleeping pill in a chunk of hamburger or something that the dog ate. Radar is moving around. He's a little groggy, but he's moving." Tom saw her wipe her eyes. "Jessie, what the hell?"

"Matt's life is in danger. Every minute counts, and here we stand. They're getting away. Don't get me wrong, I'm thankful Radar is okay. He's not only a valuable dog, he's Frank's friend. I wish we could give him time to recover, but Radar's the only one that can lead us to where they've taken Matt. I feel so helpless." She pushed away from the counter and began to pace.

"We'll find Matt." He poured cream into his coffee and spit it out in the sink after the first sip "They're working the dog outside to see how he's doing. They have one of Matt's shirts. We'll know soon if he can track. Frank had Radar out last night before ten, so the vet seems to think the drug should be wearing off soon."

"Let's hope. I've seen what those men are capable of." Jessie gulped back the sob inching its way up her throat. She walked back to the bedroom and leaned her forehead against the wall. "Matt, I'm sending you my thoughts. We're coming, sweetheart. You'll know what to do. Amir, Ryan, and Shara are with you. Roth may have surprised us, but we have a few surprises of our own. Come back to me, please come back."

"Jessie, it's a go. Let's roll!" Tom shouted at her. "We still have a couple of hours before daylight."

"I'm ready." She followed him out the door.

When Tom turned on Main Street, he stopped, and Frank took Radar out of the car to see if could track which direction the car carrying Matt had left town. He picked up the scent, and they followed the route. Several times, Radar's tracking ability assured them that they were heading in the right direction. The final turn took them to a heavily wooded area a few miles from where they had found Owen Marshall. Tom called in their location and Sanders and a few others were a few miles from the targeted area and on their way. Radar was fully awake and ready to go.

Jessie moved away from Tom and Frank. Matt was somewhere out there in the darkness. She was sure of it. The thought sent shivers running up and down her spine. He was calling her name.

****

Matt's eyes opened. What happened? Struggling to recall any small detail, he reached his hand toward his pounding head. The vehicle stopped suddenly, and he braced himself to keep from slamming into the side of the van. "Damn," he groaned, his heart racing. Two voices were talking, but he couldn't understand a word. The door opened, and hands reached to pull him out. Yanking his arms behind his back, one of the men pushed Matt against the side of the van while the other tied his wrists. Fighting to keep his eyes open, Matt took a quick survey of his surroundings. There were two men, and they were armed. No landmark was recognizable; the bag seemed to descend over his head in slow motion until the light of the moon went out. Darkness settled over him. Surprise—all their planning now meant nothing. His shaky legs fought to hold him upright. Despair crept into his mind, but he fought it, holding on to a glimmer of hope in Jessie's words. He would be all right.

Was she still alive? Fear clutched him as he remembered the silent house...

A shove in his back caused him to stumble and fall. The men argued as one of them hauled him to his feet. How far had he walked? Suspended animation, slow motion, his brain was foggy, and his feet felt as if they were encased in concrete. They came to an abrupt stop just as his legs buckled. A door opened, and the men grabbed him under the arms and carried him inside, dropping him on the cold ground. Tension filled his body. A heated exchange passed between his abductors, and then a few well-placed kicks to his back and stomach left him writhing on the floor. Matt curled on his side and waited for the next blow. A few more curses and blows to his head and side followed. Footsteps grew distant and silence fell. Yet he knew he wasn't alone.

"We meet at last, Parker." The man's raspy voice broke the silence.

"Who are you?" The bag muffled his words.

"My secret for now. All you need to know is it will be a pleasure to watch you die."

"Roth," Matt mumbled. "This must be my lucky night," he added sarcastically.

"So my fame precedes me."

"I wouldn't call it fame—more like a failure." Matt felt cold steel against his leg. The first jolt hit him, and the pain ripped through him for an eternity, finally releasing him and leaving him limp. He couldn't stop the groan that burst from his mouth.

"I thought you might enjoy a small demonstration of what those kids went through and what you have to look forward to. We'll be in no hurry." He chuckled. "I'll leave you to your thoughts." Roth's sinister laugh could still be heard after the door slammed.

Matt was alone. Acid surged into his throat, and he almost vomited. His hands were sweating. His wrists ached from the wires that bound him. It didn't stop him from working to free his hands. There was zero chance of survival if he didn't get them free. He pictured how Lewis had removed the binding from the victims' hands. The wire gave a little. He moved them back and forth, the sweat lubricating his wrists. He gulped, holding his stomach at bay. How had they got to him? He didn't want to travel the road where his thoughts were trying to take him. She couldn't be dead. One girl he had loved had already died. He couldn't lose another. He loved her too much. *Jessie!* His fingers found the twists in the wire, and he worked to unwind them. What was the strange sound? Ringing in his ears? Man, everything hurt, but he kept working at it. *Hurry, Matt.* Hope was the sound of her voice in the distance. Jessie was coming, and he wanted to live.

Chapter 43

It was her dream all over again, only she was living in it. The fog swirled among the trees and hovered along the ground like an evil mist; the full moon cast its eerie light through the woods, giving enough illumination to see the treetops swaying in the wind. She didn't recognize the area. Apprehension gripped her. Trees and fog seemed to go hand in hand to make the darkness scarier. She stood on the edge of the woods waiting, wanting to go in but equally not wanting to. Matt was in there, no doubt about it. Jessie pulled her jacket tightly around her as chills raced down her spine.

"What do you think? You're so quiet." Frank walked up beside her.

"I know he's in there." She pointed into the woods. "I want to help, but I have no idea what to do."

"We all want to help, and we'll do our best to get him out safely." Frank patted her arm. "I can't believe they were able to abduct him without us hearing. Matt isn't a small man. They drugged him; that's obvious, but they still had to move him. We should have heard something." Frank shook his head.

"We didn't though, and that *why* may never be answered." Jessie leaned against the front of the car. I saw the ghosts last night. They were at the house."

"Matt's house? Have they ever been there before?"

Frank asked.

"No, not that I know of."

"I wonder why they were there last night." Frank turned at the sound of the approaching car.

"You and me both. I don't know them well enough to know if they're around to help or to cause problems."

"One question I can't answer and know nothing about. Looks like reinforcements are here, and we'll be starting soon. I'd better get Radar ready." He turned to walk away.

"Is he okay?"

"More alert as time passes. He'll be ready to find Matt. Radar likes him."

"I'm happy he does." Jessie followed Frank over to the group of men standing near Dylan's cruiser. They had a map out, and several flashlights were shining on it.

"How are you holding up?" Dylan squeezed her hand. "Matt knows what he's doing. He has great instincts."

Jessie gave him a wan smile. "Yes, he does."

"Kip sent me a text message. This is where the old abandoned flour mill is." Dylan pointed to the area on the map. "We're looking at about five to seven miles on foot. We can't drive in, or we'll alert them and take away the element of surprise."

"We walk in pairs and spread out across this area." Sander's hand moved across the area on the map. "They might be with him or watching us right now. Be careful and look out for your partner. With any luck, we'll surprise them the same way they did us. If you see anything, call it in. You all have your radios."

Frank put the line on Radar. He bent down in front

of him with Matt's shirt. "Find our friend, fella. Let's get to work." Frank followed his dog, and Jessie and Dylan walked with him, guns ready.

After walking a few miles, Jessie saw Amir straight ahead. Towering above him moved a magnificent creature of light. Amir's hands rose to halt them. The angel flew back and forth blocking their entry deeper into the woods. "Something's up. We aren't supposed to move forward."

"What do you mean? We have to keep moving. Matt's in there." Dylan gave her a puzzled look.

She explained about Amir, leaving out a few details. "It's a warning to stay where we're at. Matt would get it, but I don't know how to tell the others."

Dylan called Sanders and explained what Jessie had told him. "What should we do? It's your call, sir."

"We'll wait." Sanders put the call out on the radio to the others to hold in place until the all clear was given.

****

Matt worked his hands free. It was almost as if someone had loosened the wires, but how could that be? Jessie had said the same thing to him in their last case. Damn, it was chilly. He rubbed his arms. Lifting the bag from his head, he squinted around the dark room. Faint moonlight filtered in through the cracks between the boards that had been nailed over the windows, and a thick shaft jutted down from the ceiling to end above a broken circular stone nearly three feet across. The old Cove Gristmill. He knew it. As a kid, he and his best friend Chad had explored this place many times. He pushed up slowly from the floor. His legs were shaky, and he stumbled several times on his way to the hidden door Chad had discovered years ago. He hoped it was still there.

The pain in his side was terrible. His body trembled, but his mind screamed for him to get out quickly. The humming sound was louder. Matt rubbed his forehead. The ache in his head didn't help. What was that sound? He should know it. He searched his memory in vain. Pain racked his body with each step. Instinct told him to get away from the mill and stay hidden but remain close enough to see them when they returned. Where had his captors gone, and why had they left him alone? He found the place where the plank siding of the mill was rotted and loose and slipped through it into the overgrown brush around the building. *Think, Matt.* Either Roth was stupid, or he was walking into a trap. He closed his eyes for a moment. It wasn't making any sense. If Harry wanted him dead, he would be dead already. The delay was for a reason.

Matt hunched down behind some bushes. By now, Sanders and the rest should be looking for him.

Unless they'd moved back for safety...

Hell! He jumped up to run. The explosion knocked him off his feet and rained pieces of the gristmill down on him, covering him with debris. In slow motion, his life marched in front of him. His past flittered like a ghost through his mind and crumbled into the brilliant light around him. Fear and worry dissolved into peace and that's when he saw the beautiful creature. He must be dead. If this was heaven, why did he feel like hell?

****

The ground moved beneath their feet, and a fireball brightened the early morning sky. "My God, we would have all been there when it blew," Sanders called to

Dylan over the radio. "Let's move in with caution. Watch for our suspects in the area. Keep your eyes out for Matt. I'm not holding out much hope, but you don't need to tell her I said that."

Jessie was stunned. He was there. An anguished cry escaped her lips before she could stop it. "Matt." She took off running.

Dylan caught up with her, grabbed her, and held her to his chest. "You can't run in there Jessie. The suspects are waiting to pick us off. Use your head. You would know if Matt were dead. What is your heart telling you?"

"I don't know." She shook her head. "How could he survive? You can still see the fire from here." Jessie fought to hold herself together.

"In your dream, did he die?" Dylan asked her.

"No, but there was no explosion either." The wail of sirens was getting closer. Sanders had called in the blast.

"Listen with your heart. Matt is stronger than you think." Dylan gave her a gentle nudge. "Let's go find Matt. But carefully!"

Dylan was right. Matt was still alive, and they had to find him. He could be injured. The acrid smell of the burning wood mixed with the stink of sulfur was strong in the air. Thick black smoke made the night seem darker.

"Will Radar be able to pick up Matt's scent with all the smoke in the air?" she asked* Frank.

"I don't know." Frank shook his head. "We'll see how he does as we get closer. We'll find him, Jessie, don't worry."

Dylan motioned for them to stop. "There's a

vehicle ahead. Stay back." The agents checked it out and gave them the all clear. Two agents remained with the van in case the suspects returned.

After walking several minutes more, they rounded a curve. Ahead, it looked like a war zone. What was left of the mill smoldered, and small fires burned among the broken boards. Shattered timbers and shingles littered the ground. How could he have survived? Roth had expected them all to be killed in the blast, Jessie was sure of it. He would have taken out Matt along with Sanders, Dickerson, and those who had been tracking him if Amir and the angel hadn't stopped them.

The angel and Amir had saved them. Jessie stopped. The scene in front of her was overwhelming. The air was oppressive, and there was an eerie silence except for the crackle of the burning building. Then, gunfire erupted, and Jessie dove for cover.

Chapter 44

Matt opened his eyes. The sound of gunfire was too close for comfort. The blast had sent him flying, and things were still a blur. Could he sit? He pushed rubble off his upper torso and managed to lift his body into a sitting position. He cleared the debris off his legs and moved them. They worked, but whether they would hold him upright was another question. He would know soon enough. Damn, everything hurt. Each breath was agony. He crawled over to a nearby tree. Holding on to the trunk, he pulled himself to a standing position with his one good arm. The pain that hit him made him briefly dizzy. Something had broken for sure. He rubbed his eyes with his good hand and blinked, trying to clear the image. The light temporarily blinded him.

Rapid pops of gunfire erupted. It was close, too close. Matt took cover behind the tree. He grabbed a wooden slat from the ground and used it as a crutch. The tree helped to hold him upright. He could see a shadowy figure running toward him. The man fired off a round as he ran.

If only he would come a little closer. *Come on, man, just a little more.* Matt waited, bracing himself against the tree and swung the plank full strength like he was swinging for a home run. It cracked against the shooter's head with the solid sound of a base hit, and the man staggered to his knees. Slamming the man's hand against the tree with what little strength he had left, Matt grabbed the gun and held it on him. A few more bursts of gunfire sounded before it was silent.

"Don't move." The man froze on hands and knees. "I'd be happy to shoot you for what you've put me through tonight."

"Hell, you're supposed to be dead." The man lifted his face to look at him.

"You move again, and you will be." Matt couldn't see the man's face in the shadows, but from his size, he was sure it was Roth. "This night might turn out okay after all." He bared his teeth in a grin. Give me just one reason not to shoot you." He hoped someone got here soon; he wasn't sure how much longer he could stand.

"You'll never make it. I can see you sweating." Roth laughed hoarsely.

"Shut the hell up." Matt's legs were shaking. "If I go down, you'll die first." His shoulders wanted to sag, and the hand holding the gun trembled.

Radar rounded the tree, pulling Frank with him. "Matt's over here. Jessie, over here."

"Hi, big fella, help me keep an eye on him." The dog growled at Roth and Matt handed the gun to Frank before his legs buckled. Jessie tried to soften his impact as he dropped hard to his knees and knelt beside him.

"Hi, sweetheart; it's good to see you." He grimaced as fresh pain spiked through him. "I wasn't sure if I'd ever see you again."

"I never doubted you for a minute." She brushed the tears from her eyes. "It's all in night's work for you. I see you got your man."

"I did. Hold me, would you?" His head dropped back against her arms. Jessie saw the light moving in and around Matt as she held him. He would live.

"Frank, where are you?" Dylan called out.

"Over here, we need some handcuffs and an ambulance." Frank waved to him. "Matt's alive, and he captured one of the suspects."

"I'll be damned." Dylan cuffed Roth. He radioed Sanders to tell him the news. "How are you?" He squatted down beside Matt.

"I've been better, but I'm glad you're all here." Matt closed his eyes. "Take care of this scum, will you? I can't wait to question him." Matt squeezed Jessie's hand. "What happened to the rest of them?"

"Three are dead, and Sanders has the other one." Dylan motioned for the paramedic.

"Let's take a look at you, Chief." One of the medics held a light while the other inserted a drip line. "We'll get you on your feet in no time, sir. The hard part will be to get you out of here to the ambulance." Several of the officers lined up to help.

****

By the time, Jessie had talked to the doctor and gotten to his room, Matt was sound asleep. She pulled the chair over by his bed and laced her fingers through his. He didn't stir, and she didn't want to let go. "I came close to losing you." Her eyes roamed over the contours of his face, and her finger traced his lip with a feather touch. "I don't know how you survived." Jessie kissed his forehead. "A narrow escape is how the doctor described it." She sighed. "How did you do it, sweetheart?" she whispered.

Frank and Dylan walked into the room. "No ordinary day at the office," Dylan said. "How is he?"

"Sleeping and hasn't stirred. Did you talk to the

doctor?" Jessie glanced at them.

"Yes. The doctor wants to keep him for a couple of days. I already know he's going to fight it. He'll want to question Roth. He's lucky to be alive, and we'll make him stay put." Dylan leaned against the wall.

"What else did he tell you?"

"He has a couple of busted ribs and a broken collarbone. Painful, but not life threatening."

Jessie winced. "Painful is right. Is there anything else?"

"He had one blow too many to his head this week. He has a concussion and will have a nasty headache for a few days. With his proximity to the blast, his hearing might be jacked up for a while. Add to all that the bruises and cuts from falling debris—you can see where I'm going with this."

"I can. I'm grateful he's still with me." She glanced at his sleeping face. "Where's Tom?"

"He's at the station with Sanders. Tom still can't believe they got in Matt's house to get him."

"None of us know how they did it without one of us hearing him," Jessie replied.

"Roth hasn't said much, but the other guy is singing like crazy. We had to get an interpreter. Once he got to the station, the suspect said plenty."

"What have you learned so far?" Jessie asked.

"The idea was to use Matt as the bait to get the agents tracking them to the mill in time for the bomb to go off while they were near. They never thought Matt would get away—he was in a bad way when they left him."

"They didn't account for Amir stopping us from moving forward."

"True, And the suspect said that some really scary things happened to them in the woods. I guess that's why he's talking. He's afraid those *demons* are going to come after him again. The man was freaked. Honestly, I can't wait to hear the rest of the story." Dylan checked his text messages.

"Sounds like our ghostly friends helped." Jessie yawned. "I still wonder how they were able to carry Matt out of the house without us hearing them."

"The suspect was surprised no one put up a fight. They were ready to start shooting if anyone came out of their room." Dylan shifted from one foot to the other. "The one having the hardest time is Tom. He thinks he blew his assignment, and there's no talking him out of it."

"Maybe we weren't meant to hear. One or all of us would be dead if we had." She ran her hand through her hair. She had no idea if it was a mess. "How's Radar?"

"He's good to go. Matt's face lit up when he saw Radar. Matt was about done, and we arrived right on time." Frank rubbed his chin.

"I'm going take Frank back to get some rest. Tell Matt that his theory is proving to be right. We're only beginning to scratch the surface of their main plan." Dylan squeezed her shoulder. "I'll be back later, if you want to go home to rest."

"I'm not leaving. I want to be here when he opens his eyes." Jessie walked them to the door.

"I figured you might. The doctor ordered something for pain and sleep. He's going to be all right." Dylan gave her a brief hug.

"I know, but it was close, and I don't want to let him out of my sight for a while. Be sure to fill Katie in on the details. I turned my phone off." Jessie went back to Matt's bedside.

"I'll take care of it."

The nurses checked his temperature and blood pressure with the change of the hospital shifts, and Matt slept through it all. At some point, Jessie did, too.

****

"Good morning, beautiful." His hand pushed her hair out her face. "You didn't need to stay here all night, but it was nice to open my eyes and see you."

"I must look a mess." She attempted to straighten herself.

"Well, that would depend on how you define mess." He grinned. "You're one mess I wouldn't mind waking up next to every morning." He reached for her hand. "Could you kiss me? My movements are a little clumsy and tend to make me groan."

"I'd be honored to." She leaned over him and kissed him, careful not to bump him.

"You call that a kiss?" He wrapped his good arm around her and pulled her close. "I want a real kiss." He proceeded to show her. "Now, I'm good."

She blushed, fanning her face. "You're something, to coin a phrase from you. How do you have the energy?"

"I'm alive, and happy to be. You haven't seen anything yet. If you don't want to embarrass a nurse when she walks in on us, you'd better go home and come back rested. I have plenty of surprise moves. I'm alive, in love, and damn happy to see you."

Jessie smiled. "I'm happy to see you, too." She kissed him again.

"I don't want to put a kibosh on this heartwarming

scene, but you're about to be joined by several agents and officers." Dylan chuckled as he stuck his head in the door. "Although I was touched by the display, they might razz you a bit."

"See you later." Jessie grabbed her phone and left the hospital room.

"She's a keeper." Dylan sat in the chair by Matt.

"She is what kept me going last night." Matt glanced at his friend's face. "I know you get it."

"I do." Dylan tugged on the collar of his shirt.

Matt adjusted his position and groaned. "I swear last night I had help getting my hands free."

"You're going to hear many things in the next hour that boggle the mind."

"Like what?" Matt studied his friend's face.

"We would have all been at the mill when the bomb went off, but Jessie saw Amir ahead of us giving a sign not to move forward. I know there's more to the story, but she's not telling it. And Sanders let her stop us. Good thing! I'm still shaking my head over that one, and it's the tip of the iceberg. Eat your breakfast." Dylan stood as the nurse brought in his tray. "You'll need your strength for what you're about to hear." He gave Matt a mock salute. "I'll be back. I need to grab some coffee."

"Before you leave, thanks for keeping Jessie safe for me. I never realized until last night how afraid I've been of losing her."

"We all had someone looking out for us last night. Now get better so you can marry that girl." Dylan chuckled and left the room.

Matt finished his breakfast and laid his head back. No one needed to tell him it had been a strange night.

He was alive, and he couldn't begin to describe what had happened to keep him in one piece. He didn't know how the kids had endured all the times the weapon had been used on them and whatever else was done to them. He winced when he changed positions. All he knew was that the strength to keep fighting had come from deep inside him. Reba was right—it had been there when he needed it.

Chapter 45

A nap, shower, a fresh set of clothes, and she was ready to go. Audrey was at the store, one less thing for her worry about. She wanted to spend the afternoon with Matt. She twisted the ring on her finger. He had told her she'd beg him to marry her. She smiled at the memory. "No, Mr. Parker, I believe you'll be begging me, and the way I feel, you won't have to beg for long."

Jessie ran by the store to check on things. "How's it going, Audrey?"

"Steady, which is nice. I had another call from a book club that would like to meet here. I told them you'd have to check the calendar and would get back to them. The name and number are on the pad near the phone."

"I love the idea of book clubs meeting here. It keeps the place filled with people and conversation. I think it gives business to Molly, too." Jessie tore the page with the phone number, off the notepad. "I'll call them later."

"Sounds good. By the way, how's Matt? It's all everybody is talking about this morning."

"He's banged up, has some broken ribs and collarbone, and is fortunate to be alive." Jessie's eyes got misty. "As soon as I have lunch, I'm headed to the hospital. When I left earlier, he was waiting for the agents and his officers to arrive for a meeting. It's hard for him not to be involved." Jessie walked through the open doors into the coffee shop.

Audrey followed her. "He's a great chief of police."

"You won't get any argument from me. I think he's the best." Jessie smiled. "If you need anything, you can call. I'll have my phone with me." Jessie walked into the coffee shop

"I will. Tell Matt I said hi, and I hope he feels better real soon." Audrey waved at Molly.

"Jessie, what a pleasant surprise. What can I get you?" Molly asked.

"I want a bowl of your broccoli soup, and I'll take six of the brownies Matt likes, to go."

"Do you want the soup to go?"

"No, I'll eat it here." Jessie gave Molly a twenty and waited for change.

"I didn't expect to see you here today. I thought you'd be at the hospital."

"I was there overnight. I'm headed back as soon as I finish eating. I thought I'd take Matt a treat while I'm at it."

"How's he doing? Better yet, how are you doing?" Molly squeezed her hand.

"He's hurting, but it could have been so much worse. Let's just say I'm happy to have him with us today." Jessie put a few dollars in the tip jar.

Molly handed Jessie a tray with the soup and a slice of thick crusty bread on it. "Do you want something to drink?"

"Water with lemon would be nice."

"Go sit down. I'll bring the rest to your table. I want to hear all the details."

Jessie recounted the events of the past several hours to Molly. "We're all fortunate to be here today. The suspects had some diabolic plans to kill as many law enforcement officials as they could."

"It scares me to think of Kenny in this line of work. Blue Cove always seemed like such an idyllic sort of town. I can't believe all this stuff is happening here." Molly toyed with a lock of her hair.

"These guys didn't originate in our town. They were passing through to kill Matt on their way to some other dastardly deed they were planning. I guess we'll know soon enough what that was." Jessie took a taste of her soup. "Oh, Molly, this is so good. I'm hungrier than I thought." Jessie buttered her bread and took a bite.

"Enjoy. I have a special treat for dessert, and you're going to eat it. Something tells me you haven't eaten in a while. Am I right?" Molly stood.

"You're right, the past twenty some hours has been a bit of a blur. I was too worried about Matt to leave his side; no wonder I'm so hungry." Jessie spooned up more soup.

Molly brought a cup of tea and a hot blueberry turnover over to the table. "I want you to eat every bite. Look, there's Reba." Molly waved at her. "I'll bring your tea to the table, Reba."

"Thank you, Molly dear." Reba arranged herself in the chair, crossing her ankles as she sat. "Well, girl, our fine chief of police got through his ordeal with flying colors, didn't he?"

"He did." Jessie wiped her mouth with her napkin.

"Word is, he's a hero. He managed to capture one of the suspects even while injured." Reba stirred sugar into her tea.

"No exaggeration, he's a hero." The first bite of her blueberry turnover was perfect. "It was as you said—he was tried, but he found a way on his own to survive."

"Not entirely alone." Reba winked at her. "He had help, but I'm not sure he's ready to hear about that yet. Tell me all about what you know so far."

Jessie retold the story to Reba. "When I finally got to his side it was just as his knees buckled. I don't know how he did it. He had several broken bones from the beating and the blast." She shivered. "I'm happy to still have him with me today."

"It's amazing how facing the possible loss of someone you love makes you appreciate everything about them, including the things that annoy you. He's our town hero." Reba dabbed at her eyes. "You should go to him. Give him my love."

"I will." Jessie picked up her brownies. "Speaking of love," Jessie said, "I feel that way about you." She kissed Reba's cheek.

Reba wiped her eyes again. "Thank you, dear, the feeling is mutual. Tell Sadie hello from me." She grabbed Jessie's arm to keep her from leaving. "I know you saw more than the usual out there. We'll talk when you're ready." She patted Jessie's hand. "You may not see it right away; Matt will be a stronger and more loving man because of what happened to him in those woods. It will mean another adventure for you, but I think you're up for the challenge."

Jessie walked to her car. Another adventure? She shook her head. One thing at a time, please. She looked up to the heavens. "Angels or ghosts; I'm not ready for anything else at the moment," she whispered.

****

Matt glanced at the clock again. The meeting had been over for a while, and he had plenty of facts to keep his mind busy. His parents and brothers had called. It was great to hear from them. The doctor had even been in and told him he could go home in a couple of days if he promised to take it easy. He wanted to see her. Where was she? The elevator doors opened and closed several times, and she still wasn't there. It pinged again, and he grimaced as he straightened up in the bed. Shoes clicked on the tile floor; this had to be her. He took a quick breath as the sound paused at his door and then she was standing in front of him. He could breathe again.

Chapter 46

Matt wasn't following the doctor's orders, but it shouldn't surprise her. He was committed to his job. As with each of the cases before, he was busy tying up all the loose ends, and she didn't see him as often as she would like. Jessie knew he was feeling better, but not much else. Her birthday was tomorrow, and he had told he had something special planned for tonight and tomorrow night. He said tonight was casual and tomorrow was dressy.

"Be ready at five," Matt had said the last time he called.

She pulled her favorite slacks off the hanger along with an icy-blue silk blouse. Jessie looked at her reflection in the mirror. It would have to do. Matt was always on time. A glance out the window told her that his record was intact; he was just pulling into the spot beside her car. She smiled. How could she not love the man? Handsome and always on time.

She opened the door and waved at him. "I'll be right there." She grabbed her purse and locked the door. "Where are we headed?" She slid into the front seat when he opened the passenger door. "Do you want me to drive?" She pointed at the sling on his left arm.

"No, it's annoying, but I'm good." He backed out of the parking space. "We're going to the marina to talk, and then I have something else planned. You'll know soon enough." He waited for her to latch her seat belt. "I figured you'd want to know what has gone down the past few days. It's big, Jess. We're talking major."

"I'm intrigued but not surprised. I mean, look at the murder victims—outstanding students, making an impact on others' lives—there had to be a reason for their murders. Their parents are all well-known and strong members in the community. There was no way it could have been random."

"I can see you haven't stopped thinking about the case." He smiled at her. "I'm of the opinion that even you'll be surprised by where this case is heading."

"Okay, you can't keep me in suspense." Jessie turned in the seat to look at him.

"In a minute. We're almost there. I can't talk about this and concentrate on driving." He made a turn off Main Street onto Blue Cove Drive and toward the marina.

"I've watched the changes to the marina over the past few months. That's where I turn around when I run this way. It's hard to believe there was ever a bomb blast there."

"I know. It's ready for the tourist season to begin." Matt pulled into a parking space.

"I love this spot. It's a perfect view of the cove. It's such a peaceful place to reflect." She reached for his hand. "It's kind of sad that the historic old mill is a total loss, though. I kept hoping someone would renovate it."

"Chad and I used to hang out there a lot. I'm glad I remembered our secret way to get into the mill. It probably helped to save my life."

"Chad?" Jessie unlatched her seat belt.

"He was my best friend from elementary school through high school." Matt frowned and stared out at the ocean.

"Where is he now?" Jessie wondered why she hadn't heard of Chad before.

"I have no idea. We drifted apart after graduation. We were inseparable growing up though."

"Did he move out of the area?" Jessie asked. Out of sight, out of mind, she guessed.

"The last I heard he was living in Rocky Pointe, but I have no idea if he's still there. At some point, I'll have to tell you what separated us." He laced his fingers through hers.

It was beginning to make sense. "Another time. Right now, I want to hear about this case." She turned in the seat to face him.

"I figured you might." He grinned at her. "Do you remember when you told me that every conflict has a flashpoint?"

"Yes, why?"

"It got me thinking about the flashpoint in this case. There were so many possibilities and all of them came into play in minor ways." He stared out the window into the night. "The three men who traveled with Roth were extremists with very radical beliefs. They were easy for him to recruit and to control with the right tools. The fourth man they recruited from the protestors on campus. He was also the one who sent the note to Amir and monitored the kids' activities for a few weeks before they abducted them. He was a loose cannon. The four students and their friendships were the fuel by which Roth ignited one of the fires."

"In what way?" Jessie watched a boat making its

way to the dock.

"Their unlikely friendships and relationships were a challenge to the men's simple core beliefs and ideology. Roth could and did manipulate the facts to control the men he had with him."

"Are you saying Darsha and Amir's relationship was a flashpoint?" Jess asked.

"One of many." He frowned in concentration. "It's hard to know where to begin because the case is bigger than we could have imagined in the beginning. The FBI and CIA have taken control of the next phase, and we won't be hearing much about it until indictments are handed down."

"You mean the case doesn't end in Blue Cove?" Jessie grabbed her notepad out of her purse along with a pen.

"Some of it is top secret and will never hit the papers. I will share what I can. The rest of the details you may or may not read in the paper someday."

"I want to know why *those* kids, and why you?"

"Roth had a connection to Amir's father from years ago and I was linked with Mr. Baz through the FBI investigation at the time. Amir's father had shut Roth down when he tried to sell illegal weapons in his country. He embarrassed Roth publicly and Harry lost his reputation. He wanted revenge. Irwin from our Palm Spring case had met Roth on a trip overseas. He tried to peddle those goods to several countries. Roth also was a contact for the Harvest Club in India. He has had his hands in many illegal endeavors."

"I can see why he was upset with you. You shut down two of his operations. But why the kids?"

"Amir was a way to get at his father. A payback of

sorts. The other kids were in the wrong place at the wrong time. None of them was supposed to die. Roth wasn't able to control the newest recruit. When Amir died they had to kill the rest. They knew too much. We found out during the interrogation that Harry had tried to enlist Amir using the false pretense of dealing prescription opioids to the students on campus. Amir wouldn't do it." Matt changed his position to see her better. "Although Roth wanted to make a contact to move drugs more than anything, he wanted to get back at Amir's father through his son. What he didn't want was Amir dead. He planned to collect the ransom and hand their brutalized son back to them. I suspect that if Amir had become a willing pusher, Roth would have outed Amir to get him arrested. That would have been a huge humiliation to his father and family. In his mind it was the perfect retaliation; money and the humiliation of his enemy. Instead he botched another mission and will land in prison for the rest of his life."

"Amir obviously refused; he was a reputable young man." Jessie smiled to herself.

"Remember Darsha told us about the man in the limousine?"

"Yes, how does he fit in?"

"He's a mafia boss from a country currently under U.S. sanctions. Roth found people willing to launder money through their businesses for him. He contacted Roth a few months ago about a special mission. A friend of his wanted a group to stage a terror attack on our soil. It was planned for a major city, and they had a dirty bomb. I can't tell you the reason, but let's just say it was to move public opinion."

"The loss of life could have been astronomical."

Jessie rubbed her arms against a sudden chill.

"Right. And the FBI knew some of the possible players behind the scene who ordered it, but they are only beginning to put the links together."

"What are you saying?" Jessie was shocked. "This man was only a contact, but Roth was ultimately hired by someone from our own country?" She saw him nod. "You mean like a traitor willing to see people die for some cause?"

"You're catching on, Jess." Matt let his breath out slowly. "It's mind-blowing."

"Who? And how far up does it go?"

"Out of our hands, and we won't know until we know, if ever. This only came to light because Roth decided to come after me out of revenge. The failure of his operation averted one major catastrophe for now. Is there a backup plan? We have no idea. We do know that someone in our country is a traitor. We may never know who it is."

"I don't know what I expected to hear, but I wasn't expecting this." Jessie shivered. "It's scary to think about."

"In the kids, we see what we're up against. We have good people with different ethnic backgrounds, religions, and sexual orientation. Hatred against them is expressed every day. Hate groups, rhetoric, intolerance—there is always someone willing to exploit our fears, even those we might trust. Words matter. In this case, our own fears became the final flashpoint."

"I'm stunned." Jessie gazed into his face.

"Stunned is a good description. Sanders and Dickerson deal with these high-level threats all the time. Me, I've been asleep, thinking everything is normal."

"I'd say this is a wake-up call. It hit too close to home." She snuggled against his side.

"That night out at the mill, strange things were happening. I heard about Amir's ghost stopping you, but there were other things going on. Harry didn't say much, but the other suspect couldn't stop talking through the interpreter about what he saw. I think we may have had more than a little supernatural help that night." His voice took on a serious note. "My life passed in front of me revealing some areas I had buried deep inside of me. Jess, I thought I was dying and I would never see you again. It's amazing what is important when you think you aren't going to make it. You will be the first one I talk to about it when I'm ready. I want you to know everything about me with no secrets between us." Matt swiped at the tears on his cheeks. "I remember seeing a bright light around me right before I passed out."

"I will be there when you're ready to talk." Reba's words came to mind. She laced her fingers through his.

"Harry meant for the bomb to take out all of those who had been tracking him along with me. He had some grand plans."

"He wouldn't have had to worry about those who knew him the best. Thankfully his plan failed."

Matt nodded. "I can't explain how I got free or out of the mill in time. It happened, that's all I know."

"I'm glad it did." She stroked his cheek. "There were moments when I wasn't sure I'd ever see you again. Dylan helped me at one point."

"How?" Matt brushed her hair away from her face with his hand.

"He told me I would know if you were dead. Dylan said what I needed to hear." Their eyes met, and a knowing look passed between them. "It helped a whole lot more when we found you." She took his face in her hands, taking her sweet time to look at him. The air crackled around them. He was alive, and it was magic when she leaned toward him, and their lips met in a perfect kiss.

Chapter 47

Matt pulled away first. "As much as I want you all to myself, and believe me I do, I have a birthday surprise for you. I'm happy to be here to share it with you. He opened his door and walked around to her side. He took a large triangle of fabric out of his pocket. "No questions. You'll have to trust me on this, and I'm afraid you'll have to help. Here, hold this end." He lifted her hand to hold the blindfold in place while he clumsily tied it.

She tried to stop him, slapping at his hands. "What are you doing?"

"I'm following instructions. You may as well resign yourself and go with it." He closed the door and got back in the car.

"What is that supposed to mean?" She frowned, tugging on the blindfold.

"Oh, no you don't." He pulled her hand away and held it. "Be a good girl and don't make me tie your hands behind your back." He chuckled and patted her hand. "This was hard enough."

"At least you can tell me where you're taking me." Jessie tilted her head.

"No peeking." He reached over to make sure she couldn't see. "I can't tell you where, but you'll find out soon enough.

She lifted her hands in surrender. "If you must.

Lead on. I'm at your mercy."

He drove for at least fifteen minutes, turning several times. "We're almost there." He grinned to himself. He had been circling Blue Cove for a while. Jessie was too quiet.

"I sure hope so. I'm getting motion sickness. I'm not kidding. All this driving and turning without being able to see is making me lightheaded."

He pulled into a parking space and helped her out of the car. "I'm sorry sweetheart; you'll have to wear this a little longer." He grabbed her hand to stop her from pulling the blindfold off.

"I don't understand why I have to wear it at all." She held tightly to his arm as she stumbled.

"You will, soon enough. We have a few stairs to go up. I won't let you fall." He placed her hand on the railing, and they took the stairs slowly. They walked through the door Katie was holding open. He stopped in the center of the silent room, waiting for Katie's signal. With a flourish, he removed the blindfold as everyone yelled *surprise*.

****

Jessie looked around at the sea of smiling faces. She hadn't suspected anything. How had Matt managed it? Sadie and her mom and dad were standing in front of her along with new friends and old friends. She was overwhelmed. The beautiful Inn was glowing with candlelight and party decorations. The balloons made her feel like a kid again.

"How'd you pull this off?" She gazed into Matt's face, feeling happiness shining in her eyes.

"Do you like my little surprise?" He leaned close to whisper in her ear.

"It's perfect, thank you." She smiled when his hand at her waist pulled her closer. Together they greeted family and friends.

It was a magical night for her. The food was wonderful. Between Katie and Molly's amazing creations, the guests enjoyed every tasty morsel including an awesome birthday cake. The gifts and well wishes were only a few of the evening's highlights. Jessie's dad kept telling her how much he liked Matt. She assured him that she felt the same way. Her mother spent the evening talking to Katie's parents and gushing over Katie's wedding plans. If she asked her once, her mother asked several times if they would be planning their own wedding soon. Jessie danced around the question without ever answering her. Conversations flowed, laughter spilled out often, and Jessie's heart was full. This is what gave life meaning—family, friends, and enjoying the special moments when they were handed to you.

Her eyes often strayed to Matt. Surrounded by Dylan, Liam, and Kip, he was talking, and they were laughing. Her heart fluttered. She shuddered to think how close she had come to losing him, which made this moment all the sweeter. He winked when they made eye contact. Slowly he made his way toward her. She watched him every step of the way.

"Are you happy?" He tucked her hand in his.

"Yes. How did you find time to plan this? You've been a little busy the last few weeks."

"I had help from some friends. Remember you still have another surprise waiting for you."

"Matt, I love this! You don't have to do anything else. Seeing Sadie and Reba and my parents tonight is the best gift of all. You can't possibly top it."

"You have to take both nights as a package deal. Tonight, it's about celebrating with your family and friends. Tomorrow is our private celebration." He kissed her cheek.

"I can't wait."

When the last of the guests were either in their rooms or on their way home, Matt walked Jessie to her cottage. He carried her gifts, and she carried the cards.

"Sadie looks good, and she wants to move here. She likes Reba—they seem to hit it off." Excitement tinged her voice. "I would love for Sadie to be near."

"Your parents seemed happy to see you."

"It was good to see them. My dad likes you, Matt. He told me several times tonight."

"I'm growing on him." He smiled. "At least I wasn't nervous this time."

"This ranks up there among my best birthdays ever. I loved every minute of this night." She rushed ahead to unlock the door.

"I'm happy that you're happy." He placed the bags on the couch. "I'll be here at five-thirty tomorrow for round two." He gave her a quick kiss and went to the door.

She stopped his progress. "I want to properly thank you for everything." She pulled his head down and kissed him until they were both breathless. She leaned against the door, finally, a bemused look on her face.

"Get some sleep." He nudged her to get her moving. "You need your beauty rest."

"I'm not sure how to take that." She tilted her head to look at him.

He smiled and walked out the door. "Sleep tight."

****

In the morning, Jessie showed her parents her bookstore. Sadie tagged along. Her dad was impressed by how well the store was doing when he looked at her financial records.

"You're making a nice profit for a new business. The town doesn't seem big enough to sustain it."

"I did my homework, Dad. This town has many tourists year round. It's quite capable of turning a nice profit."

"I wasn't sure when you first told me you were buying it, but you knew what you were doing. I think you were smart to connect it to the coffee shop. Audrey is an asset, too." He beamed at her. "I'm proud of you, kiddo."

"Thank you." Jessie was stunned. Her dad didn't compliment her often.

"What are you girls going to do today?" He sipped his coffee.

"You know, girl stuff and shopping. Jessie has a big date tonight." Sadie grabbed Jessie's hand.

"You know where to find me when you're ready. I'll be at the Inn, watching the game."

After being pampered at the spa, they went shopping at the new boutique in the next town up the highway. Her mother handed her a red dress to try on. "Every woman needs a red dress for a special occasion," she said. "I'm sure Matt will love you in this."

"You know, dear," Sadie added, "a sexy red dress that shows off your figure to perfection without giving away all its mysteries. Look at you." Sadie turned her toward the mirror. "This dress does what it's supposed to and a whole lot more. Your mother's right. This is the dress." Sadie and her mom laughed like young girls.

Jessie had bought the dress. In her mind, she could still hear them laughing. She smiled. Her hair did what it was supposed to do. Picking up the perfume bottle, she sprayed her wrists, then dabbed a bit in her cleavage and behind her ears. Jessie glanced at the clock. He would be here in ten minutes. She took a deep breath and released it. Her mother knew what she was talking about. She turned one more time in front of the mirror. There was a lot to be said for a little red dress.

****

Matt knocked on her door. "It's me," he called out and walked in.

"I'll be right out; make yourself comfortable," she told him.

Matt sat in his favorite chair and stretched out his legs. He thumbed through a magazine while he waited. "Jess." The whistle came out before he could stop it. Jumping to his feet, he moved toward her. "Wow, sweetheart." He gulped as his mouth went dry. "You look…stunning."

"Mom and Sadie took me shopping. They taught me the importance of having a special red dress. I take it you approve." She turned to give him the full effect. "I don't believe you've ever whistled at me before. It's a first." She grinned at him.

"It's not because I didn't want to. Remind me to thank them." Matt held her coat for her. "You smell good, too." He turned her around. "Are you ready?" Matt wasn't sure what he was saying or how he was going to get through the evening with small talk.

"Damn, Jess, you look smoking hot."

"I may be wrong, but I think hot was the reaction Sadie was hoping for." Jessie walked through the door he held open. "Is it a surprise, or can I ask where we're going?"

"It's a surprise." He glanced at her every few minutes.

"You're quiet. Is everything all right?" His cologne smelled wonderful. She inched closer to him.

"Everything is fine. I like the way Sadie thinks. I bet she gave your grandpa all that he could handle."

"She did and a few other men along the way." She placed her hand on his arm. The aroma of his cologne filled the air.

Matt turned off the highway. "I heard this place was voted the most romantic restaurant several years in a row. We are about to find out." Matt opened her door.

She looked perfect in the setting. Matt noticed others noticing too. Built in the eighteen twenties, the inside was rustic but elegant. The tables were set up in private sections throughout the restaurant. White linen tablecloths and candles on each table added to the ambiance. A grand piano stood in front of a floor-to-ceiling window with amazing views. The pianist was incredible. He was playing *Unchained Melody*. Matt grinned. Luck—along with a little romance magic—was on his side tonight. She had told him once the words and the melody made the song romantic. It was near the top of her list. He whispered in her ear. "He's playing your song, sweetheart."

"I know." She smiled as he pulled her closer. The host seated them at a table in a private alcove.

The sommelier went over the extensive wine list

with Matt and helped him make his choice. The waiter took their orders of lobster and shallot-crusted beef tenderloin.

Matt reached across the table to take her hands in his. "Happy birthday, sweetheart."

"Thank you. You've made this the most amazing birthday ever." She held his hand up to her lips and kissed his fingers. "This place is beautiful."

"You are beautiful. This place suits you." He smiled at her.

They dined, talked, and discovered new aspects of each other. When the waiter removed the last plate, Matt placed a card and small box on the table. "I realized something in the last few weeks. You gave me back my life, and I'm grateful." He rubbed his thumb across the palm of her hand. "Years ago, my girlfriend was murdered and it wasn't until I found myself facing death that I fully comprehended how much it had affected my life. Something inside me had died slowly until you moved to town. You made me believe I could have it all and believe me I want it. I'm a new man." He leaned toward her with his lopsided grin.

"I don't know what to say." Her eyes were misty.

"I love you, Jess, every part of me does. There's room in my heart to love again because of you." He pushed the box toward her. "You can open your gift."

Jessie read the card first. "Oh, Matt." Her hand trembled as she unwrapped the box. She held up a ruby necklace with two small diamond chips. "This is exquisite. Thank you. I'll never forget this birthday or the words you wrote on my card." She gazed into his eyes repeating a few of his words back to him. "You are my love, my life, and the inspiration for every good thing I accomplish. You mean the world to me."

"I meant every one of them." He grabbed his wine glass. "To you, sweetheart." He toasted her, lifting his glass. "Little did I know when you walked into my life that night almost a year ago, Heaven was sending an angel to watch over me. You've brought out feelings I thought were dead. I love you, Jess, and always will. You're home to me. If I learned anything through all this, it was, wanting to see you again that gave me the will to fight. Life can be over in a moment and I don't want to waste any time that I can spend loving you. We both have dragged our feet in this relationship, but no more. I will chase you to the ends of the earth if necessary to win your heart. I love you that much.

She raised her glass clinking it against his. "To us." She smiled and sighed. "Put away your running shoes, I'm not going anywhere. My heart already belongs to you." He could see the love shining in her eyes. "I love you, too, Matt." She leaned across the table and kissed him.

A word about the author...

I enjoy writing fiction. The character development, their stories, and the twists and turns in the plot intrigue me. Once I let the characters loose I can't wait to see where they take me. I'm hooked from the first words on the paper and I have to keep writing to see how the story ends. Layer by layer it builds until I come to the happy conclusion.

I live in Colorado with my husband and family who have supported me in this chapter of life. I am a member of the RMFWPAL (Rocky Mountain Fiction Writers Published Authors League) and have enjoyed becoming involved in my community as one of the many authors living in Colorado.